"**Fast-paced** and funny." —*Library Journal*

"Bares the comic underbelly and social injustices of small-town life." —*U.S. News & World Report*

"A very funny writer who also manages to make a point with his outrageous humor . . . His characters are well-drawn and believable . . . He can easily share the shelves with any of today's best satirists." —*Tulsa World*

"A **hilarious** parable about alienation, God, and growing up." —*Richmond Times-Dispatch*

"**Humorous and touching** . . . The tale gets funnier and funnier but is surprisingly gentle and inoffensive. Instead Welter tells a tale of concerned and caring human beings willing to use their resources, their intelligence and their energy to do the right thing. He gets his message across in hilarious fashion just as Mary Poppins taught us that a spoonful of sugar helps the medicine go down." —*Southern Pines Pilot* (NC)

"**Like [John] Irving**, Welter stuffs his book with gaggles of endearing eccentrics . . . Like [Carl] Hiaasen, Welter displays a wicked sense of humor . . . *I Want to Buy a Vowel* gives Welter the chance to make some genial social criticism and tell a good fast-paced story." —*Orlando Sentinel*

"In the long tradition of *Gulliver's Travels* . . . *I Want to Buy a Vowel* finds innocence in an illegal immigrant from Guatemala who believes simple hard work will bring him the American dream . . . **funny**." —*San Antonio Express-News*

"Often hilarious, sometimes poignant, always **highly entertaining**." —*Chattanooga Free Press*

"Entertaining . . . **offbeat** . . . sprinkled with wry, comic moments and a steadfast awareness of social injustice." —*Publishers Weekly*

"A **delight** . . . thought-provoking." —*Oak Ridger* (TN)

"Gentle and downright charming . . . **you'll laugh out loud**." —*American Way*

W9-BBZ-782

I WANT TO BUY A VOWEL

*a novel of
illegal alienation*

JOHN WELTER

BERKLEY BOOKS, NEW YORK

This is a work of fiction. All names, characters, places, and incidents are either products of the author's imagination or are used fictitiously. No reference to any real person is intended or should be inferred.

I WANT TO BUY A VOWEL

A Berkley Book / published by arrangement with Algonquin Books

PRINTING HISTORY
Algonquin Books edition / January 1996
Berkley edition / November 1997

All rights reserved.
Copyright © 1996 by John Welter.
Author photo © by Leslie Takahashi.
This book may not be reproduced in whole or in part, by mimeograph or any other means, without permission.
For information address: Algonquin Books of Chapel Hill, Post Office Box 2225, Chapel Hill, North Carolina 27515-2225.

The Putnam Berkley World Wide Web site address is
http://www.berkley.com

ISBN: 0-425-16081-5

BERKLEY®
Berkley Books are published by The Berkley Publishing Group, a member of Penguin Putnam Inc., 200 Madison Avenue, New York, New York 10016.
BERKLEY and the "B" design are trademarks belonging to Berkley Publishing Corporation.

PRINTED IN THE UNITED STATES OF AMERICA

10 9 8 7 6 5 4 3 2 1

This book is dedicated to all of the people who founded America without visas or green cards.

This book is also dedicated to Betsy for reasons I don't have to explain.

I WANT TO BUY A VOWEL

John L. Welter

1

"I want to buy a vowel," Alfredo Santayana said to the first American he met, a pleasant-looking old white woman standing outside of a convenience store in Waxahachie, Texas. It was one of the very few English expressions Alfredo had memorized, one that might be followed by a wondrous gift.

"A new car!" he said.

The pleasant-looking old white woman looked a little bit less pleasant then. She squinted through her glasses at Alfredo and readjusted her grip on a six-pack of Lone Star beer.

"Jackass," she said, then got into her car and drove away.

"Jackass," Alfredo repeated, happy to possess a new American word. He knew he'd have to learn English. First, though, he'd have to find a job and a place to live. Standing in the shade of the store's wall, Alfredo looked around the area. He saw a construction site a few hundred yards away, where some workers were framing new houses along a cul-de-sac. Happily, Alfredo approached some of the carpenters at a house because they looked Mexican.

"Pardon me," Alfredo said in Spanish. "I've decided to

live here. How soon will the house be ready?''

The carpenters did know Spanish, and one of them said, ''Kiss my ass.''

''Is that an American custom?'' Alfredo said. ''Could you explain it to me?''

''It means you put your lips on my butt,'' the carpenter said, and all of them laughed. ''Boy, what country are you from?''

''Guatemala.''

''So you think you can come to Texas and get a new house just because you want one? Well you can't. You have to *pay* for the house. You got a hundred thousand dollars? You probably don't even have a green card. You better not let the police see you, amigo. You better go find yourself a pig shed, or live in a tree. Immigration will send your ass back to Guatemala if you don't hide. And here,'' the carpenter said, putting down the two-by-four he held and reaching into his pants' pocket. He pulled out some coins and gave them to Alfredo. He said, ''This is American money. Go back to the store and get yourself a Coke before you sweat to death.''

''Thank you,'' Alfredo said as he accepted the coins.

''And you better go find yourself a job.''

''Can I work here?'' Alfredo said.

''We don't want no illegals here,'' the carpenter said.

''Jesus was a carpenter,'' Alfredo said.

''Not without a green card he wasn't,'' the carpenter said, and all the carpenters laughed.

''Go on down that road,'' the carpenter said to Alfredo, pointing to the paved road in front of the house. ''You walk about two miles that way and see a Chinese restaurant. They might hire you to wash dishes.''

At the convenience store, where Alfredo drank a cold Coke in the shade, he looked at all the cars and pickup trucks, of every possible color, that came to the store or drove by on the road. It seemed as if everyone in America was born with a car, as if, on the day that they were baptized, the priest gave them a set of car keys. It was nice just to be near the endless wealth of America, even if none of it was his. It would be, though. He was in such an excellent mood that it didn't disturb him to realize he might walk past the restaurant without knowing it was a restaurant because he couldn't read.

"I'll smell it," he told himself, and set out down the road, sniffing the air as he walked. Not trusting his optimism, Alfredo decided to pray.

Dear Jesus: Please help me to find a job, and a place to live, and a vowel.

c · h · a · p · t · e · r

2

Sometimes Eva Galt prayed, too, but not to God. She prayed to Ted Williams, who had a lifetime batting average of .344. Whenever Eva tried to pray directly and exactly to God, she couldn't help thinking that no one knew what God looked like. God didn't have a face. There weren't any photographs. Her father sometimes said in his sermons that God was in all of us. That was pretty strange. But she couldn't pray to someone without a face, so because her father loved baseball and had a baseball card signed by Ted Williams, Eva decided to pray to Ted Williams, just because she knew what Ted Williams looked like, and also because she once heard her father say, "Maybe Ted Williams couldn't walk on water, but then Jesus never hit .406. I'd say they're about even." Her father was an Episcopal priest, so she figured he ought to know.

Usually she prayed in the evening, when she and her little sister, Ava, got ready to go to sleep. Like tonight. At a little after nine o'clock, in their upstairs bedroom, they kneeled side by side at the edge of their bed with their hands clasped in front of them.

"Dear Ted Williams," Eva prayed. "Hi. It's me again. And Ava."

"Mom said you aren't supposed to pray to Ted Williams," Ava said.

"No she didn't. She said Ted Williams isn't a god. I already know that. I'm just praying to Ted Williams because God doesn't have a face."

"He doesn't?" Ava gasped.

"Well no one's seen it. But be quiet. I'm praying," Eva said, trying to think of a prayer again.

"Dear Ted Williams," she said, imagining him in his baseball uniform and holding a bat, even though Ted Williams was still alive and couldn't be in Heaven. "Thank you for all of our blessings and our parents and our house and our food and our clothes and our underwear."

"Our underwear?" Ava said.

"You have to be thankful for everything," Eva said, and started praying again. "Help us to be good people who care about each other," she prayed, which seemed to be too short of a prayer, so she remembered part of another prayer and said, "And if I die before I wake . . ."

"We're gonna die?" Ava said.

"Well not right now," Eva said, and put her arm around Ava's back so she wouldn't be scared, because Ava was only eight, and Eva was eleven.

"Are we through praying?" Ava asked.

"No. You interrupted me," she said, and resumed her prayer. "And if I die before I wake . . ." She tried to think of something new that would rhyme, then said, "I'd like a piece of chocolate cake."

"I never heard that prayer before."

"It's new."

Eva made the sign of the cross, and because she was praying to Ted Williams, she also made the sign to "hit away."

In the morning, Eva and Ava got their fishing poles and went off down the street toward the sewage treatment plant. It was forbidden to go there, of course, and a large chain-link fence surrounded the treatment plant and its huge concrete ponds. But Eva and Ava and sometimes a few other children went there anyway, getting in under the fence where it was cut in a big curve to fit over a huge concrete water pipe that emptied into the pond. Someone had bent the fence there, and Eva and Ava could lie flat against the concrete pipe and hold the fence up with their hands and squeeze under it. There was a little stream near there, so they could tell their parents they were going to the stream to fish, and be telling the truth, although the biggest fish Eva had seen anybody catch there was about four inches long. One day about two weeks ago, Tommy Dillo, who was ten but didn't act that old, took a fish out of the freezer at home and secretly put it in the stream and tried to hook it, which didn't work because the fish was dead, so Tommy just stood in the stream and picked the fish up with his hands.

"I caught one!" Tommy said.

"It's dead," Ava said.

"What kind is it?" Margaret Hawlings asked.

Tommy carried the fish up to everyone and said, "I think it's a lemon-pepper trout."

"What's a lemon-pepper trout?" Ava asked.

"It's what you get in the store," Eva said.

Ava was mystified. She studied the fish in Tommy's hands for a few seconds, and then she pointed at the stream and said, "You mean, the fish in the store come from here?"

"No," Eva said. "He probably got that from his freezer at home." She looked at Tommy and said, "I'll bet you get in trouble."

"Not if no one tells," Tommy said. And no one was going to tell because everyone thought it was funny. Not everything had to be ordinary or regular. You could maybe invent part of the world you were in. Like praying to Ted Williams. So of course Eva wasn't going to tell. Besides, it was the biggest fish they'd ever caught in the stream.

Inside at the sewage treatment plant, where Eva and Ava

sat on the edge of the concrete lake with their fishing lines resting in the calm, greenish water, Ava said, "Do you think there's really any fish in here?"

"Tommy Dillo says so," Eva said uncertainly, as if it might not be a fact. "He says some high school boys snuck in here one night and dumped some catfish or something in here. He says the poop would kill them. I don't know if it would."

"I don't see any poop," Ava said, squinting into the water around them.

"That's because this is a sewage *treatment* plant. They treat the poop, and then it . . ." Eva realized she didn't know what happened when poop was treated.

"And then it what?" Ava asked.

"Well," Eva said, trying not to sound ignorant. "I think they suck it out."

Ava grimaced. "With a straw?" she said.

"Of course not," Eva said. "They use machines. Who would suck poop with a straw?"

Ava giggled. "Suck poop!"

"Don't say that when we get home," Eva warned.

"With a straw," Ava said, and started laughing.

"Stop saying that. Remember what happened when we saw all those boy dogs chasing a girl dog, and then Tommy called them butt-sniffers, and you went home and told Mom we saw some butt-sniffers? You'll get in trouble again."

"Why?" Ava said.

"Because of morals," Eva said.

Ava looked puzzled and serious. "What's morals?"

"Morals," Eva said. It was a word she'd heard people use dozens of times without anyone ever explaining it. Like Tommy Dillo was always saying, "Well, shit!" and if you had morals you were supposed to get mad at him for saying it. "I think it's when you know something's right or wrong. Only you don't know how you know it. Someone just says so. Dad says you have a conscience."

"I do?" Ava said.

"*Every*one has a conscience. It's like this voice in your

7

head. Well, not really a voice. A conscience is this thing in your soul that kind of gets you upset if you're getting ready to do something bad."

"You mean like if I said 'suck poop with a straw'?"

"Like that."

"It doesn't upset me. Poop, poop, poop."

"Well it'll upset Mom and Dad if you say it."

"Is that because they have morals?"

"Yes. And some day, you'll have some, too."

"Like breasts?" Ava said.

"What?" Eva said.

"Mom told me some day I'll have breasts. Do you get morals and breasts at the same time?"

"Well I think you're supposed to get morals first."

"What'll I do with breasts, Eva?"

This was something Eva wanted to know, too.

"You feed babies," Eva said.

Ava tilted her head and frowned at Eva with perplexity. "You feed *babies*?" she said. "You mean they eat your *breasts*?"

"No, stupid. You get *milk* in your breasts. That's why you have nipples. And then the babies suck the milk from your breasts."

Ava pulled the top of her blouse open and pressed her chin against her chest to look at herself. "Which grade do you get breasts in?"

Eva frowned at her sister and said, "Well it's not like you get in school and someone gives you some breasts. Breasts just grow on you."

It made Eva think of why some of the junior high school and high school girls at the mall all walked around in gangs of pointy bras. And then in magazines, like *Cosmopolitan*, the women all had such big breasts smashed together so hard it looked like your butt. Ava even said so at the grocery store when they were in the checkout line and Ava and Eva were looking at the magazine covers. Ava said, "Why is that woman's butt on her chest?" Some other people started laughing, and Eva walked out to the car to be embarrassed in private.

Secretly, Eva wanted breasts. She didn't know what she'd do with them, though. Being a girl hadn't been explained all that well.

After about half an hour of fishless fishing, the girls headed back home, stopping to loiter for a while and stare at the old warlock's home that had been there since before the Civil War or the Revolutionary War or maybe the War of 1812 or possibly World War II, since no one really knew how old the warlock's house was. It used to be the old witch's house, but when Eva was talking about the old witch's house one time, her mom said it was sexist to think that only an old witch could've lived there. She said a male witch was called a warlock. You might as well say a warlock lived there. So Eva started saying that.

The walls of the old warlock's house had faded gray shingles with some peeling brown paint left on them, under a sloping tin roof that looked like the air might cave it in. The rotting shingles were arranged in long rows that looked like the scales on a snake. The front door was permanently open, maybe broken that way, but no one ever went onto the sagging wooden porch to find out, since the house looked like it might be filled with monsters, banshees, ghosts, poltergeists, murderers, satanists, demons, and really big insects. Through the front door and two of the broken windows, wasps and hornets and a few birds sometimes flew in and flew out. A crooked stone chimney rose up at one end of the house, which could have been where invisible demons floated into and out of the house, although they could've also used the front door. Eva had argued with Tommy Dillo about that, saying demons wouldn't have to use a chimney or a door. They could just walk right through the walls.

While she stood next to Ava, thinking about death and demons, Eva saw a small patch of something white moving through the trees and bushes ahead of them, and a few seconds later she saw through an opening in the trees that it was a woman or a man, she couldn't tell which, walking quickly ahead of them toward the house.

"There's somebody up there, sneaking along on the trail," Eva whispered.

Whoever it was was wearing a white shirt and dark pants and seemed to be carrying a bag. The person hurried up the steps of the house and went inside, and the girls breathed in suddenly, as if the person would surely be killed, or maybe have their soul sucked out by demons. In an astonished, troubled silence, they remained hiding in the trees, staring at the house and waiting for horrible screams. But nothing happened. There was no noise at all.

"Do you think they're dead?" Ava whispered anxiously.

"I can't tell," Eva whispered. Even in the full sunlight of midday, the house was covered in shade from the tall trees around it, so it still looked like the house itself was trying to hide and withdraw into darkness.

"Do you think that's the warlock?" Ava asked in a voice even more hushed than before.

"How could it be? *I'm* the one who started calling it the old warlock's house."

"Is it Satan?" Ava said.

"I don't know who it is in there, and we're not walking up there to find out," Eva said. "We'll just have to loop over there through the woods so he won't see us."

Walking as quietly as they knew how, which meant stepping on dry leaves and old branches that snapped under their feet as if to alarm every demon in the house, the girls sneaked past the house and hurried on through the woods toward the safety of their neighborhood.

"Should we tell Mom and Dad?" Ava said as she walked next to Eva on the trail and glanced behind her.

"I don't think so," Eva said. "They'll just say Satan doesn't exist, and then tell us we can't go back in the woods anymore."

c·h·a·p·t·e·r

3

Eva's father, Daniel Galt, sometimes got annoyed that his congregation expected him to be constantly involved in nearly every part of the church's existence simply because he was the priest. Like the damn Human Rights Committee—and why couldn't he think "damn" without feeling he'd committed a minor sin? He'd never been convinced that swearing was a genuine violation of anything that mattered to God. He pictured God saying on Judgment Day, "We can't allow you into Heaven because you uttered a total of seven thousand, three hundred, and forty-two obscenities, profanities, and assorted vulgarities in your life. Because of those linguistic violations, you are condemned to Hell. Sorry."

And now the damn Human Rights Committee was due to arrive at his home to discuss their latest mission: the need to be "proactively" involved in the plight of the homeless. He hated that damn word *proactive*. All the right-thinking liberals at church used it now. Like *diversity* or *empowerment*. He wanted to say, "Would you please stop using that damn word?"

And now the damn Human Rights Committee was showing up to change the world over dinner. Of the thousands of ways to change the world, why did so many require committees?

There were six—five women and one token man, as if the only people who cared about changing the world were women (and one man, for diversity).

Daniel remained outwardly cheerful and gracious and interested during dinner as his wife, Emily, made certain that all the committee members and Daniel and Eva and Ava had a steady supply of meatloaf and mashed potatoes and green beans, and for the more devout vegetarians on the committee, a mysterious kind of squash and cheese casserole.

"I'm afraid I could go on and on about the moral conflict of meat versus plants," Beverly Holdman said at the table. Then she paused.

"Are ya?" Ava asked. She was only curious, but it made Beverly shut up, and Daniel was secretly pleased to have such a tactless daughter.

Soon enough, the committee launched into passionate and frequently incoherent ramblings about the homeless. They kept repeating the word *homeless* so often that Daniel became thoroughly distracted and wondered if, instead of always saying "homeless," people could use different words, such as *houseless. Apartmentless. Townhouseless. Duplexless.*

It wasn't that he didn't care about the homeless and poor. He did. He was just so tired of fashionable language. Maybe the Bible said, "The poor are always with us," but it seemed like today that verse would be altered to read: "The unempowered are always with us." Jesus wouldn't be helping the poor. He'd be helping the economically challenged.

As the committee members droned on, Daniel wished a poor person would come to the front door and say, "Stop calling me homeless. I'm poor, dammit. I'm *poor.*"

• • •

Eva found it mysterious and astonishing that a roomful of adults could be so thoroughly boring. She tried to pay attention and be interested in what they said, but it was too hard to care about it, and her thoughts strayed far away, the way they did when she'd daydream in church and get lost in the liturgy. As she heard everyone in the church suddenly making the sounds of standing up to sing a hymn, she would quickly reach into the book rack in front of her for a hymnal and pretend to start singing whatever she heard everyone else singing, even if she didn't know the song, which she usually didn't.

But no one would be singing. Everyone would be kneeling on the little padded benches, so Eva'd quickly put the hymnal back and kneel down beside Ava as their dad prayed something aloud from the altar. When that was over, and everyone shuffled and coughed and cleared their throats again as Eva sat back down on the pew, nobody else would sit down. They'd be standing up with hymnals. The liturgy was as complicated as chess to Eva, who never memorized enough of it to ever know where she was supposed to be.

When everyone sang a hymn that Eva didn't know the page number for, she'd hold the closed hymnal to her chest and pretend she'd memorized the song that she pretended to sing. She wondered if God ever got upset about people not singing hymns right or if he was pretty tolerant. Usually when the song was over, Eva kneeled down on the bench, then realized everyone else was just sitting down in the pews. So she pretended she was fastening the strap on one of her shoes and then sat down like everyone else to listen to her dad. Her dad said there was some system to it, some way to figure it out, but she kept forgetting. It was Sit, Stand, Kneel. Or sometimes it was Kneel, Sit, Stand. Or otherwise it was Stand, Kneel, Sit.

When her dad would say, "Let us pray," Eva didn't know if that meant you were supposed to pray whatever you wanted, or you were supposed to pray in silence, or you were expected to pray in unison with her dad, or if it was one of the extremely complicated parts where her dad read part of a psalm and then everybody else prayed another part right back at him. It made Eva think of tennis. She could never find the right page in the prayer book, either, unless her mom bent down and showed her. Usually by then the prayer was over, and Eva didn't know whether to sit, stand, kneel, or what. Church was pretty hard.

Sometimes, while she was thinking that, the prayer would end before Eva had a chance to pray anything, and so in an attempt to catch up or at least let God know she was trying to pay attention, she would pray silently, *Dear Ted Williams: I'm trying to pay attention. Amen.*

The thing that Eva really wondered about prayer was if it worked. You were supposed to believe it did, which was why anybody even prayed. But sometimes at church there'd be someone from the congregation who was really sick with something, and everybody prayed for the person, and then they died anyway. Or there was that war in Bosnia, where everybody prayed for peace, but you didn't get any. Or like the floods along the Mississippi River and all over the Midwest and in some places in Texas. Her dad asked everybody to pray, and they did, and then the floods went right on. It was the most perplexing thing.

So far, Eva had never gotten what she asked for. Sometimes she would look up at her mom beside her in the pew and wonder if she'd been praying wrong, and if that was why her parents were unhappy with each other and would maybe get a divorce. Eva prayed at least once a day for her parents to be happy again. Sometimes she prayed to the unknown God without a face. Sometimes she prayed to Ted Williams. Sometimes she prayed to Jesus. That was three different people, so that if two of them weren't paying attention, maybe the third one was. Although, at the end of every day when Eva had said whatever prayer she could think of and her parents still weren't happy again, Eva had to wonder if prayer worked at all. Maybe it was technical difficulties, like when a TV show suddenly stopped. So maybe certain prayers malfunctioned. But there wasn't some number you could call and say, "Is God paying attention to my prayer this time, or are you having technical difficulties?''

You just never knew. And there inside the big church, with the organ playing and the choir singing and everyone trying to communicate with the God who you couldn't tell ever heard anything no matter how loud you were, Eva still sometimes thought that possibly one of her prayers would get answered one day. So she still said them, and sent them off floating past the Earth's atmosphere and out into the darkest radioactive space where, if the prayers didn't get sucked into a black hole, someone might hear them.

c · h · a · p · t · e · r

4

Waxahachie police chief James McLemore usually liked protecting the public, but it pissed him off that some old woman who lived just barely inside the town limits had reported possible satanic activity in her barn. McLemore stood in front of the town map on the wall in his office with his finger on the approximate spot where the old woman lived.

"God*damn* it!" McLemore said, looking across the room at Sgt. Gloria Mondesi. "She probably lives just a hundred yards inside the town limits. If we could just move her goddamn farm a hundred yards, we wouldn't have to go looking for any goddamn satanic activity. We could call the sheriff."

"I know," Sgt. Mondesi said. "I don't look forward to arresting Satan either."

"And which town ordinance prohibits Satan from coming to town, anyway?" McLemore said, shaking his head. "I don't think we *have* an ordinance covering fallen angels. I just *hate* this. First we have all those religious zealots in Waco having a shootout with federal agents on live TV. Now we have Satan in a barn."

McLemore sighed and put on his gun belt and cowboy hat.

"Let's go look at the barn," he said in a sullen tone.

"What do we do if we find Satan?" Sgt. Mondesi said.

"We'll do what we do with any suspect," McLemore said. "We'll ask for his driver's license."

In Dorothy Eldrid's barn someone had arranged a few dozen large rocks into the shape of a five-pointed star on the dirt floor. The blackened remains of a small wood fire were in the center of the pentagram. Mondesi and McLemore squatted next to it and used pieces of charred wood to dig through the ashes, where they found the partly charred jawbone of a small animal.

"I *told* you it was Satan," Mrs. Eldrid said as she stood behind McLemore.

"No. It's too small to be Satan. I'd say it's a raccoon," McLemore said while looking at the jawbone.

Mrs. Eldrid looked perturbed. "I wish you'd take me seriously," she said.

"We do," McLemore said. "I'm just releasing a little investigatory tension."

"Well I keep a loaded shotgun with me wherever I go now," Mrs. Eldrid said, resting the butt of the shotgun beside her in the dirt. "And if I catch any satanists out here in the barn, I'll shoot their damn heads off."

"You should call us before you shoot anyone," Sgt. Mondesi said.

"Fine. I call you, *then* I'll shoot 'em," Mrs. Eldrid said.

McLemore stood up and used a Polaroid camera to take a few pictures of the pentagram.

"What're you doing that for?" Mrs. Eldrid said.

"Christmas cards," McLemore said, smiling. "Not really. It's just routine to take pictures of a crime scene, so we'll have a record of what we're talking about. We're going to ask your neighbors if they saw anything suspicious. And we want you to keep your eyes open and call us immediately if you see anyone out here who doesn't belong here. Just try and get a good description of 'em, and don't shoot anyone, please. If they require being shot, that's our responsibility. And as for the possibility of satanic activity, well, I haven't been trained to recognize satanic signs, so I'm not sure what this pentagram means. It could just be some boys out fooling around. I'll be in contact with authorities on the subject of satanism, and if I find anything out, I'll let you know all about it.''

Actually, McLemore didn't think the pentagram and the burned jawbone meant very much at all, but he called the FBI office in Dallas and explained to an agent there what little he knew about the supposed evidence of satanism.

''Maybe you should call directory assistance and ask for the X-Files,'' the agent said.

''You mean there really *is* an X-Files?'' McLemore said.

''On TV there is. We watch that show every Friday night, just to see what stupid shit Mulder and Scully will do again. Investigating aliens from space is far more interesting than what *we* do in the FBI. Most of the aliens we investigate are from Colombia. And they don't have green skin. They have green backs. Anyway, as far as your satanic campfire goes . . . and that'd be interesting, wouldn't it—Satan cooking hot dogs in a campfire? But I wouldn't worry about what you saw. It might mean something, it might mean nothing. I wouldn't spend too much time investigating it, unless whoever's doing that starts damaging property or mutilating livestock or things like that. Frankly, chief, from the point of view of the FBI, if people want to worship Satan, that's their business. It's not illegal.''

''That's what I thought,'' McLemore said. ''But I don't want to tell that to the newspaper. Folks would get pretty upset if they found out satanism isn't illegal. They'll probably have an emergency meeting of the town government to outlaw Satan. Then it'll go to the Supreme Court and we'll all be embarrassed to find out the Supreme Court says Satan can be a registered voter like anyone else. I'd rather keep this quiet.''

"Good idea."

He did keep it quiet, but Mrs. Eldrid didn't. She called every local newspaper and TV station she knew of, and within a day there were newspaper and TV reports about the possibility of satanic activity in Waxahachie. Even if there hadn't been any satanic events in the first place, the publicity guaranteed that there would be. Calls started coming in to the police about suspicious campfires and darkly dressed people doing ominous things. It also created a new interest in geometry. The local newspaper reported in several stories that a few town residents claimed to have seen suspicious pentagrams, pentagons, hexagons, and polygons around the community, which prompted McLemore to say that he should bring in all of the local geometry teachers for questioning. He got so annoyed with it all that he told a reporter that, based on all the geometric evidence so far accumulated, it wasn't Satan they should be looking for. It was Euclid. "Euclid who?" the reporter asked. "Is he a known satanist?"

"Off the record," McLemore said, "I don't think you better put Euclid's name in your story."

"You mean it might interfere with the investigation?"

"It might interfere with your career."

"Is that a threat, chief?" the reporter said, looking combative.

"It's a joke. Believe me, Euclid's not a suspect."

c·h·a·p·t·e·r

5

Eva was lolling on her front porch when she saw Hookey walking across the front yard with a big long bone in his mouth. Hookey was part German shepherd and part something else pretty big, and the bone was maybe a foot long and all darkish, like maybe it'd been buried in the dirt somewhere and Hookey had dug it up.

Dinosaurs, Eva thought. That was it. She and Ava could go looking for dinosaur bones. She went into the kitchen, where Ava was still eating cereal and her mom was reading the paper.

"Mom? Do we have a pickax?" Eva asked.

"Why on Earth would you want a pickax?" her mom said.

"To look for dinosaur bones."

"Well, do you know where some dinosaur bones are?" her mom said pleasantly.

"No. But I thought I'd go look for some in the woods. Do we have a pickax?"

"We certainly don't. How would you even know where dinosaur bones might be?"

Eva gave an exasperated sigh and looked at the floor.

"Well, we do have a shovel in the garage," her mom

said. "You could use that if you promise not to go very far."

Eva smiled and ran out the side door to the garage.

"Can I go?" Ava said, looking anxiously toward the garage, and then jammed one last spoonful of cereal in her mouth as she slipped from her chair.

The girls went off gleefully down the street, with Eva carrying a shovel approximately two inches taller than she was, and Ava carrying a hand spade.

"Where'll we look?" Ava wondered.

"In the sediment," Eva said.

"What's the sediment?"

"Dirt."

"There's dirt everywhere. How do we know which dirt we want to dig in?"

"You want dirt near a riverbed or a stream or something."

"What for?"

"Because that's where the dinosaurs fell down while they were drinking in the water and died."

"They fell down?"

"Well some of them did. I learned that in school. If dinosaurs died in a river, their bodies got covered with silt and sand and stuff from the water, and after millions of years, they were completely covered up with sediment."

"You mean dirt?"

Eva decided they should go to a spot along the stream that was farther away than where nearly anyone had gone before, so none of the kids who might go fishing or exploring would come and see them digging and then get in the way or call them buttholes. Practically anytime you did something different, someone called you a butthole. As far as Eva could tell, that was just how most people were, always ridiculing anyone who wasn't exactly the same as they were. She figured that when Alexander Graham Bell invented the phone, people made fun of him, even if they probably didn't call him a butthole. Or maybe they did and it just wasn't taught in school.

As the girls walked along one of the trails in the woods, Eva decided to explain part of her knowledge of dinosaurs to Ava.

"Do you remember in *Jurassic Park* where the *Tyrannosaurus rex* ate the lawyer?" she said.

"I didn't like that part," Ava said. "I was scared."

"Well there weren't lawyers millions of years ago, so a *Tyrannosaurus rex* wouldn't even know what they tasted like. The movie wasn't that real. All dinosaurs lived in the Mesozoic Era, and that included the Triassic Period, the Jurassic Period, and the Crustacean Period."

"Okay," Ava said.

"There were two kinds of dinosaurs—plant eaters and meat eaters. A plant eater was like *Stegosaurus*, and they ate plants. A meat eater was like *Tyrannosaurus rex*, and they ate plant eaters. Some dinosaurs weighed fifteen or twenty tons. But you couldn't weigh one. They're all dead."

"Why're they dead?"

"I don't know. They just all died one day."

"In one day?" Ava said with amazement.

"Well no one knows that. They died millions of years ago, before people even existed."

"Well then how'd *Tyrannosaurus rex* eat the lawyer?"

Eva sighed impatiently and said, "Because they brought the dinosaurs *back*, using mosquito blood. Weren't you paying attention during the movie?"

Ava shook her head no. "I had my popcorn tub over my eyes. My eyes started stinging, and then Mom took me to the bathroom to wash the salt from my eyes."

"All right. Never mind. Let's just hurry up and find a place to start digging. I think we've walked far enough."

They stood in an area near the stream that Eva regarded as a clearing. Not that anything had been cleared there. It just didn't have as many trees and weeds as every other place nearby.

"We'll dig here," Eva said.

"What for?"

"Well we don't know ahead of time where the dinosaurs died. The only way to find out is to just start digging," Eva said, tapping the metal end of her shovel experimentally into some hard dirt. There was a rustling noise in some bushes nearby, and out came Hookey, sort of prancing toward the girls to greet them, and then he walked off a little ways and began excitedly sniffing the dirt and digging there with his paws.

"*Hoo*-key!" Ava said cheerfully. "What's he digging for, Eva?"

"I don't know. Let's go look."

They walked over beside Hookey and watched as his big paws threw up an almost endless stream of dirt.

"He's digging a lot faster than we could," Eva said.

"And he doesn't even have a shovel," Ava said.

"Maybe he discovered something," Eva said.

"Probably something dead," Ava said. "I hope it doesn't stink. I get sick."

Hookey dug furiously for a little while longer, shoved the dirt around some with his nose, and then stuck his head down in the hole and began yanking at something. It was stuck.

"Get back, Hookey," Eva said, and lightly pushed the dog aside so she and Ava could look at the thing in the hole. They couldn't tell what it was. Squatting over the hole, Eva used her fingers to pull and wipe the dirt and dog saliva from the thing, which had a knobby, rounded tip and a more slender end that was still submerged sideways in the earth.

"I think it's a bone!" Eva said cheerfully.

"Is it a *dinosaur* bone?" Ava said, squatting beside Eva.

"I can't tell what kind of bone it is until we get it out. You have to dig around it. Gimme your spade."

Hookey pushed his head back down into the hole and began yanking on the bone with his teeth again.

23

"Stop it, Hookey," Eva said. "This is an archaeological bone, not a chewing bone."

She pushed Hookey away again and began scraping and hacking and pounding at the dirt surrounding their potential treasure until most of the earth had been cleared away. By holding the upper end of it in all four of their hands, they were able to yank the dark object from the ground, and then fell backward together, with Ava briefly rolling across Eva's head as Eva lay on her back with the precious grimy thing held victoriously above her in the air. Hookey grabbed the bone with his teeth and tugged at it as Eva tugged back.

"Will you *quit* it?" Eva said and pinched Hookey's nose, which caused Hookey to let go of the bone, but he still stared at it, grinning with anticipation.

The girls sat up in the dirt and studied the bone, which was so discolored and dirty that Eva took it to the edge of the stream to wash it off and get a better look at it.

"I think it's a leg bone," Eva said.

"A leg? It must've been a pretty short dinosaur," Ava said.

"It might not've even been a dinosaur. All we know is it's a bone. It could have come from anything, like a cow or a wolf or a deer. It could even be from a person," Eva said, staring somberly at the bone, then at Ava.

Ava's eyebrows rose up. "A person?"

"Of course. Lots of people lived all over the place before we came here in modern times, and they just died everywhere, like explorers and Indians and cowboys and Civil War guys and even Lewis and Clark."

"Who's Lewis and Clark?"

"They were these two explorers who went all across America in the 1800s, discovering the wilderness and killing beavers."

"So you think maybe they died here?" Ava wondered, staring fretfully at the bone in Eva's hands.

"Maybe."

The girls were silent, wondering about the bone and its meaning.

"Well is that Lewis's leg, or Clark's leg?" Ava said.

"Why would I know?"

Ava shook her head. "How do you know what kind of bone it is?"

"Well I don't. I'm not a bone scientist."

"Do you think it could still be a dinosaur bone?"

"I think so, but probably a real short dinosaur."

"What should we do with it?"

This hadn't occurred to Eva, that if they found a bone, they'd have to do something with it. "Well," she said, "we could take it to a museum and ask someone there what it is. I bet Mom or Dad would take us."

"What if it's Lewis's or Clark's leg?"

"Well," Eva said, thinking, "if Lewis or Clark died here, and somebody buried him, they wouldn't bury just one of his legs. People don't bury you one leg at a time. So it's probably not a person."

"I'm glad. I want it to be a dinosaur bone," Ava said happily. "Will we be on TV if it's a dinosaur bone?"

"Probably. Last night they had a man on TV just because he grew two tomatoes that were grown together and looked like Siamese twins."

c·h·a·p·t·e·r

6

The museum in Dallas was so gigantic and old-looking that to Eva it resembled some fantastic piece of ancient history itself, as if the building couldn't have been built in the twentieth century but was magically retrieved from the far-away past and crunched down in its present spot in the downtown. Eva's mom knew some guy at the museum who knew the head guy at the museum, so Eva and Ava and their mom all went inside the museum, which was almost as tall as the outdoors and had a gigantic skeleton of a *Tyrannosaurus rex* just standing up right in the middle of the room when you walked in, like it could kill everybody there, except it was just bones. But pretty *mean*-looking bones. Ava was afraid of the skeleton, so Eva said, "It can't hurt you. Unless the bones fall on you."

They had an appointment with Mr. Gobb, who was a paleontologist. Eva took her dirty bone into Mr. Gobb's old office filled with drawings and color posters of dinosaurs Eva had never seen before.

"This is it," Eva said, and handed the dirty bone to Mr. Gobb at his desk. Everyone smiled as Mr. Gobb put his glasses on and looked at the bone.

"Where did you find this?" he asked.

"Out in the woods by our house," Eva said.

Mr. Gobb looked very seriously at Eva, then at Eva's mom. He stared back down at the dirty bone in his hands and said, "This isn't a dinosaur bone. It's a human bone."

"Good Lord," Eva's mom said.

"It looks reasonably old. Not ancient. But fairly old," Mr. Gobb said as he moved the bone around to stare at it from every angle. "I can run some tests on it myself, but I'll have to get some other people involved in it, in case the bone has some archaeological significance. And if the bone isn't quite as old as it looks, we'll contact the police."

"Do you think someone was *murdered*?" Eva's mom said.

"I see that as a slight possibility. But the bone could have any number of explanations. It could be from an old cowboy or settler or an Indian. We'll know more after we examine it better."

"Could it be from Lewis and Clark?" Ava said.

"Not from both of them," Mr. Gobb said, smiling. "Actually, I don't know if Lewis and Clark ever went through Texas. Maybe Lewis and Martin did."

"Who's that?" Eva said.

"Jerry Lewis and Dean Martin," Mr. Gobb said. "They were in the movies. But anyway, I'll get things started here, and we'll need your phone number, Ms. Galt, so we can have some people go out to the spot where the girls found this bone, in case there are other skeletal remains there to be examined."

"Skeletons?" Eva said, starting to feel scared.

"Yes. Bones usually don't get buried one at a time."

Eva was a little bit dizzy, realizing the dirty bone she'd held in her hands was from a person. Bone hunting wasn't so much fun then.

The bone men had on hiking boots and blue jeans and T-shirts, dressed just like boys, even though they were archaeologists. They had shovels and backpacks filled with tools that sometimes clanked into each other as they walked along through the woods with Eva and Ava and their mom to the exact spot where Eva and Ava found the bone. The girls and their mom stood by while the two men slowly and carefully dug through the earth, almost as if the skeleton might whimper if you hit it.

"Here it is," one of the men said as he scraped away some dirt and found the first knobby part of one more bone. The men worked even slower then, digging away with little spades and chisels, uncovering more and more of the bones in slow motion, until Eva's mom said she and the girls would go back home while the men finished their digging.

"Can't we watch?" Eva said.

"I don't think we really need to see that poor person uncovered," Eva's mom said, and it seemed like she was right. Finding a dinosaur skeleton would have been fun, but finding a real human skeleton was just sad and frightening to Eva.

"Is it Lewis and Martin?" Ava asked as they walked back home.

"We don't know yet," Eva said.

Mr. Gobb called Eva's mom the next day and told her everything he knew. It was on the TV news and in the newspaper, which meant that Eva and Ava and their mom's names were on TV and in the paper, too, like Eva and Ava were famous discoverers. Except nobody interviewed them. They just interviewed Mr. Gobb and the other guys and found out that the skeleton was from a man who had a big hole in his skull that probably killed him. They were using some kind of scientific tests and dental records to find out how old the skeleton was and who it was, but they didn't know who it was. They only guessed that it was a man in his forties who was killed in the 1920s. He was probably murdered with some big object, like a rock or something that caved his skull in. And then somebody buried him until Eva and Ava found him. So it wasn't archaeology anymore. It was evil.

Someone also started a rumor that got in the paper, saying the police found a pentagram marked on the ground beside where the skeleton was found. The police chief said it wasn't true, but no one believed him.

Having considered all of that, Eva went into the bathroom to wash her hands over and over, trying to get the dead man off her hands. She was afraid the skeleton would come to her, or that satanists would know where she was because she touched the dead man's bone, and they'd find her. Her mom and her dad sat down on the couch in the living room with Eva sitting between them as Eva held her hands in front of her and stared at them, as if they weren't clean enough.

"Nothing will happen to you. I promise," Eva's mom said.

Eva stared at her fingers and the palms of her hands. "Will the dead man leave me?" she said.

"He's gone," Eva's dad said. He raised Eva's hands up and bent over to kiss both of her hands. "Your hands are clean, Eva. You're safe. There is no danger to you at all."

"What about the pentagram?" Eva said.

"That's all make-believe and foolishness," her dad said. "A pentagram is just a five-sided star. You'll find dozens of pentagrams in the sidewalk on Hollywood Boulevard, related to no one more satanic than Groucho Marx."

Eva seemed slightly less anxious.

"It's just a star, Eva, like the star of Bethlehem, which some people say wasn't really a star but was possibly a meteor or a comet or maybe one of the larger planets in the solar system aligned in an unusually rare position visible above Palestine in . . ."

"Get to the point," Eva's mom said.

"Yes. Excuse me," Eva's dad said. "A pentagram, Eva, is a completely powerless geometric figure, also called a pentacle, which sounds like 'tentacle.' "

"And 'testicle,' " Ava said. No one knew why. But it took everyone's minds off of pentagrams.

c·h·a·p·t·e·r

7

Kenlow Schindler had drawn a pentagram on the back of his hand so he'd never again start to draw a hexagram by mistake. The mistake could've screwed up his campaign of urban terrorism that very first night in that old woman's barn. After going to the trouble of carrying a dead and nauseating raccoon into the barn and putting it in a fire like a satanic burnt offering, he used a stick to draw a pentagram in the dirt around the fire. While admiring his work, he realized he'd drawn a Star of David. He quickly scratched that out and drew what he believed was a pentagram, then couldn't be sure which was which. He spent most of the next day anxiously waiting for a TV news report to see if some stupid reporter would announce that satanists had drawn a hexagram in the barn. He was thoroughly relieved to see that he'd drawn the right thing. The sense of fear that this created in Waxahachie finally made Kenlow feel that he'd had some effect on the world.

So he was angry and disappointed that the police chief said there was no pentagram drawn in the dirt where they found that skeleton. In fact, Kenlow had put one there after the bones were discovered. The spot was described in a newspaper story, and it would have been the most perfect place yet to have a pentagram, next to the skeleton of some murdered man. But then the damn police chief denied it all. Even so, if the police chief was afraid of how the public might react to one more pentagram, then Kenlow had real power. That was new.

Actually, they had no idea who he was. He was anonymous. He'd always been anonymous, just an ordinary boy who couldn't play football or do anything that might make him seem valuable and desirable to anyone at all. What made it more unbearable was being the son of a minister. People always assumed that because his dad was a minister, Kenlow would be some kind of a religious fanatic, so most people avoided him. But now he could go to school or hang out with his friends or go to church and get almost anyone to talk about the suspected satanists in town, knowing at last that he'd achieved for himself an identity that everyone knew about. Not that he wanted to *be* a satanist. He didn't think what he was doing was evil—just a kind of joke. In fact, every time he went somewhere to leave behind another pentagram, he always got scared and looked around in the dark to see if a real satanist might be walking up behind him to punish him for being an imposter.

But it was a pretty good joke, he thought. He, one guy, could affect the entire town by drawing some stupid star in the dirt. And then he'd be in church the next Sunday listening to his own father condemn the satanists in a sermon. It was a bit frightening, thinking how his father might react if he found out what Kenlow was doing, and it was satisfying. The problem was, if anyone *did* find out, he might get arrested. So he had to enjoy his bad reputation without anyone else knowing it was his. But being an unknown satanist was better than being an arrested one.

That night he returned to the woods. The archaeologists had laid out a grid of strings around the site. Kenlow figured they were looking for more skeletons. He wore all black, including a black ski mask pulled down over his face. It was uncomfortable, because Waxahachie got pretty hot in the summer, but he didn't want to be identified by anyone. He put black electrical tape over the front two thirds of a flashlight so only a small amount of light would help him find his way through the bushes and trees, and so no one else was likely to see the light.

Kenlow carried with him an empty Miracle Whip jar partially filled with chicken blood and giblets. There hadn't been enough chicken blood in the chicken his mom fried for dinner earlier that night, so Kenlow added the giblets. In case that might not seem satanic enough, he also added the contents of a small can of pork brains he'd bought at the store. It seemed pretty strange to him that you could use fairly ordinary human food to make people think of satanists. Still it seemed effective, and when Kenlow arrived at the spot where the archaeologists had been digging, he quietly set about gouging a huge pentagram in the dirt. First, though, he checked the drawing of a pentagram on the back of his hand.

In the humid, warm darkness, Alfredo Santayana sat on the front porch of his abandoned home, with only a single candle burning to provide light and attract the various large bugs that kept biting and fluttering near him. He was watching a small light in the woods. It was about two hundred yards away. Sometimes the light moved, but only a few feet, as if whoever was carrying the light was moving it only a little bit. He wondered if it might be the same people he'd seen digging around some spot for a few days. He didn't know who the men were, but he'd snuck near them one afternoon and peeked at them from some bushes. The men were digging up something very slowly and carefully, like the foreigners Alfredo had sometimes seen digging for Mayan relics and bones in Guatemala. It was strange how people acted as if cemeteries should never be disturbed, but then they'd go and dig up ancient burial sites and yank the bones out for public display.

Alfredo thought it was too late in the day for archaeologists to be there, so he worried that it was border police looking for him, even though he wasn't anywhere near the border. He blew out his candle and noticed that, even without light, the flying bugs still found him and bit him. His eyes grew accustomed to the dark, and he could still see the distant light. Whoever it was hadn't moved toward him. He had to know who it was, in case it was someone looking for him. He decided it couldn't be a normal American, because what normal American would give up the comfort of their home to be outside with flying, biting bugs? For that reason, Alfredo suspected it might be another illegal like himself, an illegal looking for a place to hide. If it *was* an illegal, Alfredo planned to tell him to get the hell out and to find his own woods. He said quietly to himself, ''These are *my* woods. This is *my* abandoned house. Go live uncomfortably somewhere else.''

Walking as silently as he knew how, Alfredo snuck up behind a big tree just about twenty feet from where he saw the flashlight on the ground, its little stream of light pointing at some man using a big stick to scrape in the dirt. The man was on his knees, dressed all in black, with a black thing pulled down over his face. He looked evil, like in some American movies Alfredo had seen on TV where people called ninjas ran around all in black, kicking the shit out of everyone. The idea that he'd discovered a ninja in the dark scared Alfredo. He was afraid to leave, afraid to move at all, since any slight noise might alert the ninja, who could shove a spear or a sword through Alfredo's stomach and then do a backflip.

Alfredo remained completely still, forcing himself to breathe slower, more quietly, as he watched the ninja scraping the dirt with his stick. The ninja had made a very big design in the dirt, like a star. Alfredo had never seen such a star, but surely it had some horrible meaning. Ninjas never did anything that wasn't horrible.

Feeling fear and sweat all over his body, Alfredo watched from behind the tree as the ninja picked up a glass jar. He opened the jar and poured some gooey red stuff inside the center of the star. It looked like blood and animal flesh. Maybe it was from someone the ninja had killed. Alfredo suddenly felt nauseated and horrified, imagining his own flesh being poured in the middle of the star. He wobbled dizzily and lost his balance behind the tree. As he stumbled backward, he grabbed onto a small limb, which broke free with a loud crack. Alfredo fell to the ground with the limb in his hand. Instantly he stood back up, violently swishing the limb back and forth in front of him to keep the ninja away and yelled, in Spanish, "Stay back, you devil!"

Kenlow heard the crack just as he was appreciating the grossness of his giblets and pork brains and chicken blood inside the pentagram. Something that sounded like a large animal landed on the ground nearby. He reached frantically for the flashlight to see what was happening, but with the tape over its lens, he could barely see anything—then he saw in the distance an upright figure with a grotesque arm slashing toward him. The figure yelled something in what sounded like Spanish. Satan!

He grabbed his jar and the flashlight and took off running faster than he'd ever known was possible, running as nimbly through the dark as a deer being chased by a grizzly, so overcome with fear and adrenaline that it seemed he might soon be airborne.

Standing by the tree in the quiet night, Alfredo remained still, feeling his heart slowing down again. He held the limb tightly, thinking the ninja could unexpectedly jump through the sky at any moment and do two or three somersaults before landing directly in front of Alfredo with a sword to cut his head off. But there was no sound. No movement, except a big, flying bug that landed on his nose. He brushed the bug away with his hand and began walking back to the safety and comfort of his uncomfortable home.

God had spared him. Or possibly the Virgin Mary. It could have been Jesus. Or a patron saint or a guardian angel. Possibly *all* of them had spared him, all gathered around him in the dark. The night was getting very crowded.

Ever since the apocalyptic Waco cult shootout in which the minions of Satan succumbed in a fiery battle against the Kingdom of God and the Bureau of Alcohol, Tobacco, and Firearms, Rev. Kyle Schindler felt exonerated in his continuous mission to alert the world to the existence of Satan. Membership in his congregation at Christ's Unfurling Grace Church in Waxahachie had slightly increased in the last year, and he thought of it as a renaissance of spirituality that he had nine new members.

True, there were doubters and infidels, as always. But Rev. Schindler believed that would soon change, especially now that he had one more newspaper story providing worldly proof that Satan was more active than ever. He cut the story out of the paper with scissors and reread the first part of it.

State archaeologists digging in Waxahachie near the site where a skeleton was found last week said they discovered a large pentagram carved into the dirt near the excavations Wednesday morning.

The archaeologists said there appeared to be fresh blood and mangled animal flesh poured into the middle of the pentagram.

Waxahachie police chief James McLemore said police evidence technicians recovered some of the blood and flesh to have it analyzed.

"Right now we can't say much about who might have done this pentagram business," McLemore said. "We have no suspects and can't even call it a crime, really. And preliminary reports from the police lab say that the blood was chicken blood and the small amount of flesh appeared to be chicken giblets and pork brains.

"So if it was satanists who did this, it appears that their black mass was made possible by the existence of grocery stores," McLemore said.

Rev. Schindler refused to accept the grocery store theory. Surely the police would lie to avoid panicking the public with factual evidence of the real and looming existence of Satan.

He put the story in his manila envelope that held all the other recent stories about satanists in town and put a piece of typing paper in his typewriter to make some notes for his next sermon.

1. Why Satan might make his presence known through pork brains
2. Theological evidence of Satan as regards grocery stores
3. Pentagrams, geometry, Euclid, the square root of evil
4. The end of the world has been imminent for thousands of years

He scratched out number 4. That was one of the parts of the Bible that he secretly wondered about. Thousands of years ago, the earliest prophets announced that the world would end soon. So it sometimes seemed a bit distressing that the world still existed. And that itself could be shocking—to have the faithful hope that the world would end and then to seem disappointed that, unfortunately, the world kept existing.

Thus it was possible for Rev. Schindler to feel awful either way.

He shook his head, as if to dislodge his sinful doubts, as if to knock some sense *out* of himself.

"The wisdom of man is foolishness unto God," he said, which was the Scripture he always used when he wanted to suggest to someone that trying to make sense was ungodly. But the problem *there* was that he was using Scripture to sensibly argue that being sensible was a waste of time . . . as if humans were given reason in order to understand the uselessness of reason.

He shook his head again, trying to fling all reason from his head.

Then he resumed typing his sermon notes.

4. Satan and the apocalypse, as manifested in giblets

Looking at that made him think that sometimes his ideas were too mystical, too disturbing. But the world was plainly a battleground between God and Satan. That was necessarily disturbing, and it did no good to ignore it.

He heard the front door open, and he got up to see who it was. It was Kenlow, and Rev. Schindler immediately felt himself frown, just looking again at Kenlow's disgraceful haircut. It was that new and reprehensible style where the hair was completely shaved off all around the sides and back of the head, while the hair on top of the head was left shaggy and uncombed. It continually distressed the reverend that his own son was trying to look like a social outcast. He wanted to think that the usual rebelliousness of teenagers could somehow be avoided here in a Christian household. But the haircut and the baggy jeans with the knees worn out were just a standard uniform for teenagers now. Rev. Schindler knew it was superficial and temporary. His son had been baptized years earlier by the Holy Spirit. And regardless of how offensive Kenlow's haircut and clothes might be, he regularly attended church and Bible classes.

He sat back down at his desk to write notes for his sermon.

Kenlow went into his room and shut the door. He sat on his bed and began looking through the book he'd just checked out from the library: *From Hindu to Voodoo: A Concise History of Religions, Cults and Fringe Groups*.

Kenlow was hoping to find useful instructions for satanic rituals that might be affordable and wouldn't require actually killing anything or becoming friends with Satan. He intended to just be a recreational satanist.

For two days Eva stayed around the house, never wandering farther than the edge of her yard. Sometimes through her bedroom window, where she could get a good view of the woods and fields, she'd look toward the approximate spot where the skeleton used to be, as if the skeleton might come walking out of the trees and stop to look up at Eva in the window.

She knew that was dumb and impossible, but sometimes the impossible didn't seem that hard. Also, she was growing up in a family where her dad was a priest, and the whole Bible was filled with stories of people doing the impossible, like the Rapture, where all the old skeletons in the whole world were supposed to come alive one day and go floating through the sky. So it didn't seem so dumb to be looking out the window for just one skeleton.

But one thing her dad had told her was that "bones is bones." He used bad English, which was funny for her father. But that was what he said. Bones is bones. He meant the skeleton couldn't do anything. It wasn't all that comforting, really, when you thought about the Rapture and all the horror movies on TV where skeletons and zombies and the people in this one movie called *The Ripe Undead* wandered all over everywhere. But her dad still tried to make her feel better about it all.

"Well think about *this*," her dad said. "Do you know where that skeleton is right now?"

"No," Eva said.

"It's in Dallas. It's probably lying in several pieces in some box in a medical examiner's office. How do you think the skeleton's going to get here? Walk? Hitchhike? Take a cab?"

"I don't think so," Eva said.

"And also, why would the skeleton be mad at you anyway? *You* didn't do anything to it. Don't you think the skeleton would know that?"

Eva raised her head up to look curiously at her dad. "But why're you talking like the skeleton would know anything?"

"I'm not using my logic anymore. I'm using yours, Eva. Pretend the skeleton *does* know something. The main thing he'd know was that he'd been hidden away for years until you found him and made it possible for the police to try and investigate the murder of the man who the skeleton used to be. So in my opinion, the skeleton would be *grateful* to you, not *mad* at you."

It did make sense, in a kind of superstitious way.

As Eva tried to be comfortable with that, her mom walked into the living room where Eva and her dad were sitting on the couch. She sat on Eva's other side and didn't look at Eva's dad as she said, "Are you still afraid of the skeleton?" Her parents did that a lot, where they'd be in the same room talking with Eva or Ava but not talking to each other, or even looking at each other. It was as if they'd stopped liking each other but agreed they'd go on being parents anyway.

"I'm a little scared," Eva said. Her mom put her arm around Eva and seemed to hug her without touching Eva's dad, like there was a rule against touching him.

"Honey, skeletons don't do anything except in the movies," her mom said.

"That's what I told her. Bones is bones," her dad said.

"Your father's right," her mom said. They never looked at each other the whole time. Eva wasn't bothered by the skeleton very much. What bothered her more was how her parents could be in the same room about three feet apart and not touch or look at each other, like they were ghosts.

In the morning, when Eva was completely convinced that the skeleton was closed up in some box in Dallas, and after she looked out in the woods to make sure the skeleton wasn't walking toward the house, she and Ava went into the woods by the most distant trail they could find, carrying with them a backpack, bologna sandwiches, a Thermos of iced tea, a shovel, and a baseball bat.

"We gonna play baseball in the woods?" Ava asked.

"No. The baseball bat's for protection," Eva said.

"You mean the skeleton? Dad said bones is bones."

"I know. It's funny when he talks that way."

"Is bones bones?" Ava said.

"Let's stop talking about bones. Except dinosaur bones."

The girls were dragging their shovel and backpack and baseball bat along one of the crisscrossing trails when Eva saw through the trees ahead of them a human figure on the front porch of the old warlock's house.

"Shhhh," Eva shushed, pointing with one finger toward the figure standing on the porch, a figure that was looking away in a different direction than where the girls were. Ava obediently remained silent as they stepped off the trail and into the invisibility of the trees and weeds. Eva peeked through the tangle of leaves and limbs to spy on whoever it was on the porch. At first the figure looked ghostlike, or demonlike, or satanic; a tall and threatening being with black hair and dark eyes scanning the woods for someone to do unspeakable evil to. But as she stared longer at the demonlike thing, she realized that it had on a green short-sleeve shirt, like you might find at Sears. There was no reason for a demon to shop at Sears.

"It's a man," she whispered. "Or maybe a boy. He looks like a Mexican. I can't tell. The trees and stuff are in the way."

"What's he doing?" Ava whispered a little anxiously, because after all, it *was* the old warlock's house, and nobody ever went into it. Nobody human, anyway.

"He's just standing there. Now he's moving around. Looking."

"What's he looking at?"

"He's just looking, like anybody who'd want to see something."

"Is it the warlock?"

"Well I don't know what a warlock looks like," Eva said. "And it's just an old house, Ava. People used to say a witch lived there and I got tired of it and said a warlock lived there. I made it up. So it doesn't mean anything. So that guy on the porch is just some guy. But I don't know what he's doing there, either."

"Should we call the police?" Ava wondered.

"What for? He isn't doing anything."

"Well if he's not doing anything, then what's he doing?" Ava said.

Sometimes Ava seemed too dumb even for a little girl.

"Let's just watch for a while and find out. But don't make any noise, and don't move."

Ava nodded her head in agreement, pushing her head next to Eva's to try to peek through the same spot Eva peeked through. They were too far away to see the man or boy's facial expressions and judge anything about him that way.

"Maybe he lives there," Eva said.

"Why would he do that?" Ava said.

"Maybe he's poor and he doesn't have any place else to live. Maybe he's an illegal alien."

"What's that?"

"It's what all those people from church were talking

about when they had dinner at our house. Let's just watch the guy and see what he does.''

What he did was walk back inside the house, and they couldn't see him anymore. They listened for noise, for any walking or creaking or thumping or screaming or the chewing noise you'd expect to hear when someone was being eaten. But they couldn't hear anything at all.

"You think the warlock killed him?" Ava said.

"No. I think being killed makes more noise than that. Anyway, nothing's happening. Let's sneak out of here and maybe come back by tomorrow and see if we can see him again. But don't tell Mom or Dad we saw him.''

"Okay. Why not?"

Eva wasn't sure. "Well, if he's illegal, maybe someone will get the police. I don't think he did anything wrong. I think he just needs a house.''

"I wouldn't live in *that* one.''

"He probably doesn't have any money.''

"Should we give him some?"

"We don't have any. Let's go. We'll spy on him tomorrow.''

Then Eva thought of something that made her back and shoulders tingle with fear. "What if that's the guy who killed the skeleton?''

It seemed so sensible. An unknown man would have killed an unknown skeleton in the woods where the man and the skeleton secretly lived.

"You can kill a skeleton?" Ava said.

"I don't mean that. I mean it was a man that got killed and turned into a skeleton,'' Eva said. "Anyway, I guess he's too young,'' Eva said. "If he killed some man in the 1920s, he'd be an old man now.''

It was strange how quickly you could pass from mortal danger to safety just by realizing something. It was like you could change reality simply by having a thought. And of course, you could. You didn't change all of reality, but you changed the little part *you* were in. And now that the man suddenly wasn't a murderer, the girls could safely peek at the house and wonder if the man was just a demon or an illegal alien.

"Is he evil?" Ava said.

"Dad says evil is in the heart," Eva said.

"I thought blood was in the heart."

"That too."

Eva stared at the frightful, deteriorating old house the man was in and said, "I don't think he's evil. I think he just lives in a bad neighborhood."

c·h·a·p·t·e·r

9

When the girls got home after discovering the man in the warlock's house, they saw their mom in her downstairs office watching the noon TV news, which showed this woman who said she saw the image of the Virgin Mary in a post office stamp-vending machine in Waxahachie. There was a TV camera down at the post office with a pretty big crowd standing around trying to get on TV, not because they'd done anything or cared about the Virgin Mary, but just because they wanted to be on TV. The camera showed a close-up view of the front of the stamp machine with a woman pointing her finger right at some blurry spot on its glass front, which looked like it could maybe be the shape of *some*thing, maybe even a woman's head, although to Eva it was too blurry to really look like any particular person.

"There she is. Right there. With her hands in front of her in prayer," the woman on TV said.

Ava stared at the TV and said, "I don't see her hands."

"Who's the Virgin Mary?" Ava asked.

"Jesus' mother," Eva said, then looked at her mom and said, "Can we go to the post office and look, Mom?"

"Why would Jesus' mother be in the post office?" Ava said.

"I honestly don't think she *would* be," their mom said. "I have no idea what's going on at the post office, but I find it hard to look at a piece of discolored glass on a stamp vending machine and think it's a religious miracle."

"Can we go look?" Eva said again. "We won't do anything. We'll just look."

"Well I suppose that'd be fine," their mom said. "In fact maybe I'll take a break here from working on this stupid report and go to the post office with you. I've never seen a religious miracle before. I'm sure your father would like all of us to see one of those."

They all got in the car and drove down to the post office, which already was crowded with cars and pedestrians who'd obviously heard of the miraculous vending machine. Their mom had to park two blocks away. The girls and their mom nudged and delicately shoved their way through the noisy crowd inside the post office. There seemed to be a mood of cheerfulness and expectation that sort of reminded Eva of the time she'd waited in line to look at the two-headed goat at the carnival. She couldn't see anything right away because most of the people in the post office were adults who were too tall or too wide to allow Eva any glimpse of the vending machine, but she held on to Ava's hand behind her and used her elbows and sometimes her head to squeeze past people and gently bump them out of the way until she had moved right up within two or three feet of it. All around her, adults were saying how they either saw the Virgin Mary or didn't see her, or how they saw some stupid dark spot in the glass that was maybe just bad glass but not any miracle.

Eva and Ava had pushed up to the very front of the crowd, so close to the stamp machine that everyone pushing each other behind the girls could have smashed them right through the Virgin Mary. There was a pale dark spot on the glass, a dark spot that looked kind of blue, and it really did have the shape of what could be seen as a person's head, with maybe this small area in the middle of the dark spot that looked like eyes, if you wanted to imagine eyes.

"Is that the Virgin Mary?" Ava asked. Eva stared at it and said, "I don't know if it's anybody."

Some man right behind them said, "Well there certainly is a miracle here today. It's a miracle we got the whole town in the post office at the same time," and some other people laughed. That's when Eva looked behind and all around her, to see what kind of adults would come to look at a miracle in the post office. There was a little bit of everybody there: Mexicans, Anglos, farmers, cowboys, teenagers, and old people.

Eva looked at the dark spot in the glass some more, trying to think of who it might resemble, who in the holiness of ancient figures it looked like, and the only thing she could think of was it looked a little bit like an eggplant. That probably wasn't a religious miracle. She was puzzled why God might choose to reveal some mysterious religious secret by putting a stain on a stamp machine. Eva experimented with her eyelids and held them almost completely closed to see what the stain would look like that way.

"It looks like Sugarloaf Mountain," Eva said to Ava.

"What's that?" a tall man behind her asked.

"It's this big mountain in Brazil," Eva said, a little embarrassed that anyone heard her, and also embarrassed because just to her right a man and a woman were kneeling in front of the stamp machine and clasping their hands in prayer. Eva had never seen anyone pray to a vending machine before.

Farther back in the jumbled, crushing crowd, a woman screamed, and another woman yelled, "She fainted! Somebody call an ambulance!"

The crowd started moving around and shoving and pushing.

"We better get outa here, before we get smashed," Eva said, taking Ava's hand and squeezing sideways along the wall past the crowd and right by the big, fallen woman, who was lying on the floor in another woman's lap. Some man was using some letters in his hand to fan the fallen woman's face. At the back of the crowd they found their mom, who smiled at them a bit anxiously and said, "It's time to leave, girls. This miracle's getting a little too crowded. Did you get to see it?"

"I think so," Ava said. "There was something on the glass."

"Did it look like a face?"

"No," Eva said. "It looked like someone forgot to clean the glass."

Right through the front door then came a group of men and women carrying big video cameras and microphones that had the abbreviation CNN on them. They aimed a camera at the big fallen woman on the floor for a while, then made their way up to the stamp machine and started aiming the camera there and trying to interview people.

"Wow. We're gonna be on TV!" Eva said gleefully. A woman with a camera and another woman with a microphone stood beside their mom and asked her if she'd seen the image of the Virgin Mary in the stamp machine.

"I haven't attempted to get through the crowd," she said. "But you might want to ask my daughters here. They were both up there."

They swung the camera down at Eva and Ava, and the woman with the microphone said to Eva, "When you looked at the glass on the vending machine, did anything there look to you like the image of the Virgin Mary?"

"No, ma'am," Eva said. "But if you squint your eyes, it looks like Sugarloaf Mountain, in Brazil."

Daniel Galt walked up to the pulpit in his splendid white surplice and placed his sermon next to the Bible there and gazed pleasantly at every aisle and every row, trying to glance at least briefly at every face out there. His gaze lingered at last on the faces of Emily and Eva and Ava before he looked down at his sermon. Eva was daydreaming, but nearly everyone else was attentive and silent, as if this one man standing before them, this mere priest, was on the verge of telling them the only things worth hearing in their entire lives. That sense of power always bewildered and sometimes amused Daniel, as if no matter what he said next, it would seem spiritual and wise, just because he was a priest. It occurred to him that he could begin reading aloud the list of ingredients on a box of Coco Puffs, and at least for a few seconds, people would tell themselves it was somehow spiritual.

Pausing a little bit longer, he studied the first sentence in his sermon, then began.

"Lo and behold, there came unto the people a sign of the Lord at the post office. And the people did go unto the post office and look at the image of the Virgin Mary, and so they kneeled and did pray before the vending machine," Daniel said, and then stopped, looking into the congregation for any expressions of surprise or disbelief. And there were many.

"I think we all know what I'm talking about," Daniel continued. "We appear to have a religious miracle of sorts at the post office. Most of us have probably never seen or experienced anything we'd call a miracle, although if you've been reading your Bibles as conscientiously as I imagine you often don't care to do, you're aware of dozens of accounts of miracles, such as the creation of life, the parting of the Red Sea, the day Jesus walked on water, and the resurrection of Christ. In fact, the Jewish religion and the Christian religion are largely founded on the shared belief in a God who can provide us with miracles. Some of the miracles are wondrous, such as raising the dead. Some of the miracles are threatening, such as the destruction of Sodom and Gomorrah. And some of the miracles are at the very least—" and he paused there, tapping his finger on his chin, and then said "—curious."

He allowed everyone another moment of silence to adjust to his ideas or defend against them.

"Frankly," he said, "I thought that as a priest, I should certainly go down to the post office and personally examine the glass on the stamp-vending machine to see if there really was a likeness of the Virgin Mary there. And I did go and look at it. I admit that I went there with a skeptical attitude, doubting that I'd see anything I'd genuinely describe as a miracle. But the fact that I *went* there implied a willingness to accept a miracle.''

To add suspense and tension, Daniel paused once more.

''Well, did you *see* one?'' an old woman in the front row called out impatiently, and almost everyone started laughing. That was one of Daniel's favorite parts in a sermon, when people laughed. He waited for the laughter to die away on its own and be replaced again by the unnatural silence.

''Well I'll tell you what I did see,'' he said. ''After spending maybe ten minutes trying to delicately and politely shove my way through the huge crowd at the post office, I stood about two feet away from the stamp machine that all the religious pilgrims had come to see. I looked at it. What I saw in the glass was a sort of bluish, purplish splotch about three inches tall and wide. The splotch was formed in the shape of what could be described as a human head, with either dark, long hair, or perhaps with a shawl over the head. Within the splotch were lighter areas that could resemble, if you cared for them to, the eyes and nose of a human. Well . . . after studying the figure in the glass for about a minute, I came to a convincing conclusion.''

That was a good time to pause again, and he did, making everyone in the congregation squirm and fidget and struggle to refrain from yelling out ''What!?''

''My convincing conclusion,'' Daniel said, ''was that there indeed *was* a sort of bluish, purplish splotch in the glass. Furthermore,'' he said in a slightly louder voice as he firmly grasped both sides of the pulpit and stared across every part of the crowd, ''I had to admit to myself that if you wanted the splotch to resemble the face of the Virgin Mary, than that's who it could resemble. And from that moment on, I *knew* what we had,'' he said, and pounded his left fist into the palm of his right hand as the congregation waited for his urgent revelation. ''We had a highly

49

adaptable splotch. A multipurpose splotch. A splotch for all seasons.

"But I refrain from calling it a miraculous splotch."

You could hear a lot of people sighing and mumbling.

"Don't be disappointed," Daniel said. "Every human in the world is free to go to the post office, shove people out of their way, and assign absolutely any meaning they want to that dark spot on the stamp machine glass. If you want to find evidence of God in a piece of discolored glass, that's your freedom. And I'm not saying it *isn't* a miracle. I have no access to the recent inventory of God's miracles. I don't pretend that my intellect is sufficient to unquestionably identify the presence or absence of the supernatural in our daily lives. But I will say *this* . . ." he said, introducing another deliberately maddening pause. "If God possesses all of the limitless power and ability that we like to believe he does, I think that if he were going to provide us with a miraculous likeness of the Virgin Mary, then you'd have to look at that splotch and say, 'I think God can draw better than that.' "

Eva thought her dad was pretty funny, and it thrilled her to hear most of the other people in church laughing at his joke. He seemed to be so good at giving sermons and explaining religious things and helping people in that part of their lives. But it still puzzled Eva that while her dad could be so good at helping maybe a few hundred people in church with the huge mysteries of religion, he couldn't help himself. Eva didn't even know what the real problem was because her parents wouldn't explain it all to Eva, as if it were too complicated or too private. All her mom said one time was that sometimes men and women are just incompatible, and that was all she'd say. Eva thought *incompatible* meant you couldn't pat. That didn't make any sense, and she looked up *incompatible* in the dictionary in her room and found out her parents were not capable of blending or agreeing or achieving harmony.

It was so distressing, anyway, and it sometimes made Eva feel overrun with sadness when she thought how her dad could have everyone in the congregation pray for peace or understanding or salvation, like that was a pretty ordinary trick to do for hundreds of people at a time; but he couldn't just once pray in church to be compatible with Eva's mom. It made it seem like you were more likely to save the world than fix a marriage.

Still, Eva prayed to Ted Williams for her parents, in case they weren't praying for themselves.

c·h·a·p·t·e·r

10

The next morning Eva made a list of things she could do:

1. Play baseball
2. Ride my bike
3. Go look for an illegal alien

Looking for an illegal alien had the greatest appeal, and Eva and Ava got their usual provisions of sandwiches and iced tea, then walked off into the woods with a shovel so it would look like they were just going out on another dinosaur bone hunt. But an illegal alien seemed more exotic than dinosaur bones because it involved a living person who was somehow against the law.

The girls didn't even pretend to look for the best spots to find dinosaur bones. They walked straight toward the old warlock's house. When they got near the house, they stepped off the trail and hid behind a tree to peek at the house, and there he was. He sat on the front porch eating something that looked like a sandwich or some bread or something. When they'd seen him before, it always looked like he was hiding, but now he sat right there in plain view on the front porch. From behind the trees, the girls watched him for a while, the way you'd watch a wild animal or an escaped convict, as if he might see the girls and attack them, although Eva couldn't think of a real reason why he'd do that, except there had to be something pretty strange or maybe dangerous about someone who'd live in an abandoned house. Except maybe he just didn't have a home, and that was it. Maybe he was an illegal alien, and he had to hide so no one would send him back to Mexico.

"I think the INS is looking for him," Eva whispered.

"What's the INS?" Ava whispered.

"I don't know," Eva whispered. "I heard it on TV."

That seemed to explain it, and the girls continued spying on the man. He had something in his mouth and he was chewing it. It appeared that he was looking at some birds or looking at the trees or just doing what anybody would do on a front porch, which was nothing, really. After he quit chewing it, he stood up and went inside the broken front door, inside where it was dark and unknown, where Eva still imagined there could be ghosts or demons or something satanic, because that's what everybody always said about abandoned houses. But if Satan, who wasn't supposed to exist, lived in an abandoned house, he must not have been very magical if he had to live with broken windows and a rotten ceiling and no electricity or plumbing—it was as if Satan had the power to steal your soul but couldn't fix a broken window. So maybe it *was* just an old house.

Eva listened for howling or other satanic noises and didn't hear any. The man came back out onto the porch with a guitar and sat down at the steps and started playing the guitar. He wasn't very good. He kept missing a lot of notes, and played clumsily. When he sang, you couldn't understand what he was singing.

"What's he singing?" Ava whispered.

"It's in Spanish. I don't know Spanish," Eva whispered.

"Then how do you know it's Spanish?"

"Because I've heard Spanish before, and I didn't understand it then, either," Eva whispered. "It's the same way

Mr. Guerra talks when he talks to Mexicans at the drug-store.''

The man sang some unintelligible song pretty badly, only he didn't act like he knew it was bad. He smiled. Eva thought it was astonishing that anyone could have such a bad life and still smile. Either he was too stupid to feel bad, or he had reasons to feel good that no one knew about, which was probably true of everybody. They listened to him sing badly for a while, and smile with no reason, and then Ava whispered, ''What should we do?''

''I don't know,'' Eva whispered back. ''He looks kind of like a nice man. I don't think he's a criminal or any-thing.''

''He doesn't sing very good.''

''Well he won't get arrested for that.''

''I know.''

''Maybe we should talk to him,'' Eva suggested. ''If he's hungry or needs water or something, we could get it for him.''

Ava stared uncertainly at Eva and said, ''What if he's bad?''

''Then I'll hit him with the shovel,'' Eva said. ''I'll hit him between the legs. Mom said that hurts a man the most.''

''Not me,'' Ava said. ''It hurts me the most when I hit my elbow.''

''Okay. I'll hold the shovel in front of me with both hands, so he'll see we're ready to hurt him,'' Eva said. ''And then we'll walk out in the open a little bit so he can see us, and then we'll say hi, and see what he does.''

''Okay.''

Holding the shovel sideways in front of her, Eva walked around the trees and out into the open, with Ava behind her holding the Thermos. Right away the man stopped play-ing guitar and stared at the girls. He was young and thin, like he didn't eat very much. Everything about him looked neglected. He wore an ugly brown shirt that possibly got some of its color from not being washed. The shirt looked too little, and his gray pants looked too big. In his dark eyes, Eva thought she saw that he was afraid.

"Hi," Eva said. The man didn't speak. He stayed exactly as he was, the way a possum pretended it couldn't move. Maybe he didn't know English, so Eva tried to say hello in Spanish.

"Allô," she said, and then remembered that was French. The man remained silent.

"What'd you say to him?" Ava asked.

"I accidentally said hello in French."

"You mean he's French?"

"No. I just can't remember how to say hello in Spanish."

The man didn't make any threatening moves. He didn't move at all. It looked like he just wished the girls would go away. Eva took the Thermos from Ava and held it in front of her.

"Do you want some iced tea?" she said.

The man's eyes moved only enough to stare at both girls carefully, and wonder about the Thermos.

"Iced tea," Eva said. She held the Thermos up to her mouth and made a gulping sound. *"Gu, gu, gu, gu, gu."*

Something in the man's eyes looked a little less suspicious then, as if he understood there was something to drink and maybe he was interested. He said something in Spanish.

"What'd he say?" Ava said.

"I don't know," Eva said.

The man spoke again, and lightly gestured with his right hand, but there was no way to know what he meant.

"Okay," Eva said to Ava. "I'm gonna go up to him with the tea and give him some. If he tries anything, you run up to him with the shovel and hit him between the legs real hard. Okay?"

"Okay," Ava said, taking the shovel from Eva and holding its blade in front of her. "After I hit him between the legs, do I say 'excuse me'?"

"Don't be dumb," Eva whispered. She then walked toward the man, thinking he was too skinny to do much. He wasn't much bigger than she was. His expression was kind of somber and curious as Eva approached, like everybody was doing a ritual that no one knew anything about, so it was equally strange to all of them. He didn't look evil. He just looked like a skinny man who was lonesome and thirsty. Eva had the odd thought that this was what religion was all about—giving iced tea to strangers. She prayed: *Dear Ted Williams, make him be a nice man.* And as she got right up to the man, where he could hit her on the head with his guitar and Ava would have to be brave enough to ram him between the legs with the shovel, where all evil and horror would be alive, Eva unscrewed the lid on the Thermos and held it out to him.

"It's got sugar in it," she said, even though the man couldn't possibly understand that. So, in case he understood shorter sentences, Eva said, "It's sweet."

The man took the Thermos, being careful not to touch Eva's fingers or look in her eyes, as if maybe he was ashamed of this kindness but he wanted it anyway. He held the Thermos to his mouth and took a big drink, spilling a little bit of tea around the corners of his mouth and onto his dirty shirt. He smiled at Eva and also smiled down at Ava, who stood at the base of the steps ready to ram the blade of the shovel into him. The man nodded his head up and down.

"You like it?" Eva said.

"*No inglés,*" the man said quietly, and drank some more tea.

"He likes it," Ava said. "I guess I don't have to hit him with the shovel."

The man said something in Spanish.

"I'm sorry. No Spanish," Eva said.

"I don't have any Spanish, either," Ava said, since she didn't want to be left out of the conversation that none of them could have. The man handed the Thermos back to Eva and seemed to be thanking her, or saying something else pleasant, in a rapid and totally incomprehensible voice.

Eva looked at Ava and said, "It's like listening to a cowboy movie where they have real Mexicans and you never know what they're saying."

"How come he keeps talking if we don't know what he's saying?" Ava asked.

"I guess it's the same reason *we* keep talking when *he* doesn't know what we're saying."

The man pointed at himself and said, "Alfredo Santayana."

"I think he knows his name," Ava said.

Eva pointed at herself and said, "Eva Galt."

Ava touched her finger to her chest and said, "Ava Galt."

They all smiled at each other, as if just saying their names was the greatest possible success, and maybe it was. Because from that point on, neither side could say anything that the other side would understand.

Eva tried to think of something simple to say, as if by being simple and brief and talking slowly, like you would to a very young child, Alfredo would understand English.

"Do . . . you . . . live . . . here?" Eva said.

Alfredo had a puzzled expression and said something back, but of course only he understood it. He shook his head apologetically and added, *"No inglés."*

"Food," Eva said. She put her fingers to her mouth and opened and closed her mouth as if chewing. Then she pointed at Alfredo and said, "Food? You want food?"

Alfredo looked a little more confused and thoughtful. He said something and put his guitar on the porch and got up to go into the dark and unhappy-looking house.

"What's he doing?" Ava whispered.

"I don't know," Eva said. "I think he went to get something."

They heard him walking back across the creaking old floor of the house, and when Alfredo stepped through the doorway, he had a big bag of Fritos. He smiled and held the bag out to the girls.

"Food?" Alfredo said.

"He thinks we want food," Eva said.

"I like Fritos," Ava said.

"We're supposed to give *him* food," Eva said. "But I don't know how to say it so he'll understand."

Eva smiled and shook her head "no" at Alfredo and said, "*You* want food? Alfredo want food?"

This only continued the confusion. Alfredo looked at both girls and shrugged his shoulders, as if he didn't understand what was happening.

"Look. He did this with his shoulders," Ava said, and shrugged her shoulders. "I didn't know Mexicans did that too. Mexicans do the same things as we do. Except talk."

"Well they talk, too. We just don't know what they're saying," Eva said.

Because Eva and Ava were talking, Alfredo started talking.

"What's he saying?" Ava asked.

"He's probably saying 'What are you girls saying?'" Eva said. "This can't go on. We'll just have to say bye to him and wave bye, and then maybe bring him some food or water tomorrow without telling anyone he's here, in case he's an illegal alien. And maybe we could learn Spanish."

"Tonight?"

"It'll take longer than that."

As the girls waved good-bye and were walking away, Alfredo said something in English.

"I want to buy a vowel."

The girls stopped and looked back at Alfredo, who smiled in the friendliest way and waved at them, and then said it again: "I want to buy a vowel."

"We don't have one," Ava said.

"I think he's been watching *Wheel of Fortune*," Eva said with wonder. "And that house doesn't even have electricity."

It seemed like two religious miracles in the same week: The Virgin Mary in the post office, and this Mexican man watching TV without electricity. It made God seem more peculiar than usual.

A little while after the girls had gotten home that afternoon, having almost forgotten about Alfredo, their parents' friend Diego Guerra, the pharmacist, came by just to visit. Right away Eva realized Mr. Guerra was someone who could speak Spanish to Alfredo and find out who Alfredo was and what he was doing here and if he was an illegal alien. Eva almost ached to ask Mr. Guerra if he'd go do that, except she couldn't ask him without her parents hearing everything. It was distressing to have such a secret as Alfredo and be afraid to tell her parents. She was supposed to be able to tell them anything, except . . . now when they were hiding part of their lives from Eva and Ava, it made Eva feel that she had to hide things, too.

Alfredo wondered if the two girls would bring him back a vowel. Perhaps it would be made of silver or gold, like the chalice he saw in a cathedral one day. Sometimes he thought of it as the holy vowel. It bothered him a little bit that, because he'd never gone to school, he wasn't sure what a vowel really was. But he'd seen how highly desirable a vowel always was on *Wheel of Fortune*, and how frequently the possession of vowels resulted in new cars, so he knew there were few things on Earth as precious. And now he was in America, the land of the vowels.

As he stared absentmindedly toward the trail where the two girls had disappeared into the trees a few moments earlier, Alfredo wondered what they would bring him—a vowel or the police. He knew he should probably leave the house immediately and go somewhere else. He would have, but it had taken him a long time just to find this one abandoned house. Maybe America was the land of plenty, but it didn't have plenty of abandoned houses.

He tried remembering the faces of the two girls, and when he did, he thought they'd seemed kind. Maybe they were too kind to tell on him. And also, they were just little girls. They might not even know about illegal aliens. Maybe they'd just think he was a poor man who couldn't buy a real house, and then Alfredo would be fine. They wouldn't get the police. Still, he was nervous, and remained hidden inside the dusty, humid, stinking house that he shared with bugs and birds. Really, it made him feel like he was related to nature that way, and it wasn't so bad, except when the bugs bit him—then he didn't want to be their relatives.

While peeping out the broken window at the front of the house to see if anyone else might come by, Alfredo ate Fritos, which would be his dinner until he went to wash dishes at the Chinese restaurant in the evening. He'd get a free dinner there. He still didn't know what Chinese food was, even though he'd been eating it for several days. Chinese food had absurd names he couldn't pronounce or remember, but it tasted good. And it was free. He could afford that.

Eating the Fritos, he wondered about how the two girls seemed to be telling him they were hungry. Alfredo was happy to share his food with them, although they didn't *look* poor. Their clothes looked fairly new and clean, as if they lived in a nice home in one of the neighborhoods nearby. Maybe they *weren't* poor. But then, why would they ask for food?

Everything was a mystery. The girls were a mystery, and twice now, Alfredo had told Americans he wanted to buy a vowel, and nothing happened, as if Americans didn't know how to get on *Wheel of Fortune* either. Truthfully, Alfredo wasn't sure what was supposed to happen. Maybe you could only buy a vowel on TV. The show never explained that. In the United States, you ought to be able to buy a vowel anywhere, and your life would be better. Anything would be better than living in that hot, dusty, stinking house. He looked around him in the dark, with just enough pale sunlight sneaking into the house to reveal part of the floor and a wall. You could tell that it used to be a very nice house, long ago. It made Alfredo sad, trying to imagine a happy family who used to live there—two parents, and maybe three or four children, with nice furniture and beds and curtains on the windows and good meals cooked every day in the kitchen. Then everyone was gone. Some horrible event happened, and the whole family vanished. They just disappeared, and all the furniture and everything went with them. The house was silent, a scene of old sadness in which Alfredo now sat, like he was a part of that sadness, as well as a part of the dust and the bugs.

It worried him that the ghosts of the family who used to live there might still be in the house, and they might attack him. He glanced around uneasily through the darkness. Sometimes he'd hear the wind, or some bugs or birds, and he'd flinch and get ready to run from ghosts. But if there really were ghosts in the house and they hadn't killed him yet, maybe they were tolerant. So he spoke to them now.

"Hello, ghosts," he said, as if the ghosts were assembled in an audience. "My name is Alfredo Santayana. I'll only live here a little while, if you don't mind. I didn't steal anything from here. It was all gone when I got here. And I didn't break the front door or the windows. Somebody else did, so please don't be mad at me. I came here from Guatemala to start a new life. It hasn't started yet. That's why I'm here with bugs. I thank you for letting me stay here."

When Alfredo was through talking, the ghosts didn't say anything. Maybe they didn't know Spanish.

"Are you English-speaking ghosts?" Alfredo said, and there was no answer. Alfredo took a nap in the silence of the ghosts.

$c \cdot h \cdot a \cdot p \cdot t \cdot e \cdot r$

11

Eva's mom had bought her a *Young Person's Encyclopedic Dictionary*, and sometimes when Eva was bored, she'd skip around through it just to see what was there. Today, she started hunting for *INS* to find out which part of the government it was she might get in trouble with because of Alfredo. But she got sidetracked by a drawing of a dinosaur called an iguanodon. It looked like a real tall lizard with a sail on its back and a goofy expression on its face. She intended to look up *INS* just as soon as she looked up the New Latin root words for *iguanodon*, which happened to be *iguana* and *odon*. While she was starting to look up *odon*, she got distracted by the word *phthiriasis*, which was one of the strangest words she'd ever seen. It meant "infestation with lice, especially crab lice." So naturally she had to look up *crab lice*, and while she flipped backward through the dictionary toward *crab lice*, she came upon a little black-and-white photo of Halley's Comet from 1986. She studied that for a while before wandering on to look at pictures of a glacier, a gladiator, and a Gibson girl. She got distracted by a picture of an X ray of a dislocated thumb that went along with the word *dislocate*. The X ray made her think of the old warlock's house, which could have had skeletons in it, and when she was starting to look up *warlock*, she was distracted by a picture of a secretary bird, which was also called *Sagittarius serpentarius* and looked like an eagle walking on stilts.

"*Sagittarius serpentarius*," she said, which sounded like something a witch doctor might say. She started to look up *witch doctor* but got interested in a picture of a spiny-headed worm. She decided that would be a good name to call someone.

She never did look up *INS*.

Well, it didn't matter. It was time to get some bag lunches and the shovel and other assorted necessities, such as Ava, and head on off to maybe look for a fossilized iguanodon. The chances of finding one were pretty slim, but that never mattered before and it wouldn't matter today. It was just *fun* looking for old, extinct, discarded things, like forgotten stories buried in the earth, waiting to be told. Eva also folded up a *National Geographic* world map and put it in her backpack, in case she saw Alfredo and wanted to find out where he was from.

Eva's paleontological strategy this time was to begin digging a hole just about fifty yards from the old warlock's house, so that even if they didn't dig up anything interesting, they'd at least be close enough to the house to see Alfredo coming or going. Ava looked skeptically at the spot Eva had selected, which was an ordinary, mostly flat piece of ground that looked almost exactly like any other piece of ground you'd ever see.

"Why're we going to dig here?" Ava asked.

"Because it's where we are," Eva said.

"But how do you know if there's anything here or not?"

"Well that's the whole point of digging—to find *out* if there's anything there."

"Is that how real scientists do it?"

"Real scientists pay somebody to dig *for* them," Eva said. "We're supposed to be doing it for fun."

"When's it going to be fun?"

"I think it'll be fun as soon as you be quiet," Eva said,

and began digging. After just a few minutes of digging, the girls heard someone playing guitar, and not very well.

"Alfredo!" Eva said.

The girls lost their gloom right away at the sound of Alfredo's distinctively poor playing, because it meant they could resume their new adventure. It was strange to Eva that someone who might be hiding from the INS would play guitar in his hiding place and risk giving himself away. But then, the only people who ever went out in the woods were just kids, and not very many of those. Eva and Ava walked down the trail to the old warlock's house and saw Alfredo on his front porch again. They waved at him, and Alfredo waved back and started saying odd things in Spanish.

"Is he always gonna talk like that?" Ava wondered.

"Maybe it's the only thing he knows," Eva said.

Whatever caution or nervousness the girls had first felt about Alfredo was gone now, although they were still a little superstitious about the house itself, as if maybe Satan lived there part-time and just wasn't home now.

"We can talk to him, but don't go in the house," Eva said. "Even if there's not any demons in there, there might be snakes or scorpions or something."

Alfredo smiled a lot and didn't seem perturbed that they didn't understand each other, as if it was pleasant just to have human company. He smelled bad, though, and Ava said so.

"He stinks," Ava said.

"Don't say that," Eva cautioned her.

"Why? He can't understand me."

"Well it's still rude. He probably just needs a bath, and there aren't any showers in the house. It's not his fault."

Alfredo walked into the house and a few seconds later came back out with a bag of Fritos, which he offered to the girls. So, to be polite, they both ate a handful of Fritos and then gave Alfredo the one apple left from their lunch and some of the leftover iced tea. To Eva, this was like an international meeting of some sort, like the United Nations, except they probably didn't have Fritos at the United Nations, and more than likely, everyone there took baths. As Alfredo ate the green apple, Eva took the world map from her backpack and unfolded the huge thing and put it down on the dirt in front of the front porch, which interested Alfredo right away, because he made a lot of excited remarks they couldn't understand.

"We're here," Eva said, pointing her finger near the center of Texas, and Alfredo nodded his head and said something that sounded like *Tay-hoss*.

"Well I don't know where that is, but this is Texas," Eva said politely.

"Tay-hoss," Alfredo said, nodding his head again.

"I don't know if he can read words, but I think he can read maps," Eva said to Ava. Then she looked at Alfredo and said, "So where's *your* home?" as if although Alfredo hadn't understood English before, he did now.

Alfredo said quite a few things in Spanish and stepped from the porch to get on his hands and knees near Eva and point his finger on the map at Guatemala.

"You're from Guatemala?" Eva said, surprised that anyone could be from such an exotic place.

Alfredo nodded his head, but that didn't necessarily mean he was saying yes, because he still didn't know English and could've nodded his head for any reason at all. As Alfredo said a whole lot of Spanish things that were probably quite expressive but nonetheless were nonsense to Eva and Ava, he put the first two fingers from his right hand down on the map right on top of Guatemala, like his two fingers were the legs of a little human. Then he walked the little human up through Mexico and into Texas.

"You mean you walked from Guatemala to Texas?" Eva said, astonished.

Alfredo said something in Spanish.

"How come you keep talking to him in English?" Ava said.

"Well it's the only language I know," Eva said. "And

he keeps talking to *me* in Spanish, like I'm supposed to know Spanish, but I don't.''

''So how're we ever gonna know what we're saying to each other?'' Ava said.

Alfredo said something.

''I wonder what he said,'' Eva said.

The girls and Alfredo looked at each other in shared ignorance.

Alfredo smiled at them and said a lot of things, then paused to see if they'd respond. Ava responded.

''What?'' she said.

''What,'' Alfredo said.

''He said *what*,'' Eva said happily.

''What,'' Alfredo said, smiling.

''Well I guess we can sit around saying 'what' all day,'' Eva said.

''What,'' Alfredo said.

''This ain't working,'' Ava said.

Alfredo scratched his chin.

''Is that sign language?'' Ava said.

''I think his chin itches,'' Eva said. ''I know what we need to do. Mom has all those foreign language dictionaries she uses for her newsletters and stuff. We could just get the Spanish one and learn a few Spanish words, and Alfredo could use it and learn a few English words. I'll tell him that now,'' Eva said, and looked at Alfredo and said, ''We're gonna go get a Spanish dictionary and learn some Spanish.''

Alfredo said quite a few things and was still saying them when Ava said, ''This ain't working.''

They could hear Alfredo playing his guitar again as they started home, and they were so busy thinking about getting a dictionary that Eva forgot to be afraid of the place where they'd found the bones until the clearing opened up in front of them. Someone else was there.

•   •   •

It was dangerous to return to the same place he'd already hit once, but there was something exciting about the danger, and having no other forces in his life to attract him, Kenlow was attracted by the danger. Taking the longest route he could think of, he'd snuck back through the woods to the spot where the archaeologists used to be. They weren't there now, and he didn't know how smart it was to be there in broad daylight, but it was too hard to keep sneaking out of his home at night. He had no idea who or what he ran into the other night, but he associated it with darkness, so it seemed safer to be there now in the light.

After he'd looked around, listened for any sounds, and decided no one was nearby, he'd quickly begun his work. Since he'd already gouged a big pentagram into the dirt and nobody had messed it up or anything, he decided to emphasize it. He shook up a spray can of yellow paint real well, then rapidly sprayed the paint all along the outlines of the pentagram, as if the satanists had come back to that spot for some new ceremony. Yellow wasn't necessarily a satanic color, but Kenlow liked its brightness.

The giblets and pork brains that he'd put inside the pentagram the first time were gone. Probably the police had taken them. He reached into his grocery bag and pulled out a package of calf's liver and a can of Vienna sausages. That book on religions and cults he had looked at didn't tell you how to do a satanic ritual, so Kenlow had to resort to whatever vague memories he had of ever hearing anything about satanic things. His memories were in fact so vague that he wasn't sure he had any. His standard idea of a satanic ritual was that you killed and mutilated a cow. Since most cows weighed more than a thousand pounds, Kenlow had decided that in any struggle with a cow, it would be himself—not the cow—that got mutilated. Besides, he didn't really want to kill anything. That was the value of grocery stores. Somebody else killed the animals and put them in packages for you.

Kenlow opened the package of liver and let all the slippery meat plop down in the center of the pentagram in a gooey, bloody pile. Next he opened the can of Vienna sausages. Probably no one but satanists themselves would know what kind of meat was truly suitable for satanic rituals, so no one who might find this newest display would object to Vienna sausages. Thus he shook the can hard and dumped the little sausages on top of the liver, then examined his work. It was revolting—a satisfying sight. He imagined that satanists themselves might be afraid of it. They might even think someone worse than *them* was loose in the world. He smiled.

As he started to put his spray paint and trash back into the grocery bag, there was the sound of someone walking close by. Kenlow had just barely shoved the stuff into the bag when he saw two girls staring at him and the yellow pentagram. Kenlow stood up with his bag and simply looked at the girls. He didn't know if they'd seen him doing his work or if they had any idea what was going on. He didn't say anything. Neither did the girls. All of them took turns looking at the pentagram and the flesh in the middle, then they looked at each other. Kenlow's mouth and throat were so dry from fear that it felt like he couldn't possibly speak.

The older girl had a big shovel in her hand, and she walked forward a few steps to look at the pentagram. The littler girl followed her. Kenlow didn't know if he should run or say something or what. The older girl's face was very serious. The littler girl looked interested.

"I just found that," Kenlow said, hoping they'd believe him.

They didn't answer. Everyone was silent again.

"It's pretty," the littler one said.

"Pretty?" the older girl said. "That's a pentagram."

"I like yellow," the littler girl said.

Kenlow was upset that his pentagram was pretty.

The littler girl pointed a finger at the pentagram and said, "What's that goop in the middle?"

"I think it's animal flesh or something," Kenlow said. "I came here to look for the pentagram the satanists made.

68

I heard about it on TV. And when I got here, it was like this," he said, staring down at the pentagram. "I think satanists did this. It looks like an animal sacrifice to me."

"You mean they sacrificed Vienna sausages?" the older girl said. She stared at Kenlow's grocery bag. "And that other meat—that's liver. You can get that at the grocery store."

"Of course you can," Kenlow said, getting a little angry. "But that doesn't mean satanists didn't do this."

"You mean satanists would go to the grocery store and do this?" the older girl said.

"Satanists shop like anyone else," Kenlow said.

"I don't think satanists would buy Vienna sausages."

"How would *you* know? You ever *seen* a satanist?"

"No. And you haven't, either," the older girl said with confidence.

It infuriated Kenlow that they weren't scared by the prospect of satanic Vienna sausages.

"Well maybe I *am* a satanist," he said, standing up a little straighter and trying to put a threatening expression on his face.

It made the girls flinch and step back a little.

"You know what I have in this bag?" Kenlow said, feeling both frightened and oddly pleased with his own drama. He held the bag up in front of him to say what horrible thing he had in there, but he couldn't think of anything. The girls looked worried as Kenlow tried to think of what could be in the bag. He'd seen plenty of horror movies where people cut off human heads and hands, but he thought those were too ordinary to say. He wanted it to be something new. He jiggled the bag a little bit, to scare the girls, and then said the first strange thing that came to mind.

"A gall bladder."

Kenlow stepped toward the girls with the bag swinging in front of him, and the girls started running back into the woods. Kenlow was relieved, until he realized the girls might see him somewhere in town and say what he'd been doing there. He yelled at the girls, "You better not say you saw me here, or something'll happen to you!"

c·h·a·p·t·e·r

12

The abrupt and continual outbreak of satanic activities in town confirmed Rev. Schindler's belief that the end was nigh. The Revelation of St. John the Divine plainly described how there would be a great outpouring of evil in the final days of the world. It didn't specifically say there would be an outpouring of giblets, but the Bible didn't need to name every single instance of evil that would manifest itself in the last days before the Apocalypse. The time was nigh, and Rev. Schindler felt just a little bit exuberant about it. It would be the final triumph of good over evil, the return of Christ, the Rapture, the Judgment Day, a virtual carnival of Christian victory.

Rev. Schindler went into his bedroom and opened the closet to look for his best suit to wear on Judgment Day. He wanted to look nice during the end of the world. He wondered if that was a cold-hearted vanity to think of how he'd look during Judgment Day. During the prophecy seminar he'd attended last year, there was a friendly argument where one minister said you should always go to bed fully dressed in your best clothes in case the Rapture happened while you were asleep. Another minister argued that there wouldn't be a dress code on Judgment Day.

"If the Rapture happens while you're in the shower, up you go, naked into the sky," that minister said.

That led to a discussion of a famous Christian painting of the Rapture that showed dozens of people floating up toward Jesus while everyone else nearby who happened to be in cars and buses and jets was allowed to crash and die as their drivers or pilots got called by the Lord. Rev. Schindler worried that it was unfair to have maybe millions of people suffer like that. But then again, the whole point of constantly preaching the Gospels was to give everyone a chance to be saved and float up safely into the sky. Rev. Schindler vividly recalled an unbearable moderate minister saying, "I find it hard to preach about the Rapture, which suggests that millions of Christians will rise into the sky like weather balloons." The reverend ignored that memory. It was his belief that if you were killed in a car because the driver floated away from the steering wheel during the Rapture, too bad. It just meant you were going to Hell without a driver.

As the obedient and well-mannered minister's son, Kenlow attended his Tuesday night Bible class just a few hours after having spray-painted the pentagram and threatened the two girls. It was extraordinarily strange to sit in the church listening to Mr. Daniels quote from the Revelation of St. John the Divine as you contemplated your own satanic expedition.

"It's particularly relevant," Mr. Daniels was saying, "that as we study the prophecy of the end of the world, we see the increased activity of Satan in our own town. It fulfills the prophecy that in the final days before the return of Christ, Satan and the Antichrist will turn up their efforts full speed to spew evil across the world."

It was astonishing to Kenlow that supposedly mature and intelligent adults could believe in the end of the world based on pranks committed by Kenlow. He'd always been fairly uncomfortable with religion to begin with, since so much of it seemed like dramatic exaggeration and incomprehensible fantasy, and also because, as explained by his father, it was a religion based on threats—the threat that if you didn't do exactly as you were told, you'd go to Hell. And now, it was turning out to be a stupid religion that saw the fulfillment of prophecy in whatever weird incidents Kenlow dreamed up for his own amusement. Kenlow almost wanted to say, "There's no fulfillment of prophecy, you dumbshit. It's just *me*." But of course he'd get in serious trouble for that, so he remained silent.

Chief McLemore's normal routine of burglaries, fistfights, drunk drivers, and an occasional armed robbery had given him little experience with and no training for investigations of fallen angels and their minions. Since the first report, about Mrs. Eldrid's barn, eight other people had reported evidence of satanic incidents in less than a week. Based on the extensive and alarmist news coverage of each new report, McLemore assumed that most of the incidents were just jackass pranks by shithead teenagers who thought it would be funny to fake some satanic activities and see how the TV and newspaper reporters would flock to the scene like cows at feeding time, which would make the teenagers briefly and anonymously famous. The little dicks.

He wanted to dismiss it all as just mentally unbalanced jokes, and ignore it. Even if people who thought of themselves as real satanists were found to be responsible for any of the incidents, the only crimes they could be charged with were trespassing and damaging private property. There were no other possible crimes, unless the town or the country or the state enacted a new law outlawing satanism.

"Satanism's not illegal in Texas," Chief McLemore told a group of reporters in his office. The next day, approximately half of Waxahachie's Christian ministers called McLemore to object to his statement and request that he intensify his efforts to arrest the local satanists for crimes against God. He wanted to say God would have to come in and sign a complaint first, but figured he'd better quit while he was behind. He merely hoped people would gradually forget about satanism and quit writing letters to the local papers and saying in TV interviews that McLemore's officers should interrogate all local drifters, itinerant workers, and legal and illegal aliens, as if the only people who might be interested in satanism were the working class and the unemployed, or anyone but white people. The absurdity was that from what he knew about satanism and cults, most people involved in it were middle-class white people. But they weren't supposed to be the suspects.

And McLemore didn't want any suspects. He had no real interest in protecting the citizens of Waxahachie from pentagrams or parallelograms. Which was why it was so maddening to be out in the woods with Det. Ivan Klowosky, looking at the freshly painted pentagram.

Det. Klowosky, a good Texas boy whose family had immigrated from Poland, stood over the pentagram and snapped pictures with a Polaroid.

"Well," Det. Klowosky said. "Do you want my opinion?"

"Sure," Chief McLemore said.

"Judging from the Vienna sausages, I'd say these satanists aren't satanists."

"I'd say they're shithead teenagers," Chief McLemore said. He stared at the pentagram and said, "Yellow paint. It's like he was decorating."

"*Better Homes and Gargoyles*," Det. Klowosky said, then took another picture. "I don't know why we're investigating this. It's not a crime."

"Nope. It ain't. But you know the media will hear about this and act like it's a crime. And then the ministers will be all over us again. I think we should find the little shit who's doing this just so the ministers will leave us alone."

After they left the woods, McLemore repeated to Det. Klowosky what Eva's mom had reported about Eva's run-in with the supposed satanist. Klowosky got copies of the local junior high and high school yearbooks and took them to Eva's home to have her look at all the boys' pictures. Eva recognized the boy, whose name was Kenlow Schindler. He had been a sophomore last year. But she kept on looking at pictures, never saying she recognized Kenlow, because she was a little scared about how he'd threatened her. She finished looking at all the pictures and said, "I didn't see him," which was awful, to lie to the detective.

"Are you sure?" Det. Klowosky said.

"Yes, sir. His picture's not in those books," Eva said, trying not to look at the detective's face.

"Well, we'll keep looking. And if you ever spot the boy in town, just tell your parents to call us, and we'll go looking for him, okay?"

"Okay."

She'd never forget that name. Kenlow Schindler. But he didn't even really seem dangerous. He was real skinny, and when she and Ava first saw him putting stuff in his bag, he'd looked frightened, like two girls could scare him. And even when he started to look mean, all he could think of was to say he had a gall bladder in his bag. No one in the world had ever had a gall bladder all by itself. It just wasn't scary. But she had run anyway, because even if he wasn't a satanist, he might have been crazy. No sane person would go around painting yellow pentagrams and putting Vienna sausages in the middle of them. And only a crazy person would say he had a gall bladder in a grocery bag.

Eva didn't think anyone would believe all that anyway, so that was partly why she lied. And there was the threat. Kenlow said something would happen to them if they told on him. Eva didn't know what that something was. But she believed it was something.

c·h·a·p·t·e·r

13

When the girls went back to the old warlock's house with
a paperback Spanish-English dictionary, they were a little
skittish about the possibility of seeing Kenlow Schindler
again, so they constantly looked around and wouldn't pass
by the spot where the pentagram was until they were sure
no one was there. Not seeing anyone, they cautiously
walked up to the pentagram. It was different now. In the
middle of the star was a package of Oscar Mayer hot dogs.

"Is that a sacrifice?" Ava asked.

"I don't think so," Eva said. "I think everybody heard
about this on TV or the newspaper, so someone just put
hot dogs there."

"Makes me hungry."

"Well you can't eat those. They're probably spoiled."

The girls went on to the old warlock's house and waited
for a while, until they saw Alfredo walking up behind the
house. He was carrying a big grocery bag with something
in it, and he waved at the girls and said incomprehensible
Spanish things like he always did.

"*¡Hola!*" Eva called out.

"*¡Hola!*" Ava said, which was practically the only
Spanish word they'd memorized from the dictionary.

Alfredo's eyes opened wide with surprise at finally hearing a Spanish greeting from the girls.

"What!" Alfredo exclaimed happily as he walked up to Eva and Ava and put his grocery bag on the front porch.

"Why'd he say that?" Ava said to Eva.

"Maybe he's just repeating the word we taught him yesterday," Eva guessed. As she held open the dictionary, ready to say something in Spanish one word at a time, Alfredo reached into the grocery bag and pulled out a white plastic foam container and a plastic fork. He lifted the lid on the container. There was Chinese food in it, with rice, which Alfredo greedily began eating like it was the only food he'd eaten all day. Eva thought the food looked like moo goo gai pan, which she'd had at a Chinese restaurant a few months earlier, so she started flipping pages in the dictionary.

"Well say something to him in Spanish," Ava said impatiently.

"I'm trying, I'm trying," Eva said. "I'm trying to look up *moo goo gai pan*, but it's not in here." She tried to think of something easier than *moo goo gai pan*. She looked up *dinner*, saw its translation, and then said it to Alfredo: *"¿Comida?"*

Alfredo looked up from his food with another surprised smile.

"Comida. Sí," he said, and then jammed more food in his mouth.

"Oh, Eva! He knows Spanish!" Ava said. "Say some more words to him!"

"Well I have to look them up first. I'll look up *rice* now." She looked it up, pointed at the rice, and said, *"Arroz."*

"Sí. Arroz," Alfredo said.

"Oh, Eva! He knows what rice is!" Ava said.

But then Eva realized that as soon as Alfredo finished eating and started talking again, he'd be saying things in Spanish so fast that Eva couldn't possibly understand all the words, let alone look them up—which was exactly what

Alfredo did. He put the plastic foam container aside and instantly began speaking so rapidly that even when Eva could make out what sounded like an individual word, she didn't know how to spell it, so she couldn't look it up.

"Well, shit," Eva said.

"I thought Mom got mad when you said stuff like that," Ava said.

"Uh oh," Eva said. It had just slipped out.

Alfredo paused, then said, "Well, shit." He smiled at Eva and nodded his head.

"I think he's learning English," Ava said.

Still smiling, Alfredo said, "Well, shit. No?"

"That's not the kind of English I want you to be learning," Eva said.

"No inglés," Alfredo said apologetically.

Eva held up the dictionary for Alfredo to see and said to him, "English, Spanish."

"Ahhh," Alfredo said, then took the dictionary and looked at it for a few seconds. He gave the book back and said, *"No inglés."*

Eva thought she could at least look up the word *read* and ask him if he knew how to read. The dictionary said the Spanish word for *read* was *leer.*

"¿Leer?" Eva asked him.

Alfredo looked confused, as if he didn't know what Eva was saying.

"¿Leer?" Eva said more clearly.

Alfredo looked more confused.

"Maybe I'm not saying it right," Eva said. "It's got some kind of accent on it, but I don't know which way to pronounce it." She held the dictionary a little closer to Alfredo, as if he might read the word *leer* and know what Eva meant.

"¿Leer?" Alfredo said. *"No leer."*

"I don't think he can read," Eva said. "I didn't think of that."

Everyone was quiet, as if they all knew Eva was

stumped, like they were all trapped within their own languages.

"I know what," Eva said, and thought of a Spanish word she'd heard a few times on old cowboy shows on TV. She looked at Alfredo and said, "¿*Compadre?*"

Alfredo smiled and said, "Ahhhhh. Well, shit, *compadre.*"

"Is he always gonna say shit?" Ava asked.

"Well, shit," Alfredo said, as if he'd mastered a common American greeting.

"I hope not," Eva said. "We gotta teach him to say something else."

"Teach'm how to say howdy," Ava said.

"That'd be okay," Eva said. She held her hand up and waved it and said, "How-dy."

Alfredo waved his hand and said, "How-dy, *compadre.* Well, shit."

"It ain't working," Ava said.

"We're at least talking a little bit. That's a good start. You don't learn a whole language in one day."

She thought of some questions to ask Alfredo, such as was this his home? So she looked up *home*, and then pointed at the crumbling old house and said, "¿*Casa, compadre?*"

Alfredo shrugged and sighed and said a torrent of Spanish things, including the word *casa*, but with so many other Spanish words jammed rapidly together it was impossible to understand.

"It still ain't working," Ava said.

"I know," Eva said. "But we still gotta try. Except I'm getting a headache from not understanding him. Anyway, I'll try and ask him if he's an illegal alien." She started to look it up, then said, "Wait. I better not ask him that. He might get mad. Instead, I'll ask him if he has a job."

"Yeah. That'd be good," Ava said.

Here, Eva realized the extreme difficulty of creating sentences in a language she didn't know. If she wanted to say "Do you have a job?" she'd have to look each word up individually and try to remember each word as she looked up the next one, which would probably take about two minutes just to ask one question. And by the time she looked up the last word, she might forget the first two or three words she had already looked up.

Meanwhile, Alfredo seemed to patiently watch Eva thumb through the book, as if he realized she was getting language from it and was curious to see what she might try to say next. Eva took a shortcut and just looked up *have* and *job*. This only took about thirty seconds. What Eva then tried to say with the right pronunciation was *"¿Tener empleo?"* meaning, "Have job?"

This seemed to mystify both Alfredo and Ava.

"Did you just say a sentence?" Ava said.

Eva shortened the sentence to one word: *"¿Empleo?"*

"Ahhhh," Alfredo said. *"Empleo. Sí."* And then it was possible that he proceeded to explain his employment in fluent Spanish, although who knew what he was really saying?

"He sure talks real good," Ava said.

Eva studied the problem for a while until she had to realize the obvious truth that the only way they were going to communicate for a pretty long time was by taking turns saying things that made no sense.

Alfredo reached into the grocery bag next to him and pulled out a big bag of Fritos.

"Fritos," he said.

That was the only sentence all three of them understood: "Fritos."

Kenlow went shopping at Dave's Big Basted Hen Family Grocery for more animal flesh for his next public satanic project. As excited and nervous as he was, he still delayed going to the checkout line at the grocery store so he could watch some guy lying on his back on scaffolding while painting some weird scene on the ceiling over the produce section.

Kenlow kept his distance from the artist, not wanting to attract any attention to himself. He stood at the end of an aisle about twenty feet away from the scaffolding and the painter, and watched with fascination as the painter painted this naked man standing beside a naked woman with some kind of leaves over her groin and one of her arms crossed over her breasts. It almost looked pornographic to Kenlow, who'd never seen a picture of an actual naked woman before.

At the other end of the same aisle, Rev. Schindler pulled his grocery cart to a stop when he saw the scaffolding set up in the produce section. It startled him to see a man lying on his back at the top of the scaffolding. It shocked him to raise his eyes a little further and see a naked woman freshly painted on the ceiling. Almost instantly he recognized it as a painting of Adam and Eve, but instead of feeling pleased that some strange artist was painting Bible scenes on the grocery store ceiling, it disturbed him that the mother of all humankind was shown in nearly complete nudity. It was one thing to merely say in the Bible that Adam and Eve were naked. Those were just words. But to actually have a public painting showing Eve in her nudity, that was sinful.

"Really?" Rev. Schindler wondered aloud. It was the part of his mind that occasionally doubted what the moral part of his mind told him. The doubting part suggested that really there was nothing wrong with such a painting of Eve because in the Bible, Adam and Eve *were* naked. So how could it be wrong to paint what the Bible itself described?

Morality resumed control, though, and Rev. Schindler stared at the vile and blasphemous painting, wondering if he should walk over and knock the blasphemer off the scaffolding. It was all just more proof that the cunning and insidious effect of Satan was corrupting even their grocery stores.

In the middle of the aisle, where it intersected with a central aisle that went from one side of the store to the other, Alfredo was getting one bag each of Fritos and Cheetos, his favorite American foods. As he stepped forward to go get some apples, he saw this big steel platform with wheels on it, and some man lying on the top of the platform. Then he saw the naked woman on the ceiling and, next to her, still being painted, some naked man. Alfredo was embarrassed. Never in his life had he seen naked women, except for his sisters. That wasn't really naked, that was just sisters. As much as Alfredo was truly interested in seeing a naked woman one day—such as a wife, if he ever found one—he was afraid to look up at the naked woman on the ceiling, especially since he was an illegal and some American citizen in the store might see Alfredo staring at the naked woman and call the police. Alfredo immediately looked down at the floor and walked backward, away from the tempting and troubling woman. With his gaze down, Alfredo was backing up the aisle toward the checkout counter when he bumped into someone. A man. A very severe-looking man.

"Discúlpame," Alfredo said anxiously, not knowing if he should have apologized in Spanish, or if he should have said anything at all.

"What?" Rev. Schindler said in an irritated voice, thinking it was bad enough that obscene Bible scenes were being painted on the ceiling. Next, he had to run into one more foreigner in town, which reminded him that all of Texas was being overrun by impoverished Mexicans who believed in the pope, whom Rev. Schindler regarded as the chief executive officer for Satan.

Alfredo lowered his gaze even more and started to spin away from Rev. Schindler just as Kenlow was walking up the aisle. Alfredo spun directly into Kenlow, knocking the food from Kenlow's hands onto the floor, just as Kenlow saw his father and began to panic.

"What? *Discúlpame,"* Alfredo said, walking quickly away.

Kenlow hurried to pick up his groceries.

"Bloody calf's liver?" his father said. "What's *that* for?"

There was hardly time to think of an answer, but Kenlow offered one.

"Barbecue," he said.

"Barbecue? *Nobody* barbecues *liver.*"

Kenlow tried to think of a different lie.

"Liver has iron in it," he said. "I was watching this cooking show on TV and it said people have iron deficiencies so they should eat liver."

Kenlow's father seemed momentarily troubled by this explanation, but he then apparently accepted it because he abruptly changed the subject and said, "Well don't look up at the ceiling."

Kenlow immediately looked at the ceiling.

"I said *don't* look!" his father said. "Someone's painting blasphemous obscenities on the ceiling."

The idea of obscenities interested Kenlow, who glanced

once more at the painting of the naked woman.

The man doing the painting looked down from the scaffolding and said, "Blasphemous obscenities? This is a painting of Adam and Eve."

"It's pornographic," Kenlow's father said.

"Pornographic?" the painter said. "This imagery comes directly from the Bible."

"Don't lecture *me* about the Bible, young man. I'm an ordained minister."

"Did you say *or*-dained, or *hare*-brained?"

Kenlow was relieved that his father got into an argument with the painter. It distracted his father and gave Kenlow time to sneak away and hurry over to the meat department, where he put the calf's liver back. He couldn't use it in his next satanic ritual because his father might hear a news report about the liver and find it too strange a coincidence that his own son had just bought some liver, which he'd never eaten before. Kenlow hurriedly browsed through the meat section and selected an alternate item—a cow's tongue.

Kenlow had just paid for the cow's tongue and was walking away when he saw the two girls he'd encountered in the woods coming into the store from the door on the opposite side of the building. Kenlow sped from the store as Eva and Ava bought Cokes from the machine at the front of the store. It took them only a few seconds to spot the painter lying on his scaffolding just below the ceiling, and they instantly went down the produce aisle to investigate.

"It'a a naked woman," Ava said.

"I will *not* stand by and let the children of this town be corrupted," Rev. Schindler said to the painter. He turned toward Eva and Ava and said, "Don't look at the ceiling, girls. Don't look up."

"Cool," Eva said, staring at the fresh painting. "It's half of Adam and all of Eve."

"I don't think you girls should be staring at such an indecency," Rev. Schindler said in a voice that sounded a little bit worried and a little bit angry.

"Pardon me?" the painter said.

"I see nothing defensible about blatantly painting adult scenes on the ceiling of a public grocery store," Rev. Schindler said. "I'm shocked that you'd be allowed to paint such material for little children to see."

"Adult scenes?" the painter said. "Are you suggesting that a painting of Adam and Eve is immoral?"

"The sacred story of the creation was never meant to be mocked by such vulgar and obscene art."

"Obscene? How stupid are you?"

"If you don't *immediately* remove that painting from the ceiling, I'll have the store owner remove it," Rev. Schindler said, then looked down at Eva and Ava and said, "You girls shouldn't be seeing such an abomination."

Eva didn't know what an abomination was. She began looking around the painting to see if she could spot one.

"Go *get* the store owner," the painter said. "*He's* the one who gave me permission to paint biblical scenes on the entire ceiling, you ignorant Philistine."

"Philistine?" Rev. Schindler said. "I happen to be a Christian *minister*, you sodomite."

"Actually I'm from Albany, New York, so you should call me an Albanian, you ignorant butthead."

Eva had never seen a painter and a minister yell at each other before. It was fun. But it also seemed a little bit dangerous, like the painter might jump from his scaffolding onto the minister, so she motioned to Ava and they left the store.

As peculiar as the whole scene was, it got explained that evening on the TV news. These days Eva's dad frequently turned the TV on during dinner, which he didn't used to do. Eva suspected he did it if he didn't want to have to talk to her mom during dinner. But it was okay if there was something interesting on the news, and that night there was. The TV reporter said there was a controversy at Dave's Big Basted Hen Family Grocery Store. The camera showed the unfinished painting of Adam and Eve on the ceiling of the store, and then they explained something about how the artist, whose name was Doug Grail, had always wanted to paint a religious mural like Michelangelo had painted on the ceiling of the Sistine Chapel in Vatican City.

"Isn't there a big difference between the Sistine Chapel and a grocery store?" the reporter asked Doug.

"Yes," Doug said. "You can't buy groceries at the Sistine Chapel."

Doug said he was going to paint religious murals across the entire ceiling of the store, with the approval of the store owner, who was Doug's brother-in-law. Then the reporter talked with the minister Eva and Ava had seen. The minister was the Reverend Kyle Schindler. He said the painting of Adam and Eve without clothes on was obscene, and he was asking everyone in Waxahachie to boycott the store until the paintings were removed from the ceiling.

Police chief McLemore had been called to the store, so he was on TV, too. The reporter asked Chief McLemore if there was anything illegal about the painting.

"It's vile and obscene," Rev. Schindler said as he stood next to Chief McLemore. "Federal law says something is obscene if it violates the prevailing community standards."

"You mean a majority of the God-fearing people in this community think that painting a scene from the Bible is obscene?" Chief McLemore said. "If they think that, we'll have to outlaw Christianity. I'm not in the mood to try that."

That was all pretty interesting, but before Eva or anyone else had time to react, there was a new story about the skeleton Eva and Ava had found. They showed the same old scenes of the woods that they had used for the first story, and then they showed a reporter standing in front of a door to the medical examiner's office in Dallas, as if the TV audience would benefit by seeing a live shot of a door, since there was nothing else to show. The reporter said there was new evidence that indicated that the man whose skeleton was behind the *"exclusive, live shot of the door!"* was murdered in 1929 by members of a defunct religious cult called the Sons of Belial.

"Sons of Belial?" Eva's dad said. "No wonder they're defunct. Their acronym would be the SOBs. They probably couldn't endure the ridicule."

It made Eva and her mom smile, which Eva enjoyed because it was one of those rare times when her parents smiled at each other and seemed to be enjoying something together. But Eva got a little bit disturbed when she listened to the rest of the story. The reporter said Belial was an Old Testament name for Satan, and that the Sons of Belial had been investigated in 1929 after a man from Waxahachie named Henry Ellis disappeared. There had been rumors in the late 1920s that the Sons of Belial practiced devil worship and that they sometimes made human sacrifices to Belial. No one was ever arrested because no bodies were ever found. But according to the medical examiner's office, the skeleton that Eva and Ava found had just been identified as the remains of Henry Ellis. There wasn't conclusive proof that Henry Ellis had been murdered by the Sons of Belial. He could have been murdered by anyone. But the fact that his skeleton had been buried in a part of the county where the Sons of Belial were said to have held some of their gatherings made it possible that Henry Ellis had indeed been murdered by the cult.

Suddenly the skeleton wasn't just a skeleton to Eva anymore. It was a murdered man named Henry Ellis who might have been killed by people like Kenlow Schindler.

As a precaution, that evening after dinner Eva put on her silver crucifix necklace, which was meant to ward off vampires. She would have put on a more appropriate piece of jewelry meant specifically to ward off satanists or Sons of Belial, but she didn't know of any necklaces, rings, earrings, bracelets, or brooches used in repelling anything other than vampires. As a double precaution, she took a black Magic Marker and drew a small cross on the slugging end of her baseball bat, thinking that if any Sons of Belial approached her, she'd slug them with the bat. Even if it didn't have any magical powers, a baseball bat was still pretty effective.

c·h·a·p·t·e·r

15

The next day, when Eva walked around the neighborhood wearing her silver crucifix and carrying her baseball bat, nearly all of the children she saw anywhere had heard about the Sons of Belial, and you could constantly hear children saying, "Hey, did you hear about the SOBs?" Even though everyone knew what the acronym stood for, it just seemed like a great new sport; it was not as if anyone seemed especially worried about the Sons of Belial, it was just that it was fun to say SOB all day long.

Eva was getting on her bike to go to the library—with her baseball bat—to get a book on illegal aliens and extraterrestrials when Tommy Dillo walked up along the sidewalk across the street from her house and said, "Hey, Eva. You know the old witch's house?"

"You mean the old warlock's house," Eva corrected him.

"You're the only one who calls it that. It's the old witch's house. And anyway, I was up by there yesterday with Andy Strauss, just walking by, and he said we should go inside, since no one had ever done that before, and I wasn't going to just because it's too scary, but Andy said it'd be fun to at least walk on up to the front porch and look inside at least. And so when we did that, when we got right up on the porch, something screamed at us. Something in the house made this noise like a scream or something.''

Eva at first imagined a demon or Satan. Then she imagined Alfredo, who could have either been killed by the demon or just been trying to scare Tommy and Andy away.

''It was probably just some wild animal,'' Eva said, hoping to make Tommy feel dumb and cowardly, so he wouldn't want to go back to the house or tell anyone else what he heard.

''Like hell,'' Tommy said. ''It was a real scream. I know what a scream sounds like. There's no wild animal that makes a noise like that.''

''Hawks and eagles scream,'' Eva said. ''Everyone knows that.''

''Well maybe they make some kind of weird sound that sounds a little bit like a scream, but not *this* sound,'' and Tommy closed his eyes and bared his teeth and made a kind of screeching, howling noise real loud for about five seconds.

''Like that,'' Tommy said.

Mrs. Carlyle opened her front door across the street and said, ''If you aren't in any pain yet, you will be if you keep making that noise!''

Tommy crossed the street to where Eva was and said, ''That's almost exactly what we heard—a scream like a ghost or something. We're thinking about going back with a lot of guys and a tape recorder and guns, maybe.''

''Guns?'' Eva said anxiously. ''You don't even have a gun.''

''My brother does. A twelve-gauge.''

''You guys are just stupid. I bet if your dad catches you with a gun, he'll whip you. And you can't shoot a ghost anyway. It was probably just a wild animal to begin with. Nobody really believes in ghosts anyway, except on that stupid TV show where they have fake ghosts because they can't find any real ones.''

''Yeah, well,'' Tommy said indignantly. ''There was

*some*thing out there, and we might just go back and find out what.''

Eva forgot about the library and went back home to get the Spanish-English dictionary in order to warn Alfredo to watch out for Tommy. But Alfredo wasn't home when she got to the warlock's house, and she couldn't just stay there for hours waiting for him, so she was going to write him a long note warning him to watch out until she realized it would take her twenty or thirty minutes to translate her English into Spanish, and Alfredo had said "No *leer*," meaning he couldn't read anyway; unless all he really meant was he couldn't understand what Eva was saying, and then maybe he *could* read. It was worth trying, so Eva translated a real short note on a little piece of notebook paper: *Algunos niños oír chillido. Vigilar!*

It meant something like "Some boys to hear scream. To watch!''

She would have liked to have written a better note, but even that one took her about five minutes to write, so she had to be satisfied with it. She put it on the front porch and weighed it down with a rock.

Eva's natural impulse was to ask her parents for help with Alfredo, but she was worried that if adults got into it, someone would just call the IRA. It was awful. She was getting her letters mixed up. It was either the IRA or the IRS. So she didn't want to tell her parents, in case Alfredo would be sent back to Mexico or Guatemala. But at least he'd been smart enough to act like a ghost when Tommy and Andy came by, a trick that might keep scaring everybody away. But it also might just make them more interested in coming back. And so Eva said a prayer.

"Dear Ted Williams: Please help Alfredo not get caught. Please help him to learn English and get a good job and find a real house to live in. Thank you.''

• • •

Maybe she prayed the wrong prayer, Eva thought later that week. Her mom had been talking with Anne Dillo, Tommy's mom, and Mrs. Dillo said Tommy had gone out to the house with some other boys and a tape recorder to try to get satanic screams on tape. It made Eva's stomach hurt to think about what she knew about Alfredo and hadn't told her mom, but she didn't want to say anything yet. Her mom said it seemed like every neighborhood in the United States had a satanic cult now.

"It's interesting that whenever there's a new report or rumor about a satanic cult, they always hold their services in abandoned, deteriorating buildings," her mom said. "I guess Satan isn't very good at fund-raising."

"Did Tommy get anything on tape?" Eva asked.

"Crickets," her mom said. "And I don't imagine they were satanic crickets. Supposedly Tommy and one of his friends were out by the house a couple of days ago and heard someone screaming inside the house. I think it's all pretty stupid, but it's still possible that some teenagers are hanging out at the house, so I want you girls to stay away from there, just in case. And this doesn't mean I suddenly believe in Satan. I don't. It just means there are plenty of dangerous humans on the planet, and just to be cautious, I think you girls should control your curiosity and stay away from the house for a while at least. Someone might think it's funny to start pretending to be Sons of Belial and hang out at that house. So please stay away from there."

This screwed everything up. Not only was Eva being told to not do the one thing she wanted to do, but she was hiding the truth from her mom. She knew there wasn't anything satanic about the house. It was Alfredo. And not telling her mom about it was like lying.

And that wasn't the only awful thing to think about. Now that Tommy Dillo had heard some strange sounds at the house, Tommy and every boy in the neighborhood might go sneaking back to the house to look for Satan or for Sons of Belial, and they'd either catch Alfredo or scare him away, unless everybody was so afraid of finding Satan that maybe they wouldn't go there. As much as it all troubled Eva, she tried to comfort herself by thinking that Alfredo had been smart enough to be out there on his own for a long time already, so maybe he'd be smart enough to keep from getting caught. Still, maybe it was a good idea to stay away from the house for a couple of days, since right now would be when any boys from the neighborhood would be out sneaking around it. They'd get tired of it after a while, and Eva could go back.

At dinner that night, Eva's mom told Eva's dad about the rumors of satanists at the old house in the woods.

"The old warlock's house," Ava said, so she'd appear knowledgeable and wouldn't be left out of the conversation.

"An old warlock?" their dad said, looking at Ava. "How old is he? Is he retired?"

"I don't know. We never seen'm," Ava said, which reassured Eva, because it meant Ava was smart enough to not say anything about Alfredo.

"So we have an old warlock in the neighborhood. I guess this is turning into a retirement community," their dad said.

"I've told the girls not to play near the house, in case some teenagers or someone is hanging out there, like that boy who scared her," their mom said, and she mentioned how Tommy Dillo supposedly went out there and heard some unholy screams and then went back there with a tape recorder.

"I don't know what's going on in this town," their dad said. "We have religious miracles in the post office, and people trying to get live recordings of Satan."

"Well, did Tommy get Satan on tape?" their dad asked.

"Not unless Satan sounds like a cricket. Anne said the only thing on the tape was some of the boys whispering sometimes, and some crickets in the background."

"Crickets aren't very satanic," their dad said. "I think if Satan's going to change himself into a bug, it should be something a little scarier, like a praying mantis. Or, rather, an agnostic mantis."

"What's that?" Ava asked.

"It's a mantis with spiritual doubts," their dad said.

"Anyway, I told the girls not to go out in the woods for a while," their mom said.

"I'm not sure there's any reason for that," their dad said in the strangely serious tone of voice that Eva had come to recognize as a sign that her father was suddenly irritable. It was silent at the table. Eva felt her stomach tighten as she looked at her dad's face, seeing him look down at some indistinct spot on the table. Her mom's face got strange, like she was smiling and frowning at the same time. It remained silent too long, the way it always did before there was trouble. Eva held a single green bean stabbed on the end of her fork, unable to raise it to her mouth or put it down.

"I don't think the girls should be out in the woods right now," their mom said.

"I don't see any real danger in it," their dad said. "We can't quarantine the girls at home just because some boy thinks he heard a demon scream. There are no demons, other than the ones people invent out of ignorance and fear."

"I'm not saying they should be quarantined. I'm saying they should stay out of the woods for a while," their mom said. It seemed like her voice got a bit more serious so that it would be just a little more serious than their dad's voice. It was like their parents were trying to defeat each other by sound.

Their dad picked up his glass of iced tea and sipped from it, like he didn't have to answer right away. He put the glass back down exactly in the spot where he'd picked it up.

Eva, just as precisely, held her fork still, as if any movement might cause more trouble.

"I don't think we need to teach our girls that the world is full of stray demons," their dad said.

"And I'm not teaching them that," their mom said, staring at their dad's face with a kind of graceful and polite anger. ''I'm teaching them that sometimes they have to be careful in the world.''

''You're teaching them to be afraid of any fool who comes along and says an unexplained noise from a rotting house is Satan. It's the theology of fear. Fear is a popular religion, and a shoddy one. But if those are your maternal instincts, who am I—a mere male in a feminist tide of enlightenment—to contradict your biological judgment?''

''Don't start this,'' their mom said.

''I'm not starting anything. Women alone give birth to children, therefore women alone are capable of raising them. I apologize for the foolish opinion that I could possibly have any sense at all,'' their dad said, smiling angrily and pushing his chair back from the table as he stood up.

''My, I married a martyr,'' their mom said.

''I'm not sure the girls know what a martyr is. Perhaps you should insult me with a simpler word.''

Their mom glanced at them and said, ''A martyr is someone who suffers for a cause. I think your father suffers without one.''

''Well, that's good. I think they get the gist of your insult now. Now you girls forget what I said. I don't want you going out in the woods playing with Satan. It might upset the neighbors. So listen to your mother. She gave birth to you.''

He walked down the hall and into his study and closed the door. Their mom put her elbows on the table and rested her face in her hands.

Nothing was safe like it used to be. It seemed like Eva was supposed to take sides, but there weren't supposed to be any sides. You could hear Ava crying real quietly.

''Don't cry,'' their mom said.

Eva stared at the green bean on her fork, unsure if it was all right to move it yet. She wondered why nothing made sense anymore, and wasn't certain that it ever had.

c·h·a·p·t·e·r
16

Eva and Ava headed back out to the woods the next day to see if they could find Alfredo again, even though Eva's mom had told them not to go near the house. The main thing they found at first was a lot of flies constantly buzzing around and landing on them.

"Ms. Danner in Sunday School said if God created everything, he also created flies," Ava said while swishing her hand at a fly. "Why do we need flies?"

"I don't know if we need flies, but if we do, we won't run out," Eva said.

When they got near the old warlock's house, you could see Tommy hiding behind a big, toppled-over tree trunk across the trail from the house. A skinny, dark thing was sticking up out of his hand. It looked like a microphone. Eva and Ava spied on Tommy from behind some bushes, and Eva worried that if Tommy stayed there long enough, he'd see Alfredo coming home and then tell somebody about Alfredo and that'd be it. One thing Eva thought she could do was to sneak around behind the house and make satanic noises to scare Tommy away, although she didn't know what a satanic noise sounded like. She knew how to imitate the call of a loon. She could also imitate the South

American howler monkey. That might sound satanic. But if she did it and Tommy got it on his tape recorder and let people listen to it, it might just make more people want to come out there. And then she realized something.

"Come on," she said to Ava. "Let's go talk to him until he can't stand it, and then he'll probably go away, because he's supposed to be having a dangerous adventure and we'll show him girls aren't afraid. Then he'll feel stupid and leave."

They walked out from behind the bushes and headed over to Tommy's hiding place. He looked astonished at first, as if any noise he heard could only be the presence of Satan. When he saw it was Eva and Ava, he used his hand to gesture impatiently for the girls to get behind the fallen tree with him, which the girls did. Everyone looked at Tommy's small tape recorder.

"I told you I was gonna do this, and I am," Tommy whispered seriously.

"Why do you think Satan would be in the house?" Eva said quietly.

"We used to think that," Ava said. She was too honest.

"Maybe *you* did," Eva said, even though she had, too.

"You already know why," Tommy said. "And I'm not saying it's really Satan who goes in there, and you know it, Eva. I'm just saying *some*thing made a pretty awful noise in there. I don't know if it's ghosts or satanists or SOBs. But if anything goes back in there and makes any sounds or screams or anything, I'm getting it on tape, and then people'll *have* to believe I heard something."

"Not really," Eva said. "Just because you have noise on a tape recorder doesn't prove anything. It just means you have noise."

Tommy looked troubled, as if he'd never thought of that until now. He said, "I know that. But maybe I can take the tape to a police lab, and they could prove it wasn't fake."

"A police lab? They only investigate crimes. What crime is there?"

Tommy didn't answer right away, because he didn't have an answer.

"Well don't talk so loud," Tommy said, although Eva had been talking quietly. "You might scare away whoever might be coming to the house."

"Satan?" Eva said. "You mean he'd be afraid of *us*?"

"I mean satan-*ists*," Tommy said irritably. "And you don't have to stay here if all you're gonna do is bother me."

"We won't bother you. We just came out here to look for artifacts anyway. Come on, Ava. Let's go dig for artifacts."

Ava followed Eva out into the open between the house and Tommy, where Eva took the shovel and started digging. It bothered her that she was out there where her mom said they shouldn't go. But she couldn't be sure what was right, since her parents had that fight about the woods. It was as if she couldn't obey either parent since nobody won that fight. So she did what she wanted, which was to look for Alfredo.

While Eva dug, you could see Tommy's mad little face peeking over the fallen tree at them.

"What're we looking for?" Ava said.

"Lewis and Clark."

"Both of 'em?"

"Either one would be fine."

"Do you have to dig right there?" Tommy called out.

"This is America. I can dig where I want to," Eva said.

"We're looking for Lewis or Clark," Ava said.

"Can't you look for 'em somewhere else?" Tommy said.

"We're looking *here*," Eva insisted as she dug.

"Well fine, then," Tommy said, and stood up. "I'll come back here at night."

"You'll need a flashlight," Eva said. "And if anyone's out here, they'll see your flashlight and kill you and gnaw on your soul."

"Well if you're so afraid I'll get gnawed on, how come you're out here digging?" Tommy said.

"Because I don't believe in Satan."

"Oh you do too. Everybody believes in Satan."

"I don't," Eva said confidently, even though she wasn't sure.

"Why? Are you an atheist?"

Eva stopped digging and stared irritably at Tommy. "That's the most ignorant thing you could say, Tommy Dillo. An atheist is someone who doesn't believe in God. So if you don't believe in Satan, that's the opposite."

"All Christians believe in Satan," Tommy said.

"Well I'm not a Christian. I'm an Episcopalian."

"A what?" Tommy asked.

"An Episcopalian," Eva said clearly. She watched Tommy's lips moving, as if he were trying to say that word and couldn't do it.

"I can't even *say* that word," Tommy said.

"Pis-co-palia," Ava said, showing how easy it was to say.

"And you don't believe in Satan?" Tommy said.

"Some of us do. Some of us don't," Eva said, which she hoped was true because she just said it was.

"Well the Bible says Satan's real," Tommy said, with a slight tone of defiance in his voice. "The Bible says Satan exists, so you have'm even if you don't want'm."

"Maybe you have him, but we don't," Eva said.

Tommy looked impatiently at Eva and said, "*Every*body has Satan."

"Well if that's so, why're you trying to get him on a tape recorder to prove he exists? Huh?"

It looked like Eva had crumbled his arguments, but Tommy wasn't prepared to lose. He frowned at Eva and said, "Satan hides out. Everyone knows that. He doesn't just walk around in public."

"And why would he come here? Because he can't afford a *real* house?"

"Oh, you don't know anything."

"I know that if Satan causes all the evil in the world, he ought to be making enough money to get a *better* house than this one."

"I'm leaving," Tommy said. As he walked away, he looked back and said, "Go to hell."

"Spiny-headed worm," Eva said.

$c \cdot h \cdot a \cdot p \cdot t \cdot e \cdot r$

17

Although everything about Alfredo was already new and unusual, there was something newer and more unusual about him when the girls saw him coming to his abandoned home that afternoon. He was speaking Chinese.

Actually it could have been Japanese, Korean, or Vietnamese, since Eva couldn't tell the difference between any of them. Alfredo walked up to the front porch and placed a big bag of something on the porch as he smiled at the girls and said a few more things to them.

"It sounds like he's talking Chinese now," Eva said, and she felt a little bit confused, since she had been assuming Alfredo was from Guatemala.

"I liked it better when he spoke Spanish," Ava said.

"Well I don't know *what's* going on," Eva said. "I don't know how you can speak Spanish one day and then the next day you speak Chinese."

Alfredo then said something to the girls in Spanish, which would have been a relief except of course they still didn't know Spanish, so nothing was a relief. Alfredo opened the bag and removed a plastic foam container that he then opened to reveal another Chinese dinner of some sort, and then he spoke Chinese again.

"Maybe he's saying the name of his dinner," Eva speculated. But she knew that probably wasn't true, because whatever Alfredo was saying was a lot longer than just a word or two that might name the food he had. It sounded like complete sentences in Chinese.

Eva looked at Ava and said, "We spend a few days trying to teach him English, and now he speaks Chinese. I don't understand *any*thing."

Alfredo ate his colorful Chinese goo on rice with a plastic fork, pausing sometimes to look at the girls and say something in Spanish and then something in Chinese.

Eva tried to think if there was some part of world history she hadn't been taught yet about the Chinese colonizing Guatemala. And then an idea moved into her head from somewhere.

"I know what," she said. "I bet he works at a Chinese restaurant. That'd be how come he keeps bringing Chinese food home. And remember when we were at the Chinese restaurant over by the highway?"

Ava nodded her head and said, "The Human Palace?"

"The *Hunan* Palace," Eva said. "Remember we saw some Mexicans working there when we had dinner there a few weeks ago? I bet Alfredo works there, and the Chinese people are teaching him Chinese."

That idea seemed to explain everything without actually explaining anything, and Eva was satisfied with it. At her own home that evening, she looked up the phone number for the Hunan Palace and called to ask if they had anyone working there named Alfredo. A woman with a very strong Chinese accent said something that sounded like "To go?"

Maybe the woman thought Eva was trying to order a Chinese dinner called Alfredo. Eva finally convinced the woman she was looking for a *person* named Alfredo, and the woman said something like "Alfredo not here. Work lunch only today. Call back lunch."

So that *was* how Alfredo'd been learning Chinese. Eva was charmed by her detective work, but it still didn't settle very many questions about Alfredo. She still didn't know if he was an illegal alien, although it seemed to make sense that if Alfredo lived in an abandoned house, it meant he might be hiding so no one would send him back to his other country. She decided that even if it might make Alfredo mad or upset him, she had to ask. Sneaking the Spanish-English dictionary from her mom's office, she studied various ways to attempt to question Alfredo, and she wrote down the sentences so she wouldn't have to spend five or ten minutes looking up the words for each sentence as she stood before Alfredo.

With the written sentences and also the dictionary, Eva waited for Alfredo at his house the next afternoon. He came home with another grocery bag of Chinese take-out food and Fritos, and he again greeted Eva in Chinese.

"I don't know Chinese," Eva said.

Alfredo said something in Spanish.

"I don't know Spanish, either," Eva said. "When are you gonna learn English? I mean, *inglés*?"

"No inglés," Alfredo said, shaking his head apologetically.

"But anyway," Eva said, "I have to ask you some questions, which I've written down here," she said, pointing at her paper as Alfredo began eating his dinner. What worried Eva was the pronunciation of the words, which she wasn't very good at, so if she pronounced a word slightly wrong, it would become a completely different word, or just nonsense. She attempted a simple question: How many years old are you? What she said was *"¿Cómo muchos anos estás tú?"*

Alfredo stopped chewing for a second and looked surprised. He shook his head no and began chewing again. Eva suspected the problem there was the word *anos*. Depending on how you pronounced it—and she didn't know the right way—it could mean something else.

She gave up on that question and studied her next sentence fragment carefully, then tried to say it.

"¿Tener tú verde carda?" she said, which meant, "To have you green card?" The church committee talked about

green cards with Eva's dad, so she knew Alfredo needed one.

Alfredo swallowed some food and stared at Eva.

It sounded to him like Eva had just said, "Tapeworm you green thistle?"

She tried it again, just saying *"¿Verde carda?"*

Alfredo answered in Spanish, and the only word Eva understood for sure was "No." He could have been saying no for any reason, or he might have meant he had no green card. That was the problem with translating. Even if Eva correctly asked a question, there was no way she could understand the answer.

Alfredo chewed more food as Eva considered her difficulties. Instead of asking Alfredo if he was an illegal alien, what Eva wanted to try first was asking him if he was a political exile, since that would sound nicer. So she tried that.

"¿Político exputriar?" she said.

Alfredo started laughing. Probably another pronunciation error.

Alfredo was still laughing and seemed to be thoroughly amused with Eva, so she decided it would be okay now to ask—or try to ask—if he was an illegal alien.

"¿Ilegal extranjero?" she said.

She must have said that one right, because Alfredo contorted his face into a look of exaggerated offense and started rapidly saying Spanish things at her.

"Perdón," Eva said, which she hoped meant "pardon," or "forgive me."

"No problem," Alfredo said abruptly. Eva supposed he must have learned that American saying at the restaurant or somewhere, and she was relieved when he said it to her again.

Then Alfredo pointed at himself and said in an unhappy voice, *"Sí. Extranjero ilegal."*

For a while they looked at each other, knowing that language was mostly useless then as they each wondered what the other might do now. Alfredo looked a little sad or hopeless, as if he expected Eva to turn him in. He hadn't had to tell her, but he did anyway. He was a nice man. And the Statue of Liberty said something about "Give us your poor, your huddled masses." Alfredo was certainly poor, but Eva didn't know enough Spanish to ask him if he was a huddled mass.

Eva decided to say the one thing that might make Alfredo feel safe with her now.

"No problem," she said. "No problem."

Alfredo smiled weakly and said, *"Gracias."*

"I *know* that word!" Eva said happily. "I'm glad you didn't speak Chinese again."

But Alfredo went on and on very rapidly in Spanish, as if even though they couldn't understand each other, it was still good to have someone to talk to.

Among the many things that had confused Alfredo was when the little girl Eva asked him how many anuses he was. No one in Guatemala would have said such a thing. Just to insult him, someone might call him a *bastardo*. But never in all of his experience with insults and profanities had he ever heard anyone ask how many anuses he was.

Eva was Anglo, though. She didn't know Spanish. That was probably why she was using that book, to learn some Spanish. Probably that was why she asked him how many anuses he was, and if he was political cough-up. But they were both good girls, very nice to him, because they brought him food and iced tea and didn't tell anyone he was there. But what about those two boys? That still made Alfredo nervous. It made him go back inside the stinking, dusty, dark house with all the bugs, just to avoid being seen by somebody else walking by. It was almost cool in the house, which was shaded by trees most of the day. But only a little bit of sunlight came through the front door and windows, making it as dark and gloomy as a cave. Alfredo lit one of his candles and held it upright on the floor between some big rocks, because he didn't even have a candleholder. It depressed him to have had so little in Guatemala, and then to have come to America and have even less. America was supposed to be the land of opportunity. So far, it was the land of hiding. Ever since he first got into Texas, all the Mexicans told him he had to hide from the immigration people, without knowing who the immigration people were.

"Isn't America the land of the free?" Alfredo asked one of the Mexicans at the Chinese restaurant.

"That means they're free to ship you back home," the Mexican said.

Sitting down on a pile of old newspapers that he used as a chair, Alfredo sipped some warm Coke from a plastic bottle and wondered about the mystery of the *carta verde*, the green card. In his home, people knew about the green card in the same sense that they knew about the fountain of youth and the seven cities of gold. They were famous, and no one knew where they were. No one ever talked about the United States without mentioning life, liberty, and the green card. And then, just a few months ago when Alfredo sneaked into Texas in Laredo and got a job washing dishes, a Mexican named Andrés sold him a green card for five dollars. It looked brand new, with fresh green paint on it. When Alfredo showed the green card to this other Mexican named Luís, Luís called Alfredo a pitiable jackass. Luís used the blade of a pocketknife to scrape some of the green paint from the card to show the real words on the card.

"Western Auto," Luís said.

c·h·a·p·t·e·r

18

The news about the old skeleton and the Sons of Belial
gave Kenlow exactly the kind of satanic identity he'd been
looking for. Instead of just pretending to be some kind of
vague and commonplace satanist—which you could find in
any community—Kenlow could now pretend to be one of
the Sons of Belial. It was real and specific. It had a believable history. And most important, it offered the prestige
associated with human sacrifice.

He went out that night for his most daring act of public
terror yet. At approximately three in the morning, he nailed
a six-inch-long cow's tongue to the front door of the Elk's
Club downtown, and he used red spray paint to write the
word *Belial* on the front door. Later that day on the TV
news, Kenlow found out he'd actually nailed the cow's
tongue onto the front door of the PEO Sisterhood office.
He had no idea who they were. But when they were interviewed on TV, they turned out to be a bunch of old women
who seemed angry and afraid, so Kenlow felt he'd been
successful in at least scaring *some*body.

Kenlow was disappointed that no one got to see it on
TV. The word *Belial* was still on the door. That was good.
But he really felt cheated that the cow's tongue had been

removed. He felt better, though, when the reporter interviewed the police chief, which would make his vandalism seem more threatening and thus enhance Kenlow's alarming reputation. But then he felt worse when the police chief didn't seem to take any of it very seriously. The police chief said he thought probably it was some teenage boys who did everything, and not any real members of the Sons of Belial.

"But we'll certainly investigate it all," the police chief said.

"Do you have any suspects in mind?" the reporter said.

"Not so far. I suppose we'll begin our investigation by asking local farmers if they've noticed that one of their cows is missing its tongue."

"So you really think this represents an instance of cattle mutilation?"

The police chief took his cowboy hat off and rubbed some sweat from his forehead. He said, "Well, I will say this. You can buy a cow's tongue at the grocery store. It makes satanism so convenient."

That just ruined it for Kenlow. Most of the potential fear he'd imagined evoking had been replaced by amusement and scorn, which almost made him despair of ever becoming a reputable satanist. He'd just need to think of more convincing symbolic acts of evil—maybe look for a support group, or possibly go to an actual slaughterhouse somewhere to find something more exotic than a cow's tongue. Maybe an entire cow's head. But that might be too big to carry around in a paper bag. Also, someone might get suspicious if you tried to buy a cow's head. You couldn't just say it was for dinner.

Ideally, he'd just go out and kill a calf and cut its head off. But he could never be so brutal to an animal. So for the time being, Kenlow decided his source of satanic animal parts would continue to be the meat department at Dave's Big Basted Hen.

c·h·a·p·t·e·r
19

Eva rode her bike to the shopping center and parked it out front by the newspaper machine at the drugstore and went on in to the pharmacy, where two women waited for the pharmacist to give them pills of something. Eva stood off to the side of the counter and looked at the colorful rows of packages with names such as Trojan and Night Rider.

All the customers were gone, and Eva looked up over the elevated counter at Diego Guerra, who smiled at her.

"Well, Eva . . . did you come to visit me at work?" he asked.

"Yes, sir," Eva said. "I came here to see if you could help me do something."

"Do something? What do you need done?"

"Well," Eva said, looking behind her to make sure no one was nearby to hear her. She looked at Diego Guerra again and said, "You're part Mexican, aren't you?"

"I think all of me is Mexican."

"And you speak Spanish, don't you?"

Diego Guerra responded by saying something in Spanish. Eva was puzzled.

"I just said 'How may I help you?' in Spanish."

"Oh. Well okay. Well anyway, I know this man who

lives around here who's probably from Guatemala. He speaks Spanish, and also Chinese.''

"Chinese? I don't know they spoke Chinese in Guatemala.''

"Well I don't think he learned it there. I think he learned it at a Chinese restaurant.''

"Oh. That's understandable, I suppose. And what about this man?''

"Well, you see, I think he's an illegal alien. I'm pretty sure. I've been using a Spanish-English dictionary to try to talk to him, but it takes too long to look up the words, and I don't think I'm saying 'em right, so it's pretty hard to talk to him. And then sometimes he speaks Chinese, which makes it harder. But I asked him if he was an *ilegal extranjero*, and he said *sí*. I think he trusts me. I haven't told anybody else about this. Nobody. I think if somebody finds out about him, they'll send him back to Guatemala or somewhere because he's illegal. I don't think people should be illegal.''

"No. People shouldn't be illegal. Maybe you should come up here where we can talk privately,'' Diego Guerra said.

Eva walked up the steps behind the counter and sat on a padded folding chair. Diego Guerra sat on a big stool near Eva and smiled at her.

"You say you haven't told anybody else about your friend?'' he asked.

"No, sir. You're the first one.''

"And why did you pick me?''

"Because I thought maybe you'd know some people who used to be illegal aliens but they became American citizens, and you'd know what to do.''

"I might,'' he said. "But you have to promise me something. You have to promise me you won't tell anybody else about this, since it could lead to a great deal of trouble. But if we begin to solve this problem of yours, then you'll have to tell your parents about it. Will you promise me that?''

"Yes, sir.''

"Good. And now I'm going to tell you a little story. It's a secret. You can't tell anyone, just like I can't tell anyone *your* secret. Okay?"

"Okay."

"Here's the story. One time there was a young man who lived in Mexico City."

"Was that you?" Eva asked.

"Why, I've never even told you this story before and already you've guessed."

Eva laughed.

"I'll tell you a different story then. One time many years ago in Mexico, a young man who lived near the border between Mexico and Texas used to go look at the Rio Grande River and stand on its banks in Mexico and look over at Texas. Although he was a Mexican and he loved Mexico, he knew he could probably never get a very good job in Mexico. The young man knew the only way he could save up enough money to have a good life was if he worked his whole life, died, and then was resurrected so he could work his whole life again. That would take too long. So one day, he snuck into America and eventually became an American citizen. Coincidentally, that man is me. So, yes, I might be able to help your friend. But don't tell anyone we talked about this. You should go home, now, and I have to distribute pills for the ills. But if you come back here tomorrow afternoon, we can talk some more and see what can be done. And don't worry. There's usually a solution for every problem, as well as a problem with every solution. We'll work on this."

Eva refused to believe it when Tommy called her in the morning and said he was out by the old warlock's house the night before with his brother's camcorder and got a video of Satan or Stalinists.

"Stalinists? You mean there are Russians there?" Eva said, trying to grind Tommy a little bit for his ignorance.

"I mean *satan*-ists," Tommy said. He whispered so ex-

citedly on the phone and with such genuine belief in what
he was saying that Eva worried he really had gotten something on video, before she had had a chance to talk with
Diego Guerra again about helping Alfredo. So Eva had to
go to Tommy's house to see.

It was like what her mom and dad talked about at dinner
one night, saying that with everyone running around with
video cameras in America, getting videos of weddings and
births and armed robberies and everything, that no one
would ever need to start a police state in America.

"You'd have a video state," her dad had said. "You
wouldn't need the government to spy on you if Americans
liked doing it as a hobby. And then the country would
become like *The Gestapo's Funniest Home Videos*."

Eva was surprised that Tommy even knew how to use a
camcorder, since he wasn't especially good at anything in
school. But when she got to his house, Tommy put a tape
into the VCR and turned it on. "Now you'll see," he said.
All you could see on the TV screen at first was black.

"It's night," Tommy explained.

"So. You videotaped the night?" Eva said, trying to
sound indifferent.

"Well I couldn't use lights. That'd give my position
away. Here," Tommy said, and did something with the
remote control and sped up the tape to where you could
see a little blur of light, and he stopped the tape there and
played it at regular speed.

"See?" he said insistently. "There's the light in the
house."

There *was* a light. From the angle at which the tape was
made, you could tell Tommy took it from behind the fallen
tree, about forty feet from the front of the house. A faint
yellow light shone through the front door and one of the
front windows, making the house look spookier than normal.

"Now do you believe me?" Tommy asked.

"Believe you about what?" Eva said.

"That there's something *in* the house."

Eva couldn't pretend she didn't see the light, but she also didn't want to act like it meant very much.

"Well there certainly is a light in there," she said. "But I don't know what it means." It had to be Alfredo.

"I don't know what it means either," Tommy said. "But if no one lives in the house, how come there's a light there?"

"I don't know. Maybe it's some teenagers."

Tommy didn't say anything, like he was considering that possibility. They watched the tape for a while, which showed the same scene over and over.

"There's nothing happening," Eva said.

"But that's all there was at first."

"So, you got a whole tape of nothing?"

"No. There's some stuff. You'll see."

After a while, you could see a shadow moving along one of the inside walls.

"There!" Tommy said. "There's someone in the house!"

"Well like I said, it could be anybody," Eva said. "It could just be some high school boys."

Tommy shook his head no. "But in a few seconds, you'll hear music," he said. And he was right. The camcorder also had a microphone, and now you could hear a guitar, just barely. It wasn't a song Eva recognized. It was a pretty sloppy song, played with long pauses and bad notes, just the way Alfredo played.

"What about *that*?" Tommy said.

Eva listened to the music for a few seconds, as if trying to identify it.

"I didn't know Satan played guitar," she said.

Tommy sighed with great irritation but didn't say anything. He just let the video keep going until it was over, then pushed the button to turn it off.

"Well there's *some*body out there," Tommy said. "That's no normal person in there. It's something strange. I wonder if I should show this tape to the police."

"Yeah," Eva said, and stood up to leave. "I bet the

police are always arresting people for playing guitar.''

She hoped to make Tommy feel dumb enough to leave the whole idea alone, but it was risky. Despite all the dumb things Tommy had ever done, he never seemed convinced that he couldn't do more.

On the appointed afternoon of the appointed day, which was a phrase Eva got from a book about spies, she crept stealthily through the woods to attend the covert rendezvous. She arrived out at the old warlock's house and waited there for Diego Guerra and Alfredo. A few minutes later Diego Guerra came walking out of the woods alone and waited with Eva to see if Alfredo would come home.

"What time does Alfredo usually get here?" Diego Guerra said.

"I don't know," Eva said.

"Too bad we didn't plan this plan," Diego Guerra said.

But Alfredo did arrive, about twenty minutes later, with his usual bag of food and a deeply worried look at seeing an adult with Eva. Before Alfredo could turn and run away, Diego Guerra started saying a whole lot of Spanish things that seemed to calm Alfredo down a little bit, and Alfredo nervously walked over to Eva and Diego Guerra by the front porch and put his bag down.

"Please tell him we're only trying to help him, or he might think I'm just trying to get him in trouble and he'll hate me," Eva said.

Diego Guerra gestured at Eva and said a lot of Spanish things to Alfredo. Alfredo smiled a little bit at Eva and spoke a whole lot of Spanish. The two of them took turns speaking so rapidly that Eva thought that even if she knew Spanish, she couldn't listen to them fast enough. She thought Spanish must be the fastest language in the world.

"What's he saying?" Eva asked, and Diego Guerra just ignored her and kept talking and listening to Alfredo's answers.

"Did you tell him about Tommy?" Eva said. "You better tell him people think Satan lives here."

Diego Guerra translated that to Alfredo and got Alfredo's reply.

"He says he has no roommates."

It made Eva smile. It was Alfredo's first joke to her, or at least the first joke Eva had translated for her. Diego Guerra went on, saying to Eva, "He says he saw some boys outside one day and that he howled at them so they'd think a ghost lives here and they'd leave him alone."

"Well now they think Satan lives here," Eva said. "Tell him Tommy got a video of this house at night and he thinks satanists are mutilating cows here."

Diego Guerra told him, and listened to Alfredo's reply, and then said, "He says if a cow was in the house with him, the cow would probably mutilate *him*. Let me talk with him a while longer and find out more about him."

As they talked, Alfredo ate his Chinese dinner, giving an egg-roll to Eva and Diego Guerra. The two of them talked for about half an hour and seemed to be getting along very well when everyone heard some voices down the trail. It was two police officers in uniforms, along with Tommy and Tommy's father.

"Eva," Diego Guerra said quietly as the officers approached. "I'm going to have to say I didn't know he was an illegal alien, or I might get arrested. There's nothing we can do now. I'm sorry."

One of the police officers asked who everyone was and why they were at the house, and Diego Guerra explained in an almost true way that he'd gone there with Eva to try to help this homeless man, Alfredo. As the officer and Diego Guerra talked and looked at Alfredo, whose boyish face was pale and frightened, Tommy's father looked at Tommy and said, "Tommy, you did the right thing."

Eva didn't know how it could be the right thing to arrest a helpless man for being helpless.

"Eva? What're *you* doing here?" Tommy said.

She was too frightened to answer.

"Is he an illegal alien?" one of the officers asked Diego Guerra.

"He didn't tell me," Diego Guerra lied. "We were just trying to find out why he's been staying here and if we could help him find better shelter."

Alfredo suddenly began speaking Chinese.

"What in the hell's *he* saying?" one of the officers said.

"It's Chinese," Diego Guerra said.

"We got a Mexican speaking *Chinese*?"

"He's not Mexican. He's Guatemalan," Eva said.

One of the officers said, "Oh. Well that explains it."

"We think he learned Chinese in the restaurant where he works," Eva said, trying to overcome her fear by being factual.

"How do you know so much about this guy?" the other officer asked. "You seen him before?"

"He's my friend," Eva said. "He lives here because he doesn't have any money. He just needs a place to live, is all. We were gonna help him. You're supposed to help people who need it."

"Well that's true, young lady," one of the officers said. "And we'll see that he gets some help after we take him downtown for questioning and find out if he's an illegal."

"How can someone be illegal?" Eva said. "How can it be illegal just to be a person?"

"Well being a person isn't illegal, honey," the officer said in a kind voice. "But being in the United States without a visa is."

c·h·a·p·t·e·r

20

Having never been arrested before, Alfredo could have been overcome by fear and sadness during his car ride to jail. Instead he kept talking to the two police officers in the front seat, repeating gleefully: "A new car! A new car!"

Alfredo was riding in a new car for the first time in his life. To celebrate, Alfredo kept giving Fritos to the police officers and chewing on Fritos himself, thinking how lucky he was to smell the new smell of a new car, and feel the car sway gently around curves, and sit in the thoroughly dirtless and comfortable backseat on this wonderful American day where, even though he was going to jail, it would at least be in a comfortable room with plumbing and electricity and not quite so many bugs as he was used to. That new man he met, Diego Guerra, told him some odd things he didn't completely remember; things about getting help from a lawyer, and maybe getting a green card, and just being comfortable in jail while someone tried to help him.

So he wasn't really worried. He ate Fritos and felt the wonderful sensations of a new car and waved at people on the sidewalks in town as the police car drove to the police station, as if he were a celebrity in a parade and all the people he waved at were his adoring new neighbors in the most wonderful country in the world. After Alfredo and the police officers got out of the car, Alfredo looked at the glistening concrete-and-steel jail building and imagined he was going to a hotel where they had a *room* for him. Yes!

But it was a small room, with steel bars. The smallness of the room made Alfredo think of something Diego Guerra told him about the words on the Statue of Liberty. It was something about huddled masses. Now that he knew those words, Alfredo felt happy to be a huddled mass. It seemed so American to be huddling in jail.

His room had another guest, too—a white man wearing clothes like a farmer, who was fast asleep on a little bed. Alfredo, too, now had his own little bed, with a real mattress, and he had a toilet and a sink. And most important, most fantastic, Alfredo's new room had *a color TV!*

The TV was suspended by some brackets in the ceiling that prevented anyone from moving it. But it was facing down at an angle where Alfredo could watch it while sitting in bed.

"I didn't expect such a nice room," Alfredo said to the police officer who locked him in his room, but the officer didn't know Spanish, so he didn't say "You're welcome."

In his glee and gratitude, Alfredo wanted to wake up his guest and introduce himself and find out what time *Wheel of Fortune* came on and discuss all the other shows and movies they might watch together. But almost certainly his guest spoke only English, so there was no reason to disturb his sleep only to find out that they couldn't talk to each other. Alfredo tried to be very quiet, to avoid waking his guest. He reached up and turned the TV on, with the volume down very low, and began switching from channel to channel to see what was on. He didn't recognize any of the shows. He stood at the steel bars and looked down the hall to where he knew the police officers were and said quietly, "Excuse me. Is there a TV schedule?"

No one answered. What he could do was keep switching channels over and over every so often, to eventually find *Wheel of Fortune*.

Then he tested the softness of his very own mattress. It made him feel sleepy, and he lay down with his head on the pillow and looked sleepily up at the soothing TV with its mysterious English jabber. He couldn't help but think that now his life had been divided into two parts. The first part was where he slept on dirty rags and old newspapers in a crumbling house with flying bugs and ghosts. The second part was his unexpected rise into a new and glorious world where he had a soft bed and a color TV. In America, even being in jail seemed like a privilege.

Chief McLemore looked at all of the Galts in his office and realized there was something extraordinary about his new prisoner. The two little girls looked almost desperate, which upset him. He wanted to offer them something to soothe them, but all he had were cigarettes and bourbon. At least he could smile, and thereby seem less ominous.

"I've never had an entire family in here before," McLemore said.

"None of us have ever been in a police station before, either," Daniel said.

McLemore leaned back in his chair at his desk and said, "Well I'm sure this isn't one of your favorite family outings, so I'll try to speed things up for you.

"Originally we were advised there might be satanists out there at the house mutilating cows or something, which I personally think is a bunch of . . . well, is ridiculous. But I told the investigating officers to look for evidence of animal mutilation."

"I see," Eva's dad said.

"Yeah," McLemore said. "And what would that be, anyway? A hamburger wrapper?"

Eva's mom laughed. McLemore smiled, and everyone seemed a little bit less tense.

"I don't think we have any genuine satanists, but after all that trouble in Waco, and the news about the Sons of Belial, one thing we don't need is our very own cult here in Waxahachie. So I was pretty relieved when my officers didn't have to arrest Satan himself. I'm not sure what violation we could've charged him with anyway. Vagrancy? And as far as I know, there aren't any state or federal laws prohibiting the existence of Satan. I think even if we brought Satan in, we couldn't hold him for anything except being highly disliked in the Bible.''

"If you look at it that way, half the people in the Old Testament could be arrested for felonies and disorderly conduct,'' Eva's dad said.

"I'm just grateful they don't live in Waxahachie,'' McLemore said. "Anyway, we were relieved to go out to that old house and just find a skinny young boy from Guatemala who speaks Chinese, which isn't illegal. What *is* illegal is being here without the proper papers saying he has permission from the federal government to be here. The truth is, we got a man back there in jail for the crime of we don't know who he is. We'll have to hold him for a few days or so, until we can establish his identity and all that. Naturally, we'll have to contact the INS about him. But—in case anyone here has a personal interest in helping him get a green card or something—you should know that it might take me a while to expedite things. I can expedite real slow, if I'm in the mood. Meantime, I'll have to keep Alfredo in jail on suspicion of vagrancy or some other suspicion I can't think of. Maybe suspicion of suspicion.''

"What's suspicion of suspicion?'' Eva's mom said.

"Just a formality, ma'am. Meanwhile, someone could look for legal remedies for this situation, maybe help the boy out. Now if you'll excuse me, I've got urgent police affairs to attend to. Someone stole the Virgin Mary stamp machine from the post office.''

One of the police officers in the post office got down on his hands and knees and began using a piece of white chalk to draw the outline of the missing Virgin Mary stamp-vending machine.

"Don't *do* that," Chief McLemore said quietly, so none of the distressed and curious onlookers crowding nearby could hear him. He leaned closer to the officer and said, "This *isn't* a goddamn murder."

"Sorry," the officer whispered.

The postmaster walked up to McLemore and said, "Thank you for getting here so quickly, but you won't have to stay long. We'll have U.S. Postal Service investigators as well as FBI agents here today to take charge of the investigation. The theft is a federal offense."

"I suppose it is," McLemore said, nodding politely. "It just seems strange to call in the entire federal government to locate a stamp machine." In fact, though, he was pissed off to realize his department was regarded as extraneous. Fine. Screw the bastards. McLemore would stay the hell out of their way.

He stared at the dozens of distressed and disappointed people loitering near the spot where the Virgin Mary stamp machine once stood. There was always a chance that the thief or thieves would come back to gloat about their theft, especially in a big crowd where they wouldn't think they were conspicuous.

Kenlow always felt conspicuous. His sense of exhilaration and guilt from being the local satanist caused him to worry that virtually anyone in town could spontaneously sense that Kenlow was guilty of something. That was why he wore a baseball cap and sunglasses as a disguise there among the crowd at the post office. He tried to seem as disturbed and outraged as everyone else there that the town's only religious shrine—the Virgin Mary stamp machine—had been stolen. But he wasn't disturbed. He was thrilled, in a guilty way, because he thought he knew who stole the stamp machine. Some man in the Get It 'N Get Out convenience store, where Kenlow worked, had quietly boasted to some other men in the store about stealing a stamp machine. Maybe it was just a joke, but the man seemed pretty serious, and he looked mean enough to steal something. Kenlow's first impulse had been to do the decent thing and call the police about the man. But when he remembered he was supposed to be the town satanist, he overcame his impulse to be decent.

As he stood there in the post office, Kenlow decided he wanted to complicate the situation. He repeatedly suggested to anyone nearby that only satanists would steal the Virgin Mary stamp machine. The rumor spread like a wave and instantly reached Chief McLemore.

"Chief?" a man in a cowboy hat said. "You think satanists stole the stamp machine?"

"Could be," McLemore said. "Maybe they're planning a letter-writing rampage."

It was the kind of deeply sarcastic remark easily misunderstood by literal-minded people, such as Melissa Kidwell, a reporter for the *Waxahachie Times*, who was standing next to McLemore at the moment.

"Really?" she said while scribbling down the chief's speculation on a notepad. "Why would satanists start a letter-writing rampage?"

McLemore was somewhat stunned by the question. Rather than explain his sarcasm, he simply persisted in it.

"Maybe they're a modern cult trying to recruit members through direct mail," he said. "That would explain the need for stamps."

The next morning the *Waxahachie Times* ran a front-page headline that read VIRGIN MARY STAMP MACHINE STOLEN; SATANISTS SUSPECTED IN POSSIBLE LETTER-WRITING RAMPAGE.

Kenlow had no idea what to think about the story. Either the police chief was stupid, or possibly he really *did* have evidence that a genuine satanic cult was at work in Waxahachie. It frightened Kenlow to think that he'd been running around the area making phony satanic pentagrams when *real* satanists—maybe the Sons of Belial—might discover him and then punish him for being a phony. He'd have to be even more cautious now. But the newspaper gave him an idea. He could actually start writing satanic letters, just like the police chief said. It was perfect. He wouldn't have to risk getting caught somewhere by satanists or anyone else. He could simply mail letters with no return address, and scare people *that* way.

After finding Eva's last name in the newspaper story about where she saw the unidentified teenager near the latest pentagram, Kenlow found her dad's address in the phone book and wrote Eva a letter.

Dear Eva,
   I'm everywhere you want to be.

In a way, it seemed threatening. But it also sounded like a TV commercial. Kenlow threw that letter away and started a new one.

Dear Eva,
   The Great Horned One is aware of your presence.
Tell no one you saw me. Oh Death, where is thy stain?

Kenlow wasn't sure where he remembered that last line from, but it made the letter seem more frightening. He mailed the letter and waited for the next shocked reaction, which would make Kenlow even more of a celebrity, even though no one knew who he was.

21

Eva saw a letter addressed to her. The only other letters she'd ever gotten were Christmas and birthday cards from relatives, so she was astonished to get what looked like a real letter just for her. She gave the rest of the mail to her mom in the kitchen and said, "Somebody sent me a letter."

"Really? Who's it from?" her mom said.

"It doesn't say."

"Well open it."

She opened it with her mom standing next to her, so they both read the letter together.

Dear Eva,

The Great Horned One is aware of your presence. Tell no one you saw me. Oh Death, where is thy stain?

Sincerely,
Unidentified Teenager

"What?" Eva's mom said as she took the letter from Eva's hand.

Eva felt suddenly uneasy as she realized who the unidentified teenager was.

"It's from that boy we saw," Eva said.

Eva's mom read the letter again and said, ''What a little bastard.''

It startled Eva. Her mom hardly ever cussed. It meant the letter was pretty serious.

''What's it mean?'' Eva said.

''Not very much, I think,'' her mom said, and patted Eva's head in a way that meant she was trying to comfort Eva.

''What's the Great Horned One?''

''This is a stupid, idiotic, juvenile letter, Eva. I think the little jackass is trying to scare you, which I won't tolerate. The boy's just making up stuff with no real meaning. I'll report this to the police and go looking for that little sociopath myself, if I have to. In fact, I'm calling the police now,'' she said, and walked over to the phone.

''But Mom. It says don't tell anyone I *saw* him,'' Eva said.

Her mom walked back to Eva and kneeled down in front of her and pressed her hands gently on Eva's cheeks as she looked in her eyes.

''Well, you've already told the police. There's nothing to be afraid of. I promise you. That boy—that little idiot— is just playing a senseless little game that I intend to see stopped. You're not in danger. *He* is.''

It was the first time Eva ever heard her mom sound like she could hurt someone. It almost made Eva feel safe, except if her mom was that mad about the letter, then maybe Kenlow really *was* threatening her. She almost started to say Kenlow's name, but she was scared.

The police sent Det. Klowosky to the house to look at the letter. He sat at the kitchen table with Eva and her mom and read the letter and the envelope, then sat there quietly thinking, with an intelligent and slightly puzzled expression.

'' 'Unidentified Teenager,' '' he said. ''That was how he was named in the newspaper story. I think it means he likes the press. The publicity. He's probably doing this for thrills. I'll bet he's waiting right now for a newspaper story about this letter. My advice to you, Ms. Galt, is to keep this quiet. Don't tell anyone about it—especially reporters.''

''You think that will help?'' Eva's mom said.

''I'm pretty sure. We don't have to tell the press about this if you don't want us to.''

''Then don't.''

''We won't. I think if the boy realizes he won't get any attention, he'll stop harassing Eva,'' Det. Klowosky said. He smiled at Eva and said, ''Don't worry about this dumb letter. We'll go looking around for this boy. And there's no reason to think he's really a satanist. I don't think real satanists would try to perform satanic ceremonies with Vienna sausages.''

Eva smiled at the idea.

After the detective left with the letter, Eva's mom hugged her a little longer than normal.

''Don't worry,'' she said in a worried way.

22

Living in a town where someone had stolen a Virgin Mary stamp machine was more interesting than Eva could have predicted. She felt a little bit proud for the town that U.S. Postal Service inspectors and the police and federal marshals and everybody were all in town investigating the missing miraculous vending machine, almost as if the post office were a religious shrine. The newspaper said Waxahachie had started to become the Mecca of Texas or the Lourdes of the West. There was even a rumor that the pope was coming to the post office. Eva's dad said, ''Can't he get stamps in Rome?'' It was strange, imagining the pope licking a stamp. The pope seemed too important to have to lick anything.

Nobody knew what happened to the stamp machine. In the newspaper they said the front doors of the post office were always unlocked at night so people could go in the lobby and buy stamps from the stamp machines, so it looked like somebody just walked in when no one else was there and took the whole stamp machine out of the wall and probably loaded it into a truck or something and drove off with no witnesses, except for the tender eyes of the Virgin Mary herself. According to the TV news, the police and postal service investigators had no real suspects except practically anybody who'd ever been in the post office. Even though Eva thought the smudge on the glass looked like Sugarloaf Mountain, not the Virgin Mary, still it seemed like someone had robbed a church or a tomb, which made it terribly interesting. Eva and Ava went down to the post office to look at the spot where the stamp machine used to be and maybe look at newspaper and TV reporters and government investigators and see if maybe the pope or someone else from Vatican City was there to say special prayers and buy some stamps.

There in the small crowd of cowboys and Mexicans and farmers and postal service guys was a TV camera crew with a pretty woman holding a microphone and trying to interview a Mexican woman who didn't know English. It seemed to Eva that they almost always hired only pretty women to be TV reporters, as if no one would believe the news if a regular-looking woman said it.

The TV reporter said to the Mexican woman, "Are you upset about the stamp machine being stolen?" and as the Mexican woman answered in Spanish, a Mexican man next to her said, "No. They've still got stamps here."

Then the TV reporter said to the man, "Are you familiar with the image of the Virgin Mary that was said to be on the stamp machine?"

"*Sí,*" the man said, and now you couldn't tell if he was going to speak Spanish or English. It was fun.

"Have you heard of anyone having come here to look at the image of the Virgin Mary who later reported experiencing any miracles?" the reporter said.

"My sister Ramona looked at the thing on the stamp machine, and when she went home, her toaster broke."

"What I mean is, do you know of anyone who looked at the image and later experienced a healing of some sort, such as someone who had a medical problem and . . ."

"My mother here had a cavity, but no longer," the man said.

"And do you think that was because she went to the image of the Virgin Mary?"

"No. She went to the dentist."

The reporter finally found a Mexican woman willing to speak English about the stamp machine. The woman said to the reporter, "I came here a few days ago to look at the Virgin Mary in the glass, and I prayed, and I bought a book of stamps from the machine, and I went home and wrote a letter and put one of the stamps on the letter and I mailed it."

"Was it an important letter?" the reporter asked.

"Oh, yes. It was my entry in the Publisher's Clearinghouse Sweepstakes."

"I'm not sure I understand. What's the religious significance of that?"

"I prayed to the Blessed Mother to help me win ten million dollars."

The reporter said, "But do you know of anyone who has had a personal miracle after looking at the stamp machine?"

"My brother, Hernando, has bad vision. He came here to look at the image of the Virgin Mary."

"And was his vision improved?"

"No. His eyes are so bad, he couldn't see the Virgin Mary."

People weren't having very good miracles, Eva thought.

The whole subject of miracles, and therefore the whole subject of God, mystified Eva. Sometimes on the religious TV shows that Eva occasionally watched part of, the minister would ask some crippled or sick person to come up front and be healed. The minister would just touch his hands real hard on the person's head, kind of the way you'd get a real good grip on a lid that was stuck on a jar of pickles. It sort of did look that way, like the minister was trying to unscrew their heads. And then the person acted healed, but Eva's dad said maybe the person wasn't sick in the first place. He said possibly there really could be miracles, but there were also a lot of fakes, and it was hard to know the difference. Eva didn't understand why God wouldn't look down at a fraudulent minister in the middle of a fake miracle and say, "Stop that, you fraud," right on TV. It seemed like God was always talking to somebody during the old days, but now, he never said anything.

And also, if God thought it was a good idea to heal someone who was paralyzed and in a wheelchair, why did he do it only to people who showed up on TV shows? Why didn't God just heal *every*body? It made it look like God just wanted to be on TV. And it didn't make sense that if God could do *any*thing, that what he decided to do was put a blurry, dark image on a stamp machine that got stolen. How was that a miracle?

Maybe the miracle was that people believed in God no matter what.

Right then, a big silver tour bus pulled into the post office parking lot with a sign on the front of the bus saying it was from Idaho. A lot of women and a few men started getting off the bus and walking inside the lobby past Eva and Ava. When a middle-aged woman in the group found out from a postal clerk that the Virgin Mary stamp machine had been stolen, the woman got on her knees in front of the empty spot where the stamp machine used to be and called out, "Our lady is gone!"

The television crews rushed over to her, blocking Eva's view, and there were lots of other ladies behind her, so Eva didn't know which lady was gone, but everyone seemed terribly upset about it.

"Someone's missing," Eva said quietly to Ava, and they were both sad about the missing lady from Idaho.

Eva was afraid that when her mom's lawyer friend, Gretchen Schramm, came to the house to visit, it was so Eva's parents could be divorced. Eva knew almost nothing about divorce, but from watching parts of the O. J. Simpson murder trial on TV, Eva assumed she might be called upon to be a witness in the divorce. She desperately hoped her parents wouldn't get divorced, and when she remembered part of a movie she'd seen about some gangster on trial, she walked up to Gretchen in the living room and said, "I plead the fifth amendment."

"You do? And why do you plead the fifth amendment?" Gretchen asked.

"It's the advice of my attorney," Eva said.

"Eva . . . what are you talking about?" Eva's mom said.

"I refuse to answer on the grounds that it might tend to incinerate me," Eva said.

"I'm not here to incinerate you," Gretchen said. "I'm here to talk with your mom about helping your friend Alfredo."

"Oh," Eva said. That was better.

The first fact Eva learned about immigration laws from listening to Gretchen was that the green card was really pink. It was actually called an Alien Registration Receipt Card, and it allowed aliens to work in the United States. When the cards were first made, they were green, and no one knew why. After everybody got used to the green cards, the government decided to make them pink, and no one knew why. Eva decided the government was as inscrutable as God.

For a while, Eva listened to her mom and Gretchen talk about a hopelessly complex fog of rules inside a shower of regulations about such things as special immigrants, refugees, and political asylees, temporary protected status, amnesty, special agricultural workers, marriage to a U.S. citizen, and enough other bewildering complexities that Gretchen said that the easiest way for an alien to get into the United States legally was by an act of God. She said, "If, for example, there was a massive volcanic eruption in Guatemala that shot debris and ash and Guatemalans about forty thousand feet into the atmosphere, and some of the people were carried by high-altitude winds into the United States, I don't think they could be called illegal aliens. Probably what they'd be called is dead. The dead are excluded from immigration laws."

Alfredo wasn't dead, so they'd have to try a different category. One possibility was to try getting Alfredo classified as a refugee or a political exile.

"How could he become a refugee?" Eva's mom said.

"First, he'd have to go back to Guatemala," Gretchen said. "You can only be a refugee if you're not here."

"But if he was in Guatemala, he wouldn't be a refugee."

"Well he can't be one here, either, without permission."

"But isn't the definition of a refugee someone who has no place to go?"

"Well, Emily, yes. But I think the INS would say Alfredo has a place to go—Guatemala."

"But if he already left Guatemala and came here, why does he have to go back to Guatemala to be allowed to come here, where he already is?"

"I think what you have to understand is that the law is under no obligation to make sense."

They decided it was too difficult to make Alfredo a refugee, even if he already was one, and they looked at some papers Gretchen brought, which said you could gain status as a political exile if you were trying to escape religious or political persecution.

"Is he being persecuted?" Gretchen said.

"Yes," Eva's mom said.

"By whom?"

"The INS."

"Well that doesn't count. Is he being persecuted by anyone in Guatemala?"

Eva's mom looked at Eva and said, "Eva, whenever you talked with Alfredo, did he say he was being persecuted?"

"Well," Eva said, "one time I used your Spanish-English dictionary to try to ask Alfredo some questions. I think I asked him if he was political cough-up. It was a mistake. I meant to ask him if he was in trouble with his government."

"And what was his answer?" Gretchen said.

"I don't know. All he speaks is Spanish and Chinese. But he knows how to say 'Fritos.' "

"Well let's forget the persecution angle for now," Gretchen said. "We'll need to have someone like Diego talk with Alfredo and find out if there's any basis for claiming persecution. Meanwhile, the only other way I know of that might help Alfredo become legal is if he marries a U.S. citizen."

"Marriage," Eva's mom mused. "I don't know if Alfredo could get a date while he's in jail."

That afternoon, Eva and her mom and Diego Guerra went to the jail to have Diego Guerra speak with Alfredo about the possibilities of persecution and marriage.

"Ask him if, in the time he's been here in Texas, he's met any women who are U.S. citizens who might want to marry him," Eva's mom said.

The answer, translated by Diego Guerra, was, "He says he likes this one woman he saw on TV whose buttocks are like great fertile hills. I think he saw her in a commercial for jeans."

"He wants to marry a TV woman," Eva's mom said hopelessly.

So then they talked about the persecution part.

Using the INS documents Gretchen had, Diego Guerra asked Alfredo if he had a well-founded fear of persecution based on his race, religion, nationality, political opinions, or membership in a particular social group.

"He says he doesn't *have* any political opinions," Diego Guerra said. "He says if you have political opinions in Guatemala, you might be shot, and so most people who have political opinions quickly get rid of them. So then I asked him if he'd ever been intimidated or threatened for his religious beliefs, and he said the only religious belief he has is that God is in his Heaven and never goes to Guatemala. I think he might easily have suffered intimidation and threats in Guatemala, but to *prove* that, it's probably too hard. Also, I think Alfredo is poorly educated and something of a dreamer, so I have no way of knowing whether what he tells me is true or just a fanciful exaggeration that he likes to tell me because he enjoys talking with someone who speaks Spanish.''

''You mean he might be lying?'' Eva's mom said.

''Well, I wouldn't say lying. It's just possible that he isn't terribly familiar with reality.''

Diego Guerra talked with Alfredo for a long time, to find out more about him. Alfredo said he was seventeen years old and had lived in a slum near Guatemala City with his eighteen brothers and sisters, as well as assorted dogs, cats, and lizards. He never went to school because everyone had to work for the family. Sometimes he wanted to be a *fútbol* star—*fútbol* meaning soccer—because *fútbol* was the most popular sport in the world. On TV at a friend's house one time, Alfredo saw a movie about a brain surgeon, and he thought he might want to become a brain surgeon so he could look at a brain. He'd never seen a brain before and wondered what they looked like. He also thought he might want to become an astronaut because astronauts wore air-conditioned suits, and in Guatemala, anybody would like their clothes to be air-conditioned. The last job he had had before coming to Texas was in a souvenir shop in Guatemala City where they made and sold fake Mayan relics to tourists who thought they were buying black market relics from Mayan temples.

Because he'd seen how Americans travel from watching a few American movies, Alfredo had tried to take a cab to America.

''Where to?'' the cab driver said.

''America,'' Alfredo said.

''I don't go that far. Get out,'' the cab driver said.

Alfredo began walking and hitchhiking to America, expecting that when he finally got there, he'd see the only thing he associated with America: the Statue of Liberty. When he finally arrived in the United States, he spent several hours walking through Laredo, looking for the Statue of Liberty.

"They ain't got one here," a Mexican told him. "You in the wrong state, *muchacho*."

Alfredo couldn't recall exactly why he went to Waxahachie rather than some other town. It was just that since he didn't know why in particular he should favor one town over another, he decided to end his journey in Waxahachie because that's where he was when his journey got too tiring.

Alfredo said he wasn't mad about being in jail. The jail was actually more pleasant than the abandoned house or his home in Guatemala. And he got to watch TV every day.

Since Chief McLemore hadn't yet contacted the INS about Alfredo, Alfredo could stay indefinitely in jail, though Gretchen said it was actually illegal, since Alfredo hadn't been charged with a crime. But it also was a sort of neutral way to keep Alfredo in a comfortable shelter while everyone tried to figure out what to do about him. Sometimes in the early evening, Eva and Ava went to the jail to bring Alfredo a basket with his dinner in it, such as fried chicken or pot roast with vegetables, which was exactly the way Otis the drunk was treated in jail on *The Andy Griffith Show*. That turned out to be one of the shows Alfredo regularly watched, and he learned new English from it. When Eva and Ava showed up outside his cell, Alfredo would wave at them and say, "Hey, Andy. Hey, Barn." And the girls would say back to him, "Hey, Otis."

Of course, Alfredo had no understanding of what he was saying, so he said "Hey, Andy. Hey, Barn," to everyone who walked by his cell. Even if just one person walked by, he'd say, "Hey, Andy. Hey, Barn."

It made Eva think maybe Alfredo was kind of simple-minded. But trying to learn a foreign language just by watching TV had to be awfully hard, so Eva assumed maybe Alfredo was in fact fairly smart just to be memorizing things from TV. He was memorizing English, but certainly not understanding it. One time when Eva and Ava brought a treat to Alfredo, a police officer walked past the cell and Alfredo said to him, "Hey, Andy. Hey, Barn. See your Ford dealer today. Kiss my ass."

"I don't imagine he heard *that* on *The Andy Griffith Show*," the police officer said.

"Proud to be your Bud," Alfredo said. "Weiser."

c·h·a·p·t·e·r

23

After a few days, one of the Waxahachie newspaper reporters found out at the police station that Alfredo was in jail, and after interviewing first Chief McLemore and then Tommy Dillo, age ten, the reporter wrote a story saying the police had "arrested an illegal alien from Guatemala who originally had been involved in unfounded reports of possible satanism at an abandoned house north of town." The story also regurgitated the information about the skeleton Eva had found and suggested that the obscure group called the Sons of Belial might still be active in town, which had nothing to do with Alfredo except through the sophisticated journalistic technique of putting two unrelated subjects side-by-side in a sentence. Then suddenly they were related.

Instantly, the TV stations began doing their own stories, as well as the national TV tabloid show *Genuine Rumors*, which sent a camera crew and a reporter to the abandoned house. As the reporter walked through the dark and deteriorating building, making sure the camera showed conspicuously eerie shadows on the walls, the reporter said, "Satanism. It's a word we all know and fear. Black magic. Voodoo. Devil worship. Whatever you call it, it conjures up images of the darkest unspeakable deeds committed in the name of Satan. It was here in this very room where a ten-year-old Waxahachie boy said he saw ominous lights one night, lights that the boy captured on videotape.''

Then they showed part of Tommy's video, which indeed showed light in the house.

''We may never know what happened in this house,'' the reporter said as the screen switched back to the inside of the house, showing the reporter walking through the vacant house into the kitchen. ''This dark stain on the floor, for instance,'' the reporter said, and the camera zoomed in for a distressing view of an unidentified dark stain. ''Could this be human blood? Animal blood? We aren't likely to ever know. Investigators say they found no evidence of foul play or satanic rituals. The only man who might know what happened in this house is locked up in the Waxahachie jail awaiting an appointment with the Immigration and Naturalization Service, who might decide to deport him back to his alleged home in Guatemela.''

A TV station in Dallas also used part of Tommy's video on the news and decided to interview Tommy and show him and his video on a special weekend news program called *Texans at Random*. During the interview, which everyone in Eva's family watched, the TV reporter asked Tommy what made him suspect there were satanists in the house.

''Well, I found a drawing of a pentagon in the house,'' Tommy said.

''The Pentagon is in Washington,'' the reporter said. ''Do you mean you found a penta*gram*—a five-sided star?''

''That's what I mean,'' Tommy said. ''It looked like it was drawn with blood, and there were bones in the middle of it.''

''None of our reporters found a pentagram or any bones when they went to the house,'' the reporter said.

"They must've gotten rid of them," Tommy said.

"Did you actually see any suspicious or satanic activity in or near the house?"

"I think they mutilated a cow," Tommy said.

"You saw them?"

"No, sir. But I heard a cow one time."

"You heard a cow inside the house?"

"That's what it sounded like."

"What makes you think the cow was being mutilated?"

"The cow sounded . . . well it was making a noise like . . . I mean, the cow sounded uncomfortable."

Chief McLemore was also watching the show. At this he turned the TV off and said, "With such an overwhelming absence of evidence, the public will have no choice but to believe they have a satanist in jail."

Whatever delicate sense of order and normalcy McLemore usually felt in his job had rapidly begun to disappear. The effect of the TV and newspaper reports was that now McLemore had no choice but to notify the INS of Alfredo's existence, particularly since a small group of people from a local Baptist church were demonstrating outside the police station with signs saying WE DON'T NEED ANY MORE SATANISTS.

"Well if they don't need *any more* satanists, it accidentally implies they already have the right number of them," McLemore said as he stared sullenly at the demonstrators outside his office window.

Maj. Dan Blue stood beside McLemore and said, "Funny, how they want us to persecute an illegal alien for being a satanist, which he isn't, and which isn't even illegal in the *first* damn place. Maybe I should go out there and persecute *them*. Arrest them all. Just because I *feel* like it, just like they want us to persecute that illegal alien just because *they* feel like it. Should I go out there and persecute them?"

"Not during office hours. You have to persecute people in your spare time," McLemore said. "But you know what pisses *me* off? It pisses me off that the same people who'd

scream bloody murder if you violated their religious freedom are the first ones to say nobody *else* should have any
religious freedom, except the freedom to be exactly like
them. And you know what else pisses me off?''

''Those Chevy truck commercials where Bob Seger
won't stop singing?'' Maj. Blue asked.

''It pisses me off that even though the Virgin Mary stamp
machine was stolen in our jurisdiction, the formal investigation is being handled by postal service investigators and
the FBI, and we're told to ignore it. And it pisses me off
that something as strange and occult as the likeness of the
Virgin Mary had to appear at *all* in our jurisdiction, or even
in my lifetime, because I'm not all that religious to begin
with. It worries me that such possible miracles as the Virgin
Mary's face on a stamp machine might be proof that every
religious thing I don't care about might be true. And you
know what pisses me off about that? It pisses me off that
we have to assume that God gave us the ability to think
clearly and to reason, but then when we're dealing with the
idea of religion, we're supposed to ignore rational thought,
ignore our rational doubts, accept everything on faith, and
be completely *un*reasonable. Can you explain that?''

''I hope not,'' Maj. Blue said.

''And also, why would God, the supreme being of the
whole universe, announce his existence by a blurry, inferior
drawing on a stamp machine?''

''Maybe God's all-powerful and all-wise, but he can't
draw,'' Maj. Blue suggested.

''And it also pisses me off that such a gentle and harmless foreigner as that Alfredo boy would have to be arrested
because of immigration laws that couldn't have existed
when America was founded or the same people who
founded it would have been illegal aliens. And it pisses me
off that anyone at all in Waxahachie or the entire state of
Texas could believe idiotic rumors of satanism and then,
with absolutely no proof, suggest that Alfredo was involved
in it.''

The two of them were quiet then, just for a second.

"Does anything else piss you off?" Maj. Blue said.

"It pisses me off that my own Irish ancestors who moved to Texas in the 1840s would have been regarded as illegal aliens today. They didn't have any passports or visas or any government documents approving of their existence. They became Americans through the only process required at the time—they showed up."

He closed his eyes, leaned back in his chair, and said to the ceiling, "If my ancestors arrived here today, I'd have to arrest them."

"Speaking of arresting somebody," Maj. Blue said as he looked at his wristwatch, "I better get on out and persecute somebody, or at least uphold the law. See you later."

Maj. Blue walked out of the office, leaving McLemore to simmer in his terrible mood. He opened the newspaper to distract himself by reading his horoscope. It said, "Marital issues stressed today."

"I'm not married," McLemore said.

The horoscope said, "Mate may surprise you with romantic suggestion tonight."

"I don't *have* a mate," McLemore said.

The horoscope said, "Good deeds done for stranger could multiply benefits for everyone."

"I don't *know* any strangers," McLemore said. "Unless you count that Guatemalan boy. He's pretty strange."

The intercom on his phone buzzed and Officer Rudy said, "Chief, some INS guy is returning your call."

"I'll take it. Thank you," McLemore said. He picked up the phone at his desk and said, "Chief McLemore here."

"Yes, sir. My name is Cal Witt. I'm an agent with the INS in Dallas, and I'm just calling to let you know we also saw the TV news report saying you got yourselves another potential illegal in jail, so we might as well start the usual process, find out if he's legal or not, and take it from there."

McLemore didn't answer right away. He was annoyed that anyone in the INS could be so goddamn eager to deport someone they hadn't even seen and knew nothing about.

"I thought you guys had hundreds and hundreds of back-logged cases keeping you busy already," McLemore said.

"Oh, we do, all right. And I guarantee you I'm not anxious to add one more case to the load. Not at all. It's just that someone in our office says it was somehow related to possible satanic activities."

"Satanic activities," McLemore said tiredly. "Yeah, well, you know, that's all just part of our annual Satanic Street Festival."

"Satanic street festival?"

"Sure. Once every year, all the local churches build satanic floats and we have a big parade downtown and slaughter farm animals in the streets. It's kind of like the Mardi Gras combined with the end of the world."

"How festive."

"But anyway, yeah, we have ourselves a young Spanish-speaking boy in jail. Probably a vagrant. I'm not sure. But he has nothing to do with satanism. That's all a lotta crap. People around here get spooked pretty easy when anyone at all mentions satanism or cults. You can grow rumors down here as easy as mildew. We haven't found any serious evidence of anything that could really be called satanism. It's just unfortunate that that boy we found in some old house showed up around here at the same time that a few people started finding the remains of campfires and things that seemed to them like evidence of satanists around here. I don't take it seriously. Some do."

"Well. I didn't know *what* to make of that satanism stuff. But I just thought I'd give you a call, in case you really do have an illegal you need to dispose of."

"*Dispose* of?" McLemore said in a surprised tone. "I like to recycle all my illegals."

The INS man laughed briefly, then said, "Well, I didn't mean we intended to throw him away. But like I said, we're ready to start the process when you are."

What was curious to McLemore at that moment was how simple and abstract and professional it would have been for him to simply say yes, and begin the indifferent process of learning that Alfredo indeed was an illegal alien, and then turn him over to the INS and never hear of Alfredo again. He could just say yes. But he didn't want to. He already had thought too much about Alfredo, already saw him as an unfortunate immigrant, regarding him with the same distant but genuine sympathy he felt for his own ancestors. He wasn't going to just turn Alfredo over to be consumed and spit out by a huge bureaucracy, especially since the government was so busy not needing his help with the Virgin Mary stamp machine. The very least he could do was delay.

"Well I appreciate your offer, but right now we don't know if he's illegal or not," McLemore said.

"We can find that out for you," the INS man said.

That made it even harder to not say yes. But McLemore refused.

"We're still looking into the possibility that he has some local relatives here," McLemore said, which was a simple, straightforward lie. He didn't feel bad about it. He just felt surprised that he'd lie for someone he scarcely knew.

"Also," McLemore said, trying to sound a bit more convincing, "we still have to go through the formality of investigating all that crap about possible satanic activity."

"I thought you said there was no reason to believe any of that," the INS man said.

"There isn't. But we still have formal procedures to follow. We should probably hold him for a few days until we're through proving he's never been employed full-time or part-time by Satan."

"Well that's fine with me. And if you find out he *is* employed by Satan, please tell him we'll give him a green card if he'll fill out the proper paperwork describing his satanic employment."

"I'll let you know what happens."

It worked. The INS man didn't care about Alfredo anymore. McLemore hung up the phone and couldn't decide what kind of law he'd just violated, or upheld.

Television had always been holy to Alfredo. It seemed even more religious in his cell, where the TV was suspended as if it came from the heavens. Although Alfredo understood that TV operated with electricity, and he had a vague sense of the existence of TV towers and cameras and cables and satellites, he still thought of it as a miracle. Were it not for God, there would be no electricity. Therefore, TV came from God. Within that little box hanging from the ceiling could be found little dramas of everyone in the world, as if the eye of God saw everywhere, and his eye was the TV. And so God was interested in *General Hospital*, and *Gilligan's Island*, and *The Andy Griffith Show*, and *Rat Patrol*, and dozens of other programs on so many channels it was like seeing with the eye of God.

All of which made him feel a sort of tingling gladness and joy when he was interviewed by a reporter from *Genuine Rumors*. A translator working with the reporter explained that Alfredo could see himself on the TV, on the very same TV on which Alfredo saw the little dramas of everyone in the world—as if the very eye of God would peek briefly at *I Love Lucy*, and *Star Trek*, and at Alfredo himself.

Actually, that didn't make very much sense. But he knew everything seemed more real on TV, even when it was fake. Back in Guatemala City, everyone watched TV like it was a window into the better world that they knew was somewhere, as if the TV shows were real and those who only watched them were less real. And so now even Alfredo was going to seem more real, on the evening news.

The hour arrived and the news was on. There he was on TV. He recognized his jail cell, and his own face—like the little ghost of himself, his soul—jumped up into the TV, and he was famous. A problem was that the reporter was speaking English, and they didn't show the parts where the translator spoke Spanish and Alfredo answered in Spanish. They just showed Alfredo sitting on his bunk in the cell and smiling nervously at the camera as the translator spoke English. But Alfredo remembered the questions from the translator, and he remembered his own answers, so he knew what they were saying about him on TV. They were saying, "I didn't mutilate no cow. I had no company at all." They were saying, "I don't know how you become a satanist. I don't go to that church." They were saying, "The reason I live in an abandoned house is because I can't afford the kind you have to buy."

He was on TV for maybe ten seconds. Possibly the entire world saw him. Maybe his friends in Guatemala City saw him and said, "Look! Alfredo has a new home in an American jail!"

His little spot on the news was over, and next they showed a car wreck. Alfredo understood this to mean that, because his interview was shown first, he was advancing in the world.

c·h·a·p·t·e·r

24

A week later everybody in Eva's family got dressed up like
they were going to church or a wedding, but they went to
Alfredo's hearing in Dallas. Gretchen, the lawyer, said the
local police had finally given the INS official notification
of Alfredo's existence, and a hearing had been scheduled.
Eva thought the hearing would be held in a courtroom with
a judge and a jury, but at the INS office they just gathered
in a pretty small and ordinary room that had a long, wooden
table where everybody sat. The INS woman who was in
charge of everything asked everyone to please sit down.
Alfredo sat between Diego Guerra and Gretchen. The
sleeves on Alfredo's suit coat were so long that when he
put his hands in front of him on the table, it looked like he
was born without hands. It was Eva's dad's suit, and Alfredo was too little for it.

The INS woman smiled all the time, as if she wanted
everything to seem pleasant and social when it wasn't either
one.

"This is just a hearing," she said, and then Diego Guerra
translated that for Alfredo.

"I want you all to know . . ." she said, and immediately
Diego translated again. The woman couldn't finish a sen-

tence without Diego saying the same thing in Spanish.

"Pardon me," the INS woman said to Diego Guerra.

Diego translated that.

"Could you please translate in a somewhat quieter voice so it doesn't interfere with what I'm saying?" the INS woman said.

"Certainly," Diego said, and then he translated *that* for Alfredo, but in a quieter voice.

The INS woman explained that at a hearing like this one, all she was trying to do was find out what country Alfredo came from and how he got to the United States and if he had any documents showing his citizenship or if he had a visa or passport or anything, or if Alfredo hoped to obtain a green card. She said no final decision about Alfredo would be made at this time. She looked at Alfredo and then at Diego and said, "Does he speak any English at all?"

"I'm afraid so," Diego said.

The INS woman looked puzzled. "You're afraid so? And why would *that* be bad, that he speaks some English?"

"Well, he doesn't speak any English that would be very helpful."

"He's been studying TV commercials," Eva said.

"Well that's very admirable of him," the INS woman said.

The INS woman went on with her questions, asking Diego if Alfredo had any documents at all showing his citizenship, such as a birth certificate or a driver's license or a visa. Following the translation, Diego said, "He said he's never had a document in his entire life, unless you want to give him one."

The INS woman laughed lightly, and so everybody else felt free to laugh.

"Where was he born?" the INS woman said.

"Guatemala," Diego said.

"What city in Guatemala?"

"He says no one told him."

"He doesn't know what *city* he was born in?" the INS woman said.

Diego spoke with Alfredo for a while, and then looked at the INS woman and said, "He says he has eighteen brothers and sisters, and so maybe his mother and father forgot where some of them were born. He doesn't know."

"Well. I guess that's understandable," the INS woman said. "But, anyway, now, I'd like for you to tell Alfredo that it's possible for him to gain political asylum in the United States if he can offer proof that he was being persecuted in Guatemala for racial reasons or for his religious or political ideas."

"Yes, ma'am. We told him that. He said he doesn't have any ideas."

"None at all?"

"None that he remembers."

"Very well. Has anyone told him about the various legal requirements for obtaining a green card?"

"Yes, ma'am."

"And based on that knowledge, are you proposing a particular way that Alfredo might hope to obtain a green card?"

"Yes we are," Gretchen said. "My name is Gretchen Schramm. I'm a friend of the family and a practicing attorney, and although I have no direct experience in immigration law, I understand that the most likely way for Alfredo to obtain a green card would be if he were offered a job in the United States. It must be a job for which he is qualified, and it must be a job that no other Americans can do or want to do."

"And has Alfredo been offered such a job?" the INS woman said.

"Not just yet, but we expect a breakthrough any day now," Gretchen said.

That ended the meeting in a pleasant way without settling anything, and as everyone walked down the hall to the elevator, Eva said, "What breakthrough are we expecting?"

"One that we have to invent," Eva's mom said.

•   •   •

With special permission from Chief McLemore, Alfredo was allowed to leave his jail cell on Sunday and go with Eva and her family to church so Alfredo could be introduced to the congregation and Eva's dad could ask everyone to think of work Alfredo could do to prevent him from being deported. Alfredo had taken a shower in jail so he didn't stink, and again he wore one of Eva's dad's suits that was too big, which made it look like he was vanishing inside his clothes the way the Wicked Witch of the West did when water was poured on her.

Eva didn't know what to pray about Alfredo. She could pray that the Immigration and Naturalization Service leave him alone, but she didn't know if God interfered with federal agencies. He was supposed to be omnipotent. But if he was, he didn't seem to like using his powers very much. Like the miracle of the stamp machine. It seemed like God would at least have a miracle no one could steal.

So she didn't know what to pray. But she was going to anyway. She closed her eyes and prayed, *Dear Ted Williams, please help us get Alfredo a job that nobody else in America wants.*

Again she'd lost track of the liturgy, so when everyone started moving again, she started to reach for the hymnal and the prayer book at the same time, but she was wrong. It was time to kneel again and pray with your eyes closed. It made her wonder, as she sometimes did, if the reason you were supposed to close your eyes was that while everyone had their eyes closed, God would be in the room, and he didn't want anyone to see him. So Eva squeezed her eyes open a little bit and looked around for God.

It scared her a little bit, thinking maybe she shouldn't look, because of that thing that happened to Lot's wife, where one of those sinful cities was being destroyed by the Lord and the Lord told Lot and his wife not to look back as they ran away from the city, and Lot's wife did look back and got turned into a pillar of salt. Eva almost was afraid that if she looked around and just slightly saw God, she'd be turned into salt. Why not pepper? she wondered.

Still, she glanced behind her toward the back of the church and saw an old woman in a bright green dress standing in the doorway at the back of the room, and she thought: "Is God an old woman? And does he wear a green dress?"

But then the old woman sat down in the back row and blew her nose during the silent moment of prayer. It didn't seem like God would blow his nose. You couldn't think of God as having mucus. And so as usual, no one knew what God looked like.

During the service, Alfredo sat up on the altar next to Diego Guerra while Eva's dad stood before the congregation in his white robe and explained the travails of Alfredo: how he had been born somewhere in Guatemala that he didn't remember the name of; how he had eighteen brothers and sisters, which was actually more people than you could find in some of the small towns in Texas; how he worked on a banana plantation and worked as a butcher and briefly worked in the field of archaeology by making ancient Mayan artifacts out of broken Pepsi bottles; and how he tried to take a cab to the United States but ended up walking and hitchhiking to Texas; and how he had been working as a dishwasher and learning to speak Chinese at the Chinese restaurant when he was befriended by Eva and Ava in the abandoned house where he later was mistaken for a satanic cow mutilator and subsequently arrested for the crime of being here.

"The crime," Eva's dad repeated, "of being here."

He gazed left and right along the rows of silent people before him and said, "I won't stand here and do the easy and simple-minded thing, which is to rebuke and denigrate the Immigration and Naturalization Service for enforcing laws that the Congress passed. I won't tell you we have some lofty and mysterious duty to feel such immense compassion for all people everywhere that this nation should abolish all immigration laws and let a tidal wave of humanity sweep across the country. I think if we let every impoverished person from every sorrowful nation come to the United States, we wouldn't have to worry about third world nations anymore. We'd *be* one.''

Eva didn't know anything about the third world. The only thing she could think of was Neptune.

''But we're not talking about a tidal wave of humanity,'' her dad said. ''We're talking about one man. He's already here. The one way we can help him remain here legally is if we can help him find a job so he can be issued a green card.''

Which was really pink, Eva remembered.

''And as could be expected,'' her dad said, ''the law has made sure that Alfredo Santayana can't simply get whatever job might be available. Immigration law states that the job must be one that either no American citizens are qualified to do, or one that no American citizens want. This means, for example, that Alfredo is free to apply for work as an astrophysicist, or he can seek a career in sewage disposal—providing that no American citizens want that career. What I'm asking you to do is to help me share the task of either finding or inventing a job for Alfredo, so he can remain in this country without having to live in an abandoned house or a jail.''

He turned toward Alfredo and Diego Guerra behind him and said to Diego Guerra, ''Please ask Alfredo if he'd like to stand and say anything to the congregation.''

Diego Guerra translated that, and Alfredo, although he looked terribly nervous and shy, stood up in his drooping suit and shuffled over to the podium beside Eva's dad, with Diego Guerra beside him to translate. Alfredo's brown eyes seemed to look both frightened and grateful, and he didn't speak right away but just looked out at maybe 150 strange faces looking back at his. It was all quiet and solemn in the room, like everyone was paying the strictest attention to the most important event they'd see that day, like they were showing Alfredo through their silence that even though he was just an impoverished illegal alien standing in front of a roomful of prosperous Americans, they could still regard him with compassion and respect. Alfredo shuffled a few more steps up to the microphone on the podium, having figured out from watching Eva's dad that the microphone was the thing you talked into to make your voice loud. He leaned his face up to the microphone, staring at everyone with frightened and grateful eyes.

"I'm not going to pay a lot for this muffler," he said.

Everyone remained thoroughly silent. The congregation kept staring quietly at Alfredo, as if now he'd say some sad and hopeful truth in Spanish about how his life had hope or something.

"My broker is E. F. Hutton," he said.

You could hear his words echo a little bit through the big hall and its arched ceiling.

"The best part of waking up is Folgers in your cup," he said.

It seemed like no one was going to laugh until they heard and saw their own minister laughing on the altar, and then a great rush of laughter came up out of everybody, like they finally got it, and everybody just gave in to laughter. Someone started clapping, and then more people were clapping and they all stood up, the whole congregation got up from their pews and applauded Alfredo. This seemed to startle and frighten him, as if he'd never heard applause before, or at least not for himself. He whispered something to Diego Guerra, and Diego Guerra whispered something back to Alfredo, which made Alfredo open his eyes wide with understanding, and then he smiled and seemed to feel better, so that when the congregation stopped clapping and sat back down to see what would happen next, Alfredo moved up to the microphone again.

"For sinus, think Sinex," he said.

Eva's head wobbled and her stomach hurt from laughing. It was certainly the most fun she'd ever had in church.

c·h·a·p·t·e·r

25

Kenlow was filled with a sense of delight as he watched the evening TV news in his bedroom and listened to the anchorwoman describing his newest satanic project.

"While Waxahachie police chief James McLemore says he was being sarcastic when he suggested that satanists might have stolen the town's Virgin Mary stamp machine in order to wage a letter-writing rampage, such an event seems actually to have begun in Waxahachie.

"A total of six town residents have turned over letters to the police that were written by an anonymous person claiming to be a satanist. None of the letters contain any criminal threats, but Chief McLemore says his department regards the letters as a form of illegal harassment and the incidents are currently under investigation.

"We at TV-14 have obtained copies of the letters, and though we don't have time to read all of them on the air, we can read two of them. The first letter, which was mailed to a Christian minister, Kyle Schindler, says: 'Dear Reverend, The Great Horned One has eyes everywhere. His enemies will be devoured. Oh Death, where is thy stain?'

"The letter, like all the others, was signed 'Unidentified Teenager.' The second letter was mailed to Jimmy Ladd, an auto mechanic in Waxahachie. It says: 'Dear Jimmy, The Great Horned One is among us. He seeks new blood. Oh Death, where is thy stain?'

"To comment on the disturbing appearance of the letters, TV-14 invited the Reverend Clay Stoner to speak with us this evening. Reverend Stoner is pastor at All Souls Baptist Church in Waxahachie, and has written a book on cults and satanism called *Meet Your New Neighbor: Satan.*

"Tell us, Reverend Stoner, do the letters that we've read this evening seem authentic? Could they have been written by a practitioner of satanism?"

"Well, Jane, all I can do is speculate. Such short letters don't give any real insights into the personality of the person who wrote them. But I can say the letters seem obsessed with Satan, the Great Horned One. Some people might say the Great Horned One is really Louis Armstrong, the greatest trumpet player of the century. Others might argue that Miles Davis is the greatest trumpet player. Still others would argue that saxophonist Charlie Parker was the greatest horn player. But I think the letters plainly refer to Satan, who, although he never played trumpet or saxophone and isn't traditionally associated with jazz, is easily understood to be the Great Horned One, as might be inferred through the classic imagery of Satan as having horns on his head like a goat or a steer. Of course, the letters could just be a mean-spirited hoax. But it makes me wonder why someone would go to so much trouble to write letters to various strangers in the community, unless he really did have a satanic interest. I wouldn't say with certainty that the letters are truly satanic, but you can't dismiss that possibility."

"And what about that sentence in both letters, the

one that says 'Oh Death, where is thy stain?' "

"Well, Jane, that's a disturbing sentence indeed. It's almost an exact quote from the book of First Corinthians in the Bible. The correct quote is 'Oh death, where is thy sting?' It refers to the resurrection. But in the two letters, it says 'Oh Death, where is thy stain?' Now I don't know if that was just a spelling error or what, but it could have a separate meaning in the mind of the presumed satanist. For example—and this is just speculation, mind you—it could mean that death leaves behind a stain, and in that sense, Christ would be the stain remover. But for the letter writer, it could mean the stain of death is imminent. It could be a kind of threat, like saying the Great Horned One is about to stain you."

"Disturbing indeed, Reverend. And we thank you for being with us tonight."

That was it. That part of the news was over. It left Kenlow feeling tingly and elated. He finally had had an effect on the world, even though he dared not tell anyone about it. The most astonishing thing, of course, was that he'd written a letter to his own father. That was pretty daring. And also satisfying. It was one of the few genuinely happy times in his life, where he had a sense that he mattered to someone else. Of course, the fact that he mattered in the wrong way was a bit troubling. But only a bit. And he was embarrassed that he got that quote about death wrong. But he liked the way the reverend said maybe it meant that Satan was going to stain someone. That was a good meaning.

Kenlow sat at his desk, with his bedroom door locked so his sister and his parents couldn't just walk in, and began pleasantly writing a letter:

Dear Chief McLemore,
    The time of the Great Horned One is coming. I am his servant, his

He was going to write *lieutenant*, but he didn't know how to spell it. He didn't want any more errors in his letters, so he continued the sentence with a different satanic rank:

his servant, his kernel. I know you seek me, but in the darkness I hide. Beware the pentagram. A great stain is coming.

That seemed evil enough to Kenlow. He signed the letter as the Unidentified Teenager and folded it and put it in an envelope, wondering how soon he'd see his letter on TV and in the paper.

The most galling thing about the letter to Chief McLemore was that a mere teenager felt free to taunt anyone at all, including the chief of police.

There was still no reason to think the little shit was a real satanist or that he represented an earnest threat at all. But he *was* disturbing the public. He really *had* scared that little girl, Eva. And now he felt free to taunt the cops. It simply made McLemore more determined to catch the little bastard.

He put the letter on his desk and wondered about it. The main and possibly the only effect of the letters seemed to be that the TV stations and newspapers would publicize the boy's idiocy. He probably thrived on the attention, the sense of illicit fame. And even if McLemore hadn't yet thought of a likely way to identify and arrest the little shit, he figured maybe he could piss him off. That might make the boy reckless enough to be caught.

He swiveled in his chair to face the electric typewriter on his desk.

Kenlow took his usual walk to the convenience store to buy the morning paper and see if he was being written about again. He wasn't on the evening news, but sometimes the papers got stories before the TV stations did, so there was always hope that he'd find a story that way. He read the various headlines, page by page, until he spotted a headline that made his heart flutter with the elation of being a local star.

SATANIST SENDS LETTER TO POLICE CHIEF

He eagerly read the story. According to the paper, Kenlow's letter said:

> Dear Chief McLemore:
>   I apologize for all the pentagrams I made and for all of the satanic letters I mailed to everyone. I've had time to think things over very carefully, and I've decided to resign from the satanic army and devote my life to gardening.
>
> > Sincerely,
> > Unidentified Teenager

Kenlow's face became hot. That goddamn police chief.
He breathed heavily and walked away with the newspaper. How could a police chief be so dishonest? He didn't know how, but he'd strike back some way, and reestablish his reputation as ... well, he wasn't sure what his reputation was. But he wanted it back.

Much of the world made little sense to begin with, and very suddenly it made less. That opinion rose hopelessly in Daniel when he read a newspaper item and realized that while Alfredo probably wouldn't be allowed to remain in the United States because he was an illegal alien from Guatemala, the INS just changed its policy regarding certain other illegal aliens. He read the news item again:

The State Department has gone to bat for the first time to allow illegal aliens from outer space to enter the country.

Russian cosmonauts Vladimir Dezhurov and Gennadi Strekalov were to come back to Earth from the Mir space station on the space shuttle with American Norman Thagard in June, landing either in California or Florida.

The problem was neither Russian had a visa to enter this country. So State went to the Immigration and Naturalization Service and "for the first time ever applied for a visa waiver for aliens from outer space," a State official said.

INS went along, the official said.

So. It was true. Aliens from Guatemala without visas couldn't come to the United States, but aliens from space could.

"Too bad Alfredo's not from Neptune," Daniel said to his wife.

"Sometimes I think he might be," his wife said.

Alfredo was sad after being told by Diego Guerra that the government would allow aliens from Neptune to enter the United States, but not those from Guatemala. Until then, Alfredo hadn't even known what Neptune was. When Eva showed him a drawing of Neptune in a science book, and showed him drawings of the other planets, too, Alfredo asked if he could please be from Saturn. Eva said no.

So now the only ways Alfredo could legally be in the United States were if he married a U.S. citizen, if he were offered a job so detestable that no one else wanted it, or if he came from outer space. It was too hard. While he was normally cheerful for practically no reason at all, now he found it hard to even be interested in the unexpected letter that a police officer brought to him in his cell. Never in his entire life had anyone sent Alfredo a letter before, but he was too sad to care very much about the letter. It was written in English anyway. He couldn't read it. He gave it to the nice police officer who spoke Spanish, Sgt. Gloria Mondesi, and she read it aloud to him:

Dear Alfredo,
    The Great Horned One is pleased with your work. You will receive many rewards. Oh Death, where is thy stain?

The letter made no sense at all, and Gloria took the letter away to show it to the police chief. Alfredo didn't know what work he'd been doing, except washing dishes. He wondered what rewards he would receive: A new car? A vowel? But he couldn't imagine getting any of them anymore, now that he was only allowed to be from Earth. He slept most of the day, hardly watching any TV at all, and when it was night he stood at the little window with unbreakable glass and looked up at the stars, where he wished his home was, so he could leave there and come to the United States.

c·h·a·p·t·e·r

26

As Daniel prepared his sermon for that Sunday, he couldn't help thinking about Alfredo. For Alfredo to get a green card, the INS required that he had to be offered a job so detestable that no one would want it—not even Alfredo. It wasn't really that bad, but close. Daniel agreed with the general principle that American citizens should always have the first choice of jobs in their own country, but Alfredo wasn't a general principle. He was a particular problem.

Daniel sighed and looked down on his desk at the hand-written list of work Alfredo said he'd done.

> Helped make fake Mayan artifacts
> Cut bananas from banana trees
> Slaughtered pigs
> Busboy
> Slaughtered chickens
> Dishwasher
> Slaughtered goats

At least Alfredo had experience doing detestable jobs, in case he ever was offered one. It seemed like the only way the INS wanted foreigners in America was if they made everything so hard and unhappy that the foreigners wouldn't want to be here anymore.

On the wall above his desk was a world map, and he distractedly stared at the complex shapes of continents, oceans, and islands—places where people had wandered for thousands and thousands of years, starting out, if you believed in the Bible, somewhere in Iraq or Syria; or starting out in Africa, if you believed in science. Daniel believed in both.

Still staring at the map, he thought how all of the ancient people first made countries, then stole them from each other. And then they made new countries and stole them from each other again. In Europe, for example, people stole countries or parts of countries so often it became hard to know which country you came from. And then everybody got the idea that instead of always stealing Europe over and over, it'd be better to get in their ships and go steal North America and Central America and South America and Australia, since they'd never been stolen before.

And so they did.

Then, after everybody had stolen every country in the world at least once, rules were made just so people like Alfredo couldn't stay in the United States because they weren't *from* there. But neither were most of the people who lived in America. Even the Indians probably came over from northern Asia, when there used to be a land bridge to Alaska. And so *nobody* was really from here.

That should have been the true requirement for residence in America. You had to prove that you were nobody.

It amused Emily in a depressing way to remember the night when the girls were asleep and Emily walked into the study where Daniel was writing a sermon and she said to Daniel, "Maybe we should talk to our local minister."

It seemed like a somewhat harmless way to begin an otherwise painful talk, and Daniel accepted the joke. He looked up from his computer at Emily and said, "I'm afraid I *am* our local minister."

Emily sat on one of the chairs by Daniel's desk and said, without looking at Daniel, "It's so odd. When I was a girl, I was always told that if people had problems with their marriage, one person they could talk to was their local minister. But who do you talk to if you're *married* to the local minister?"

She couldn't remember Daniel's answer. It was something about if you can't talk to the local minister, maybe you should talk with a distant one. It was some joke like that. Emily hadn't known what to say next. She looked at all of the books in the study and said, "Do you have a directory of distant ministers?"

There was no point in remembering any more. Nothing got solved. Nothing got better. She and Daniel went on with their lives as if the healthiest reaction to a bad marriage was to feed it and care for it and keep it as unpleasantly alive as possible. They were becoming experts at pretending to have a marriage, partly so no one at church might suspect their priest was having the same kind of worldly and unbearable life that many of the people in the congregation might have and partly to protect Eva and Ava from any awareness that their family was disintegrating.

The girls knew, of course. They could probably recall any number of fights or scenes between their parents, especially the night Emily and Daniel didn't have enough strength to repress whatever anger and sadness they both felt toward each other, and had both left the dinner table to walk down the hall and fight, as if the girls couldn't hear them down the hall, as if the girls wouldn't always remember hearing Emily say, "Well then let's get divorced. At least we won't have to mail out any invitations."

Everyone in the family seemed a little more quiet after that, as if the process of disintegration required silence. And there wasn't really any way to protect Eva and Ava from that disintegration since the girls could see every day how Emily and Daniel remained distant from each other most of the time, rigidly avoiding any closeness other than maybe an accidental touch, the way strangers at a grocery store might bump into each other and immediately withdraw. And she couldn't even say what the real problem was, as if she and Daniel had grown so alienated from each other so subtly and gradually that she could no longer recall what caused it. She imagined them sitting in a marriage counselor's office and being asked what the problem was, and she and Daniel would say at the same time: "I don't remember."

It seemed what everyone was having was a dysfunctional family, although Emily despised the word *dysfunctional*. It was too formal, fashionable, and impersonal. Rather than *dysfunctional*, Emily preferred the word *traditional*. That was because, traditionally, lots of American families were dysfunctional. It was another bleak joke in a daily haze of bleakness.

And everything grew more complicated with the news about the Sons of Belial and the threatening letter to Eva and the pathetic appearance of the illegal alien in their lives. There was simply too much to concentrate on, as if it took all of Emily's strength simply to deal with one problem, let alone all of them. Sometimes her reaction was to deal with none of it. That was withdrawal, a symptom of depression.

"I will *not* have depression," Emily said to herself. "Depression isn't ambitious enough. I prefer *manic* depression."

It wasn't better, but at least it sounded busier.

Kenlow tried as hard as he knew how to appear righteously alarmed as his father forsook his usual Sunday sermon and read aloud to the congregation the letter he had received from the local satanist.

" 'Dear Reverend,' " Rev. Schindler read. " 'The Great Horned One has eyes everywhere. His enemies will be devoured. Oh Death, where is thy stain?'

"Signed 'Unidentified Teenager.' "

The anxious silence that permeated the church seemed to flash through Kenlow, like electricity buzzing through his flesh. He simultaneously felt fear and guilt and triumph while he struggled to seem as somber and alarmed as everyone else in church probably felt.

"Satan lives," Rev. Schindler said. "Prophecy is being fulfilled. Satan walks among us."

A few people looked nervously around the church, as if Satan were in the church, looking for a seat. Even Kenlow listened as hard as he could for the ominous sound of footsteps drawing near, like Satan might bend over Kenlow and say, "Is this seat taken?"

c·h·a·p·t·e·r
27

Usually on a Sunday afternoon after church, Eva and Ava might go off into the woods, but not with Alfredo gone and Kenlow possibly out there. Eva still thought she could just tell the detective Kenlow's name and have him arrested, but she didn't know what might happen after that. She was afraid Kenlow could get out of jail and hurt her. So she just left it all alone and stayed in the living room with Ava, who was putting Barbie's clothes on Ken and Ken's clothes on Barbie. Eva herself got interested in this big ad in the Sunday magazine from the newspaper that had a large announcement at the top that said FOR WOMEN ONLY: FORBIDDEN FEMALE SECRETS! It was an ad for a book called the *Women's Encyclopedia of Health & Emotional Healing*, as seen on TV. Something that puzzled Eva was if the secrets were forbidden, how did anybody get them in a book?

The list of secrets in the magazine ad included "New anti-PMS diet. Doctor 'astonished' by results."

She had no idea what PMS was. She recalled that a few times, she had heard her mom say something was postmodernist. But she didn't know what the *S* might stand for. Never mind. The *PM* could stand for almost anything. Like *postmaster*. Another thing the list said was "Why men cheat. Secret psychological reason."

She remembered Andrew Riley cheated on a math test in school and got caught. He got an F. But why boys cheated on tests didn't seem any different than why some girls did. So that didn't seem like a forbidden secret.

She read down the list a little more and saw something that finally did seem like a forbidden secret: "A man can give you a yeast infection. What to do."

This was one of the strangest ideas Eva had ever heard of. The only yeast she'd seen was in little packages her mom used sometimes to make bread or dinner rolls. She didn't know you could get an infection from that. And why would a man give it to you? She didn't think very many men made bread, except her dad, who made some long loaves of French bread one time that were hard enough for him to have driven nails through and built a chair. And if a man *did* make bread, then why wouldn't *he* get the yeast infection instead of some woman? Eva decided that the next time her mom made bread, she'd ask her about yeast infections and PMS, and then she wouldn't have to buy the book. She looked through the ad very carefully to see if it said anything about all-purpose flour.

The phone started ringing. Her mom was out gardening in the backyard, and her dad wasn't home, so Eva answered the phone.

"Hello? Galt residence," she said.

"Is this the home of Eva Galt?" some boy said.

"Yes. I'm Eva Galt," Eva said, wondering why anyone would call her.

"Do you know who I am?"

"No."

"I'm the satanist you saw in the woods."

It frightened Eva to think Kenlow knew her phone number, as if he could get to her anytime. "How'd you get our phone number?" she said.

"It's in the phone book."

That was surprising. Eva thought satanists might have

some supernatural way to locate people. But they just used a phone book. Kenlow was seeming less and less supernatural.

"What do you want?" Eva said.

"I'm calling to let you know that the Great Horned One knows who you are."

"The great horned owl?" Eva asked.

"*No*," Kenlow said impatiently. "The Great Horned *One*."

"You mean Satan?"

"Of course I do."

"I don't believe in Satan."

"You don't?"

"My dad says Satan's a fiction. He says people made him up to scare people into being religious."

"Well your dad's stupid."

"He is not. He has two college degrees."

"I don't care *how* many degrees he has. Satan exists, and I work for him."

"You mean like a summer job?"

"It isn't a *job*, stupid. I'm a *satanist*, and I'm calling to warn you not to tell anyone you saw me."

"A police detective was here. He showed me pictures of all the high school students in the high school yearbook. He asked me if I saw your picture."

Kenlow was very quiet. Eva listened to him being quiet, then said, "I know who you are. I didn't tell the detective, though."

"And you better *not*," Kenlow said, trying to sound angry and frightening, but sounding to Eva a little bit frightened himself. "You remember all the bloody flesh I put in the middle of the pentagram?"

"You put Vienna sausages there."

"Normally I'd kill a goat or a cow, and spill its guts in the pentagram. I was in a hurry, and had to go to the store. But it doesn't matter. Any animal flesh works. It calls forth demons, and the dark specter of Hell."

"My dad says you're a fake. He said you'd probably

draw a pentagram in the dirt and try to summon Satan with Kentucky Fried Chicken.''

"Well your dad's stupider than you. If you tell anyone you saw me, blood will start gushing from your ears.''

"You can't do that.''

"Find out,'' Kenlow said, and hung up the phone.

There was probably no reason to be afraid of him. He was just a boy. But Eva's heart was beating faster than it should've been.

The days went by and no one could think of the right job for Alfredo. Every day people called Eva's house with ideas, and all of them were wrong. They suggested jobs like butler, chauffeur, errand boy, office assistant, grocery clerk, ranch hand, convenience store clerk, janitor, truck driver, trash collector, security guard, and movie usher. All of them were jobs that other Americans could do, or that Alfredo couldn't do. And they weren't repugnant enough.

And why didn't God do something? It scared Eva to think that. It was like accusing God of not doing right. But why *didn't* he do something? Eva didn't mean it as a disrespectful question. She just wanted to know why, if God was supposed to be able to help everybody, it seemed like he hardly ever did. Nobody had any *idea* what God did. They didn't know what he looked like. There was that picture of him in the Sistine Chapel where he was reaching his finger out after creating Adam, and there were the paintings in Dave's Big Basted Hen. But that was just art. That was just Michelangelo and Doug Grail guessing. People didn't really know what God looked like, what kind of clothes he wore, how tall he was, how much he weighed, if he was a gas, a liquid, a solid, or *any*thing. They built churches and synagogues and temples and mosques and shrines for him all over the world, but he never showed up at any of those places. And nobody even had a picture of him. Not even a police sketch.

It was so perplexing, like it always was, that Eva went

to find her dad in his study, where he was writing something on the computer. Eva walked up to him and said, "Dad?"

He typed a little bit more, then looked at Eva standing beside him and said, "Yes? Do you have a question?"

"Yes, sir. I was wondering, if God's supposed to be able to help all the people in the world who need help, how come he doesn't just help all of them, and then they wouldn't need help anymore?"

She waited for a quick answer, but her dad looked very thoughtful and uncertain, and didn't answer right away.

"That's a very good question," he said as he rubbed his cheeks with his fingertips and sort of smiled and frowned at the same time, like he was interested in the question and wondered what to say. "Let's see if I can remember the question. . . . If God's supposed to be able to help everyone in the world, how come he doesn't just do that, and get it over with?"

"Yes, sir. How come?"

"Couldn't you ask me a question about baseball? That's easier."

"But I don't *wanna* know about baseball," Eva said, smiling.

"So. All right. What you want to know is, if God's capable of fixing every problem in the world, why doesn't he just do that?"

Eva nodded her head yes.

"All right. The answer is this," her father said, and paused to think for a second. "As your father, and as an ordained minister with advanced degrees from reputable divinity schools, I'm fully authorized to say with complete certainty . . . I don't know."

Eva grimaced and said, "You don't *know*?"

"I thoroughly, genuinely, completely don't know," her dad said as he put his hands against Eva's face and gently pinched her cheeks. "But it's a perfectly sensible and intelligent question. It's the kind of question almost anyone's bound to think of at some point in their life, and I'm a little surprised that you thought of it at age eleven. What you've asked me is an unanswerable question. I don't *know* why God doesn't just fix the whole world and say, 'There. I'm done with it. *Now* will you stop whining?' Nothing I've ever read or studied or heard or thought of can convincingly answer that. But one possible answer—and all of us get to think up possible answers—is that God doesn't just fix everything in the world because he wants us *people* to do a lot of that work. Isn't it fun when you solve a problem sometimes?''

"I can't remember when I solved one," Eva said.

"Oh sure you can. Like when you answer questions on a test at school. People solve problems all the time. If we get tired of solving problems, we *create* them. Like if there's too much peace in the world, someone starts a war. That's just a joke, Eva.''

"I know.''

"But quite honestly, Eva, I can't say why God doesn't just solve all the world's problems. Maybe he *does* want us to do it. That could involve an extremely long wait. But in general, I think . . . well look at all those books," he said, pointing to the tall wooden bookshelf beside him. "Those are all books about religion. That's about a hundred books there. And do you know how many books there are in the whole world about religion?''

Eva shook her head no.

"Maybe two hundred thousand. Maybe a lot more. You could spend your whole life doing nothing but reading books on religion. And even if you lived to be a hundred and fifty years old, you'd die long before you'd read all the books on religion. And even if you *did* read all the world's books on religion, and took all the classes in all the divinity schools, and listened to all the best sermons and spoke with all the wisest monks and nuns, it wouldn't mean you'd have all the right ideas about God. It might just mean you'd have more opinions than you'd want. I think that's why we have four Gospels. Sometimes it makes me think that when the Bible was being written, there was a short story contest, and the top four entries were chosen for the collection. Actually, there were several *other* gospels, but I think the editors sent out rejection letters saying 'We already have four gospels. That's enough.' Does that help answer your question, Eva?''

"I can't remember what the question was," Eva said.

Her dad stood up and said, ''Sometimes when you're dealing with a serious religious question you can't find the answer to, one thing you can do is this.''

"Do what?"

"Go get an ice-cream sandwich."

Eva followed her dad to the freezer.

A big story came out in the Waxahachie paper that week saying some rancher noticed that what looked like a campfire on his property and heard strange, chanting noises right above where the big government tunnel was. It had happened the day before Alfredo was arrested for possible suspicion of satanic activities. The story said Chief McLemore only arrested Alfredo as a possible illegal alien, and the chief said Tommy Dillo's belief about Alfredo being a satanist ''was just the fanciful idea of an impressionable boy.'' But the newspaper interviewed the rancher and some other people who also said they'd seen fires at night and heard people chanting out by the underground tunnel, so they thought it was too much of a coincidence that Alfredo was in town at the same time these ''eerie and inexplicable'' incidents started happening. One man in the story said Alfredo might be leading a cult from his jail cell. And in Texas, if you said ''cult,'' right away people wanted to shoot somebody.

So now people were trying to get Alfredo deported for possibly being a satanic messiah, which was the name used by the rancher's lawyer, who said he was going to contact the INS about that, and he did.

Now Eva remembered why, when she and Ava first met Alfredo, she didn't want to tell any adults about him. As soon as adults started doing the right thing, everything got worse. And now they wanted to deport him for being a satanic messiah. Eva thought that was like saying someone was a devout criminal. She thought adults were supposed to be intelligent and fair. Maybe some of them had special permission not to be.

Because of all this, Eva's parents decided to go back to the immigration office with proof that Alfredo wasn't a satanic messiah. Eva and Ava went along with them, and everyone met in the same room as before with the same immigration woman. Eva's dad said right away, "I suppose you've been told by now that Alfredo has been accused of being a satanic messiah."

"I did speak on the phone with an attorney who suggested such an idea," the immigration woman said, sounding as if she were both serious and indifferent to the idea.

"Does your office regard it as a serious accusation, one that requires investigation?" Eva's mom asked.

"Just offhand, I'd say no, it doesn't seem like a serious accusation. But as a procedural formality, we would have to investigate it, just in case anyone applying for a green card was in any way involved in illegal activities sometimes associated with certain cults."

"The only people Alfredo associated with were dishwashers and cooks," Eva's dad said. "I don't think washing dishes is generally regarded as a cult activity."

"I wouldn't think so," the woman said.

"And while it is true that Alfredo has been associating with known criminals recently," Eva's mom said, "it's only because he lives in jail."

"That *is* a mitigating circumstance," the immigration woman said, smiling.

"I think if you'll just talk with the Waxahachie police chief, Chief McLemore, he'll tell you there's no evidence to suppose Alfredo was involved with satanism. He probably can't even pronounce it."

"He can pronounce Denorex," Eva said.

"Well that's good," the immigration woman said. "And

I wouldn't worry very much about this satanism deal. It just sounds like the kind of idiotic, crackpot accusation made by people who oppose immigration for any reason whatsoever.''

As Eva and her parents drove by the police station on the way home from the INS office, they saw three women and three men carrying posters on sticks that said things such as WE DON'T NEED A SATANIC MESSIAH and DEPORT THE SATANIST.

''Who are those guys?'' Eva said, staring at the protestors as her mom decided to turn the car into the police station parking lot.

''They're misguided souls,'' her mom said.

''Oh, Lord,'' her dad said in a tired way. ''If Satan didn't exist, people would invent him as often as they wanted him.''

''Are they protesting Alfredo?'' Eva asked.

''They're just publicizing their ignorance,'' her dad said, and they all got out of the car and walked past the protestors to go talk with Chief McLemore. The chief invited them into his office and sat back very comfortably in his tilting leather chair with his legs up on his desk so you could see the worn-out spots on the bottom of his cowboy boots. He looked out the window toward the protestors and said, ''I hate to think we ratified the Constitution and the Bill a' Rights to guarantee the right to unrestricted stupidity. People don't ever seem to run out of ignorance, though. Maybe that's why they're so willing to share it.''

Eva wasn't sure what that meant, but it made her parents smile a little bit.

''Have you spoken with any of the protestors?'' Eva's mom said.

''Yeah. Yeah, I talked with 'em for a few minutes this morning.''

''Are they making any demands or anything?'' Eva's dad said.

''Naw. These people are too polite to make demands. I think they're just fired up by what they read in the paper or saw on the TV news about the possibility of satanists performing evil rituals out by the super conducting super kaleidoscope tunnel. They don't know what's going on. Sometimes I think this country was created by accident. A government of the people, by the people, and in spite of the people. I made it clear to the newspaper and TV people that Alfredo had absolutely nothing to do with satanism. Hell, you can . . . Oh, I'm sorry about my language. I apologize, young lady,'' Chief McLemore said to Eva. ''I mean you can go back there in the jail and see that young man's a perfectly innocent, harmless boy who doesn't do anything more satanic than repeat TV commercials. But people're pretty superstitious. So if they start putting two and two together and come up with negative four, it doesn't matter how plain the truth is, they're gonna believe whatever they have in their minds just because it showed up there. And none a' this means a *thing*, mind you,'' he said, gesturing his hand toward the window. ''It won't have any effect on my department. But I'm afraid it *is* time to realize that I can't keep Alfredo here much longer. I know the immigration people'll call me pretty soon to see if Alfredo has a job yet. And if he doesn't, you know they'll take'm in custody and send'm on his way back home. I am sorry about that, but I can't interfere with it. So if you can find that boy a career, you better do it pretty quick.''

c·h·a·p·t·e·r

28

A bad feeling went through Chief McLemore when he glanced out his office window and saw about a half-dozen people, including Rev. Schindler, huddled on the sidewalk in front of the police station. The people were gathered in a circle, as if they were having a prayer huddle. You could see Rev. Schindler's mouth moving as he raised a large black book, almost certainly a Bible, over his head.

Chief McLemore's sense of distress increased when he saw a TV-14 van parked across the street and a man aiming a TV camera at the people in front of the jail. Chief McLemore's first thought was that the people were about to do something distressingly religious. He not only believed in the separation of church and state, he believed in the separation of church and everything else. He put on his cowboy hat and walked out the front door toward the prayer huddle, where Rev. Schindler was saying something biblical. McLemore knew he had to be cautious about what he might say because it might get recorded for TV. But he had no inclination to be too cautious.

"Is this your new church—the sidewalk?" McLemore said as he walked up to Rev. Schindler.

The minister stared at McLemore with a somber smile.

"To Jesus, everywhere is a church," Rev. Schindler said.

"Sounds a little disorienting," McLemore said, trying to seem pleasant. "But may I ask what everyone is doing here in front of the police station?"

"We are gathered here to do God's work," Rev. Schindler said.

"Amen," several of the people said.

The cameraman, a reporter, and some man holding a big parabolic microphone to record everything anyone in the crowd said walked across the street and stood a few feet away from McLemore and the others.

Rev. Schindler looked at McLemore and said, "As I told the television people earlier, we are here as soldiers of Christ to exorcise this jail of the spirit of Satan himself, who we believe has possessed the body of the illegal alien in jail."

McLemore blinked.

"You're going to exorcise the jail?" he said.

"In Christ's name," Rev. Schindler said. "With sufficient faith, you can move a mountain."

"Why don't you do that, and leave the jail alone?" McLemore said.

"We will not be swayed from our path," Rev. Schindler said. "If you'll please stand back, the exorcism will begin."

McLemore didn't like being asked to stand back from his own jail. "You got a permit to exorcise this jail?" he said.

"A permit?" the minister said.

"Satan's not in here," McLemore said. "And if he was, you wouldn't get him out with exorcism. You'd need a lawyer or a bail bondsman. Now I won't interfere with anyone freely practicing their religion, but if this here exorcism takes more than five minutes, I won't call it religion anymore. I'll call it loitering, and I'll give you a citation. Remember that. Five minutes," the chief said, looking at his wristwatch as he walked back inside the police station.

He turned and stared out of the glass doors at Rev. Schindler and his followers.

As much as McLemore believed in freedom of religion, he wished the Constitution had been written to stipulate that religion could be freely practiced indoors only. It was an embarrassment to know his police station and jail were possibly on live TV as Rev. Schindler held his big black Bible open in his right hand while he spread his left hand open and put it against the wall of the police station.

"I have established contact," the minister said, looking back toward the sidewalk at his small group of followers and spectators. He also looked at the TV camera with a solemn and sober expression.

"Like an electrode from the Lord," he said, "my hand can sense in this building the presence of evil incarnate."

"That's not evil. It's the air conditioner vibrating," McLemore said to the various officers staring out the door.

Rev. Schindler looked at the building and held the Bible high in his right hand while he seemed to lean forward a little bit to put the weight of his body on his left hand, which was spread out on the building.

"My right hand is the lightning rod of the Lord," he called out. "My left hand is the electrode of the Lord."

"It makes Jesus sound like a battery," McLemore said.

The minister stretched his legs straight behind him and leaned forward against the building, which made him appear to be trying to knock the building down.

"Grant me, oh Lord, oh Heavenly Father, oh Lord of Hosts," Rev. Schindler said, and then paused, as if he was trying to think of every possible name to call God. But then he resumed the sentence, saying, "Grant me now your divine and eternal and righteous strength to cast out from this building that most dark and unclean and wicked spirit known by many names—known as Beelzebub, known as Lucifer, known as Satan, known as the Devil, known as Belial, known as the Prince of Darkness, and who disguises himself this very moment as an ordinary illegal alien."

The minister's body began twitching and shaking, which

possibly was supposed to be divine energy running from his lightning-rod hand to his electrode hand, but the way he moved reminded McLemore of someone having a seizure. In fact, McLemore considered calling an ambulance and interrupting the exorcism by reporting it as a medical disorder. As Rev. Schindler twitched and shook, he began swaying backward and forward, and then left and right, and his head jerked backward a few times, so people could imagine Beelzebub flowing through the police station wall and into the reverend's electrode hand. Chief McLemore briefly expected to see a hideous monster with slime on its head suddenly poke out through the reverend's stomach, like in the movie *Alien*. Maybe there was some similarity between space monsters and people without passports.

McLemore turned to Sgt. Mondesi and said, "Go get Alfredo. We might as well let him watch himself being exorcised."

Rev. Schindler was still twitching and undulating with his hand on the wall when Sgt. Mondesi brought Alfredo to the door and began quickly explaining things in Spanish.

Alfredo pressed his nose up against the glass door and watched the minister swaying and twitching.

"He's removing devils from me?" Alfredo asked, in Spanish.

"That's what he says," Sgt. Mondesi said.

"I don't feel anything," Alfredo said, touching his stomach and chest and forehead.

"It might be that you don't have any devils," Sgt. Mondesi said.

"I have so little," Alfredo said.

The two of them watched the exorcism for a while, then Alfredo saw the camera.

"Is that a TV camera out there?"

"Yes. You're being exorcised on TV."

"This is wonderful! I'm on TV again."

"Not really. The *wall* is on TV."

"Oh. That's right. So the father thinks I'm behind that wall?"

"Yes."

Alfredo watched Rev. Schindler leaning with his hand on the building.

"Should we tell him I'm over here?"

"No. Let him exorcise the wall."

Outside, the minister yelled, "I can feel it!" and then made a strange groaning sound.

McLemore knew it was irrational, but he almost wanted to see a monster slam through the wall of the police station and land in the street.

"It's going through me now!" Rev. Schindler called out in a tense, high-pitched voice. "Yes! Yes!" he yelled, and then he waved his right arm, the one holding the Bible over his head, and he yelled, "The demon *has* been sucked away! Sucked out of his haven and passed through my very flesh and bone and flung back! Back into the wretched, hideous stink of everlasting Hell!"

The minister's followers, about eight of them, began clapping and cheering when Rev. Schindler stood up straight and victorious. He turned toward the street and got on his knees on the sidewalk and held his hands together in prayer. Everyone got quiet then, and all the followers also kneeled and prayed on the sidewalk. Everything that just happened was so peculiar and occult that it seemed to emphasize the silence then. It remained so quiet out by the jail that you could hear, very faintly, a bell going *ding-ding, ding-ding*. It was like the faraway sound of a church bell. For a minute, McLemore imagined that the bell was someone in Heaven signaling that Satan had been sucked back into Hell.

The sound of the bell ringing got ever so gradually louder, as if whichever heavenly creature was ringing it would soon be in view.

Ding-ding. Ding-ding.

It was astonishing, and made the hairs on the back of McLemore's neck tingle, to think maybe there really *was* a Heaven, and some angel or someone was ringing a bell and coming this way, right now, to spread some blessed message.

Ding-ding. Ding-ding.

After a few more seconds, with everyone on the sidewalk looking off in the direction of the ringing noise, with everyone maybe waiting to get their first true glimpse of people from the kingdom of God, you could see it wasn't angels.

Ding-ding. Ding-ding.

"What's that?" Alfredo said.

"It's an ice-cream truck," Sgt. Mondesi said. "They drive around and stop to sell ice-cream bars and Popsicles."

"Now that I've been exorcised, do I get ice cream?"

"Well, why not," Sgt. Mondesi said, and walked outside to get ice cream.

There was a fire in Rev. Schindler's head. It was a burning, tingling feeling that was perhaps the spiritual sensation he might expect after doing an exorcism. Or possibly it was just a migraine. As careful as he tried to be about spiritual reality, he often wasn't sure if whatever emotions or physical sensations he felt were the true spiritual emanations of someone doing the Lord's work or if he was just having an ordinary headache. Of course, he'd never admit that to his congregation, or even his wife. Such an admission of doubt or uncertainty would seem like an absence of faith. He couldn't even remember how many years he'd spent expressing and preaching nothing *but* faith in the powers and miracles of God; so much so that he almost completely believed every fraction of an instant of his life was permeated with the mystical and infinite powers of God. And it was in fact his mission to preach such faith to all who had ears.

Sometimes it just gave him a headache. Sometimes he simply wanted to rest, and not have to find complete religious devotion in every second of his life. But he worried that maybe that was a sin, to just want to rest, so he resisted it and remained devoted. And tired.

As he chewed the first bite from his bologna sandwich and looked out the kitchen window at nothing in particular, he remembered the TV camera, and the little crowd, and the slightly painful feelings in his hand as he pressed violently against the wall to bring Satan out through his own body. Something had flashed through him then. A hot, tingling sense of motion seemed to briefly swell in his flesh and then flash away, as if the subatomic particles of Satan raced through him in the moment of exorcism.

He didn't really know. But you weren't supposed to know. You were supposed to have faith. Knowledge was for infidels and doubters. Faith was the thing. Pure faith, like God's breath.

So he knew he was doing the right thing, and remembered kneeling on the sidewalk after the exorcism, praying with his eyes closed and hearing the bells of Heaven. He almost didn't want to open his eyes then and look, as if he was afraid of whatever heavenly figures he might see. But even in the Bible, people always saw angels and were afraid, so it was a perfectly natural thing to hear the bells and be afraid that maybe this time, maybe he really *did* make miraculous contact with God. That was all. There were those long, long seconds when he kept hearing the bells, kept feeling both fear and wonder as the ringing grew louder and he wondered if he should open his eyes yet, or open his eyes at all, to see an angel of the Lord. So he kept still, remained kneeling with his eyes closed, praying to not be afraid, praying to be worthy of this miraculous moment when all the doubters and backsliders and hypocrites and unbelievers would at last see complete proof of the Kingdom of Heaven, and he was finally brave enough to open his eyes when the ringing got right behind him, where he expected to see the blazing eyes of an angel looking upon him, and it was the ice-cream truck.

He almost collapsed on the sidewalk. A feeling washed completely through his body, as if he'd been betrayed by his own faith; as if his most passionate and sacred hopes were made instantly useless by imagining that the bells on an ice cream truck were a visitation from Heaven. He felt so foolish and tired then, as he watched some woman police officer walk out of the police station and go right by him to buy some Popsicles. And it was all on TV. Everyone in town, everyone for miles, would see that scene on the TV news that night. And they wouldn't know the seriousness of his hand upon the wall. They wouldn't feel the tingling, hot motion that flashed through his own flesh. They'd just see some man leaning against the wall, and see everyone kneeling down in prayer as the ice-cream truck came by, making it all seem like meaningless farce.

But Satan was secretly at work in the world, moving about as freely as the wind, and it was his responsibility as a minister to do battle with Satan. The problem was, you never knew where Satan really was. Satan could disguise himself in any human or animal form. He could send out thousands upon thousands of individual demons to possess human souls. It made Rev. Schindler wonder how he knew that Satan himself possessed the soul of that illegal alien in jail. And the answer was . . .

And the answer was . . .

At first there wasn't an answer. For a few seconds, it was quite disturbing that Rev. Schindler might have made illogical assumptions and actually didn't know anything at all about the illegal alien. But then he remembered how he knew that Satan possessed that man's soul.

Once he saw the report on TV about possible satanic activities in the abandoned house where the illegal alien lived, Rev. Schindler felt his neck tingle and his pulse increase. *That* was how he knew it was Satan. Only the truest and most pure intuitions could make his neck tingle and his pulse increase. It *had* to be a spiritual communication from God, a warning that Satan was nigh and had to be expelled to Hell. And he had expelled him.

At least it seemed like he had. He'd never done an exorcism before. Actually, he'd only guessed on the technique and wording and so on. And so when he put one hand on the wall and the other hand in the air and summoned the devil to pass through him and go back into Hell, he didn't know if it worked. *Some*thing passed through him. It was warm and tingly. He assumed it had to be Satan. Although, actually, sometimes he felt warm and tingly when he held his wife. But that certainly didn't mean he'd exorcised his *wife* through the wall of the jail.

That little instant of doubt and uncertainty was flung from his mind, the way he always flung away any intrusion of reason, because reason led to doubt; and doubt led to . . .

Well it led to somewhere, and Rev. Schindler wasn't going there. He lived on a mountain of faith, even if sometimes it felt like he lived under it. He thought of the crucifixion of Christ and held his right hand out on the kitchen counter, remembering his occasional impulse to take a screwdriver and a hammer and slam the screwdriver through the palm of his hand. But that would take three hands, and he was given only two.

c·h·a·p·t·e·r

29

From the floor of the grocery store, where Eva and Ava looked up past the scaffolding where the painter, Doug, was lying on his back and still painting, they could see what Eva thought was a truly splendid painting of something she couldn't identify. The colors were bright and precise, and it looked like a realistic scene of hundreds of biblical people in their robes and things outside in the desert, holding their arms up in the air to catch pancakes falling from the sky.

"How come all those people are catching pancakes in the air?" Eva asked Doug.

"Pancakes?" Doug said. He rolled sideways on the scaffolding to look down at Eva and Ava and said, "Well I guess they do resemble pancakes a little. But it's supposed to be manna. I'm not sure what manna looks like. But this is supposed to be the scene where Moses and the Israelites are out wandering around in the desert and God sends them manna from Heaven so they won't starve."

"It looks like pancakes," Ava said.

"Maybe so," Doug said. "Maybe I should paint scrambled eggs and hash browns in the sky. People would say it isn't authentic, though. But I could say it's a scene from the New and Improved Testament."

The girls were smiling about that and studying the terribly interesting scene with Doug when they saw a few people walking down the aisle toward them. There were about five people at first, but more and more people came down the aisle behind them; maybe ten or twelve people. The man in the front of the crowd was Rev. Schindler, who Eva and Ava had just seen on TV while he was exorcising the jail. There were so many of them that the sound of their shoes on the floor was loud and a little bit threatening, like soldiers marching.

"Uh-oh," Doug said from the scaffolding. "I don't think they're here for groceries. Maybe you girls better step back a little bit, just to be safe."

Eva and Ava walked a few feet down the aisle and stopped as Rev. Schindler and the people with him arrived in front of the scaffolding.

"I don't know what you're here for, but there better not be any trouble. I'm calling the police," the store manager said from behind the people in the aisle. No one even looked at him, and he stayed behind them all. Everyone stared up at Doug, who lay stretched out on the wooden platform with his paint and brushes about ten feet above the floor. No one spoke right away, and it became uncomfortably silent as Rev. Schindler and the other people seemed to examine Doug's latest painting.

"It somewhat resembles Moses and the Israelites receiving pancakes from Heaven," Doug said. "Actually, it's manna."

With a severe look on his face, Rev. Schindler said, "We gave you a chance to end this blasphemy, and you ignored it. You cheapen and degrade everything sacred. Since you won't end it, we will."

Rev. Schindler and two other men began climbing the scaffolding with cans of spray paint in their hands.

"What the hell are you people doing?" Doug yelled.

The men kept climbing, which made the scaffolding wobble while Doug yelled, "Someone call the police!"

"I already called them!" the store manager yelled.

Rev. Schindler and the other men reached the top of the scaffolding, where each man held on with one hand and aimed their cans of spray paint toward the new painting with the other. Doug managed to kick the can of spray paint out of one man's hand, but Rev. Schindler and the other man started spraying black paint all over the scene of the Israelites.

"Goddamn vandals!" Doug yelled as he kicked at Rev. Schindler, who dodged the kick and then began spraying black paint on the adjacent scene of Adam and Eve. He'd sprayed part of Adam and Eve's feet black when Doug scooted on his back and got close enough to the reverend to slam his foot violently against the hand that Rev. Schindler was using to hold on to the scaffolding. Rev. Schindler screamed in pain and jerked so strongly away from the scaffolding, which was already wobbling, that you could hear things creaking and snapping as the whole scaffolding tilted toward the aisle and began falling. Small buckets of brown and yellow and white and green and red paint sloshed and sprayed long streams of paint through the air and onto the bread aisle, which was where Doug fell, landing on top of several layers of sandwich bread in the aisle as Rev. Schindler seemed to partly fall and partly dive away from the crashing scaffolding. A bright, swirling stream of yellow paint fell with him, splattering all across the back of his head and suitcoat, as the howling reverend landed into the edge of the people he'd arrived with, who then tumbled and fell in a pretty orderly fashion, as if they'd all practiced falling like that, while the other man from the scaffolding landed halfway on top of a display of nectarines, during which the shuddering form of the scaffolding finished its violent decline in such a way that three or four different colors of paint formed a brief and attractive spray in the air while large and small fragments of sandwich bread and hot dog buns and hamburger buns and several varieties of doughnuts were propelled through the immediate area like edible shrapnel as Doug dangled from the top of the bread aisle and yelled, "You stupid bastards!"

to a group of presumably sensitive and God-fearing people who might have been offended by being called stupid bastards if they hadn't already been so preoccupied with falling down and screaming as Rev. Schindler held his hand tenderly where he lay on top of his followers on the floor and yelled at Doug, "I'll have you arrested for assault!"

Doug threw a package of brown 'n' serve rolls at the reverend.

"Assault!" Rev. Schindler yelled.

Doug threw packages of light rye and dark rye at him. He threw white bread and wheat bread. French and Italian. Some of the bread had wet paint on it, and as Doug threw those packages, the minister became decorated with smears and splats of various colors, making him cover his face with his arms as Doug continued throwing pita bread and potato bread, raisin bread and multigrain bread, onion rolls and kaiser rolls, powdered doughnuts and chocolate doughnuts. A partially flattened box of glazed doughnuts tumbled to rest near Eva and Ava, and both girls picked up a doughnut and began eating it, so it wouldn't be wasted.

Two police officers soon arrived and at first simply stood behind the crowd of Rev. Schindler's followers.

"You there! Stop that!" one of the officers yelled up at Doug on the bread aisle. But Doug continued throwing whatever bread was in his reach while the reverend still held his arms up protectively and shouted scripture at Doug.

"Man does not live by bread alone!" the minister quoted.

"Or strudel!" Doug yelled, throwing some strudel.

The police finally stepped in front of Rev. Schindler, and Doug stopped throwing bread. Everyone was taken down to the police station except for Eva and Ava, who felt so guilty about eating the glazed doughnuts that Eva paid for the whole box. Rev. Schindler, the two men who were with him, and Doug were all charged with disturbing the peace.

"There wasn't any peace to *disturb*," Doug complained.

Doug was also charged with destruction of bread,

whereas Rev. Schindler and his two associates were charged with vandalism and disorderly conduct.

"Vandalism?" Rev. Schindler objected. "We were protecting the public from blasphemous and obscene art."

"Maybe we'll call it Christian vandalism, then," the arresting sergeant said.

The four men were briefly locked in a cell directly across from the cell Alfredo was in. Alfredo was so pleased to have new neighbors that he immediately greeted them.

"Give me a break, give me a break, break me off a piece of that Kit Kat Bar," Alfredo sang.

But no one answered him. They all seemed sullen and irritable, especially the man with paint all over his clothes and hair.

After several hours Doug and Rev. Schindler and the other two men were released on bond, and as they walked out of the police station at the same time, Rev. Schindler glared at Doug and said, "There's a special place for you in Hell."

"Well, thank you, but I don't think I deserve such favoritism," Doug said.

30

The town council meeting room was completely filled with curious citizens when Mayor Elizabeth Reese banged her gavel three times to signify the start of the meeting.

"I call this meeting to order, and I move that we modify the agenda to allow the council to now address a special item on the agenda titled 'Illegal Alien.'"

The motion was approved, and Mayor Reese looked at the audience and said, "I know that many of you are here exclusively for the discussion of the illegal alien question, and we'll deal with that item first. There will be a five-minute limit on how long anyone may address this council. If you can't make your point in five minutes, maybe you don't know what your point is."

The first person to walk up to a microphone at the front of the crowd was a young man in a blue cowboy shirt and blue jeans who looked uneasy about being there. He called the mayor Madam Mayor and he called the council members Madam Council. The man then apologized for saying Madam Council. He said his name was Cooley Hardwell, and that usually when he talked in front of a crowd, it was just cows he talked to. He was the rancher who reported the strange chanting noises and fire about the same time that Alfredo was arrested. Cooley Hardwell said he hadn't caught anybody on his ranch doing anything suspicious or satanic, but two different times he found the remains of campfires or some kind of fires on his land, and three different times he heard people making chanting noises out in the night.

"How do you know it was chanting?" the mayor asked.

"Well, that's what it sounded like," Cooley Hardwell said.

"And where have you heard chanting before? It's not a normal sound you'd hear in Texas," the mayor said.

"I've heard chanting in the movies."

"What movies?"

"I don't remember."

"Did the chanting sound like Gregorian monks?"

"Monks? Do we have monks around here?"

"But anyway, Mr. Hardwell," Mayor Reese said, plainly ignoring his question, "could you please tell us why you believe the peculiar sounds you say you heard and the remains of the fires you say you found have anything at all to do with an illegal alien from Guatemala?"

"Well it's just the timing. There weren't none of this happening before. It only started happening the day before the alien was put in jail. I'm not saying it was him out there. I'm only saying that, like the news said, he was originally investigated for suspicion of satanism, and even though nobody found any proof on him that he was doing anything satanic, everyone knows Satan don't operate by the normal laws of nature. I ain't saying I think Satan's inside the soul of that illegal alien in jail. In fact, on TV they showed some preacher casting out demons from the jail. It's my opinion if you did that to the whole jail, you might get a whole *slew* a' demons an' spirits and screaming meemies flying outa that jail. But what I'm saying is it seems possible that that illegal alien coulda been directing satanic activities even from inside the jail, is what I'm saying."

A lot of people in the room talked quietly to themselves

when he finished, as if discussing what they'd just heard. The next person who spoke up was a man in a suit who said his name was Lowry Fowry, which Eva thought rhymed too much to be a real name, but that's what he said it was: Lowry Fowry. He said he was Cooley Hardwell's lawyer, and he said, "Regardless of what anyone might care to speculate about the possibilities of the supernatural in our daily lives—which no one can prove or disprove— I think the real point is that the city jail was not built to hold illegal aliens for the federal government. I suggest that the mayor and the council use their authority to advise the chief of police to arrange for the immediate transfer of the illegal alien into the custody of the Immigration and Naturalization Service. This way, the city frees itself of any public anxiety over demonic guests in the jail."

Then some woman in a green dress that looked like it used to fit her but didn't anymore, since it drooped across her and sagged like she'd lost some weight, got up to the microphone and said, "As a Christian taxpayer, for whom Christ died—"

"Christ died for taxpayers?" the mayor interrupted. "Never mind. Just go on."

The woman said, "Well what I want to say is I think our jail was meant for respectable criminals, and not satanists."

"I imagine our criminals are as respectable as anyone else's," the mayor said. "But there's no reason to believe the man in jail you're referring to is a satanist."

"No reason?" a man in the back of the crowd said. "Well then why'd that reverend exorcise the whole jail?"

Everybody looked to where the man was, and the mayor banged her wooden hammer on her table real loudly and said, "Anyone who interrupts the orderly process of this meeting will be escorted outside. We're not here to discuss religion. This part of the meeting is about any city matters pertaining to the lawful operation of the jail, and nothing else. So if anyone came here to enforce their religious beliefs, you came to the wrong meeting."

Whispering and quiet talking broke out across the room. Eva turned her head to see some man walking quickly up the center aisle toward the microphone. The woman in the green dress stepped aside to let the man stand there in his solid black suit as he seemed to lean forward severely toward the mayor and the council.

"I am the Reverend Kyle Schindler, of Christ's Unfurling Grace Church."

He glanced slowly across both sides of the room as one of the TV guys walked up closer to hold the camera just a few feet from the reverend's face.

"I am," the reverend said, and paused, as if he liked getting everyone's attention and then making everyone wonder why he got it, "sure in my heart that when the founding fathers established this great nation based on the Judeo-Christian principles stated clearly in the Holy Bible . . ."

And he stopped there, paused again, as if he were allowing everyone to consider what he'd said so far. Or maybe it was such a long sentence already that by the time he'd said the first part, he couldn't remember what the second part was.

The whole room was quiet, all the people waiting to see if the reverend would remember the rest of his sentence. Then his mind apparently overcame the great difficulty of remembering what to say, and he continued: ". . . that they never envisioned a government of the people, by the people, and for the people that would require God-fearing citizens to allow their hard-earned taxes to . . ."

And he stopped again, like a train going up a steep hill. Mayor Reese thought it was as if the sentence in his head was so long that he'd misplaced part of it and was trying to see where it went. But he seemed to have located the misplaced sentence. He said, ". . . be used to pay room and board for an illegal alien described in our very own free press as a satanic messiah."

"Would you repeat that?" someone in the crowd said.

"No, no," someone else said.

"Everything worth saying at all is in this book," Rev. Schindler said, holding up what looked like his Bible.

"Well don't start reading all *that*," someone else said in the crowd, and the mayor whammed her gavel down and said, "Let's not have any snide remarks. I think we can all be uncomfortable with each other without that."

The mayor looked at the minister, who didn't bother to stare back at the people taunting him, and said to him, "Reverend, would you answer me one question, please?"

"Surely."

"Do you believe that in your ritual outside the jail this week that you truly deported any evil spirits from the jail?"

"I firmly believe that, yes, ma'am."

"Well then, if that's so, you can't complain that anyone in jail is a satanic messiah, because you apparently deported Satan."

Rev. Schindler didn't answer. The whole room was quiet as everybody thought that over and waited to hear what he would say.

"Well my immediate response," he said, even though his immediate response took him about ten seconds, "is that if you admit I deported Satan, then I was right that he really *was* in jail."

"I admit no such thing," the mayor said. "I'm simply reporting your own logic to you. And your logic—not mine—makes it clear that if you believe you expelled Satan from the jail, then you have absolutely no reason to come here and complain that there's an evil spirit in the jail."

"But what you don't *realize*," the minister said quickly, "is that no victory over evil is complete until the return of Christ. Satan could return in an instant," he said, and snapped his fingers.

"Well if he does, we'll arrest him and assign him a lawyer," the mayor said. "As for now, your time is up. Next speaker, please."

Only three other people got up to say anything about Alfredo. One woman said she liked foreigners just fine, but she didn't think all our ancestors came over here just so other people could sneak in illegally. One man said that Alfredo was an illegal alien, and it was wrong to keep illegal criminals in jail, since the jail was meant for legal criminals.

Then the old Comanche named Distant Cloud walked down the left side of the room toward the microphone. He looked just like an Indian you might see in a movie or a TV documentary. He wore old blue jeans and a black cowboy shirt and, instead of cowboy boots, a pair of Reebok running shoes. Mayor Reese had never heard Distant Cloud talk, and she wondered if he'd speak Comanche. She wondered if he'd start singing a Comanche song filled with words nobody understood, like the last living Comanche singing the last Comanche song. And finally, after the whole room seemed to swell or ache in its own silence, Distant Cloud spoke.

"If you send everyone back to where they used to be, you all will be gone. This building will be mine. This town will be mine. I'll wave to you as you leave."

Distant Cloud put the microphone back in the stand and walked down the center aisle and out the door into the night. Even for a few seconds after he was gone, everybody was still quiet, as if they all knew they could be sent back to Europe or somewhere. Mayor Reese imagined them all, including herself, being sucked away like ghosts, everyone in the world being sucked right out of where they were, yanked high into the air and magically returned to whatever distant and strange country their ancestors first came from thousands and thousands of years ago, so that everyone was rightfully sent back into the full and frightful wilderness as ancient as the Olduvai Gorge in Africa, without passports.

It didn't happen. Everybody got to stay. Except Alfredo.

Even after Eva's mom and Chief McLemore and Eva's dad defended Alfredo and told about everyone trying to get a job for him so he could be a legal alien, the council voted to urge Chief McLemore to turn Alfredo over to the INS as soon as possible. Mayor Reese voted against it. Then Alfredo stood up in a badly fitted seersucker suit and looked toward the council and the mayor.

"Aetna, I'm glad I met ya," he said.

31

In his random and uneven attempts to learn English, Alfredo realized that Diego Guerra had actually taught him an American saying that explained Alfredo's situation in America.

"I'm screwed," Alfredo said, pleased that he'd spoken English, but sad that he was screwed.

The green card. That was the problem. It was all so confusing. The government took his dishwashing job away and then said he couldn't stay in America because he didn't have a job. And then they kept him in jail so he couldn't look for the job they said he needed.

He practiced his English again: "I'm screwed."

It made Alfredo sit down on his bed and try to think of jobs. As Diego Guerra had told him, the jobs had to be so repugnant that no other Americans would want them. *That* wasn't very nice. It was like saying "Welcome to America, you stupid bastard."

He saw Sgt. Mondesi down at the end of the jail hallway and called to her to have someone to speak Spanish with. Sgt. Mondesi walked up to Alfredo's cell and said, "What can I do for you, Alfredo?"

"You can try to help me think of a job," Alfredo said.

"Diego says the government will give me a green card only if the job I get is so repugnant that no one else in America wants it."

"Those are the rules, I'm sorry to say."

"Well, which job would that be?"

"I don't know, Alfredo. It's not like there's one particular job that everyone knows about that's so awful that nobody wants it."

"Then how will I know if the job I want is awful enough?"

"The immigration people will tell you."

"Okay. And what awful job would you recommend?" Alfredo said optimistically.

"Well, let me think," Sgt. Mondesi said, and thought a moment. Then she said, "Maybe you could get a job with the border police, arresting people like yourself as they try to sneak into America."

"That'd be awful."

"Awful enough. But probably a lot of Americans already have those jobs, so you'd have to think of another one."

"Which one?"

"I really don't have much time, now, but let me think," Sgt. Mondesi said. "Okay. I know one—convenience store clerk. Like at Get In 'N Get Out."

"Really? Why's that so awful?"

"Because they get robbed all the time. Sometimes they get shot."

Alfredo nodded his head and thought about the job. Then he said, "Getting shot is too hard a job. Is there a job where they just beat you up?"

Wheel of Fortune had just started on TV when they brought in the drunk to Alfredo's cell. His former cellmate, the white man, had been gone for two days, so Alfredo was glad to have more company, especially since the drunk looked like a Mexican, and Alfredo could finally talk with someone in Spanish.

"You got here just in time to watch *Wheel of Fortune*," Alfredo said in Spanish.

"Eat my butt," the man said.

Maybe there wasn't going to be much conversation. The man stretched out on the bottom bunk and immediately went to sleep, breathing out a faint fragrance of alcohol that slowly filled the room. Alfredo watched *Wheel of Fortune, Beverly Hills 90210, Home Improvement*, and *Gunsmoke* as the drunk slept. The easiest shows to learn any English from were *Wheel of Fortune* and *Gunsmoke*, where a few sentences were short enough or repeated so many times that Alfredo had memorized them fairly easily. So now he could add sentences together from each show to form entirely new sentences. When one of the guards walked by the cell, Alfredo happily said to him, "I'd like to buy a vowel, Marshal Dillon."

As many times as he'd watched *Wheel of Fortune* in Guatemala, he had never fully understood it. Whenever one of the contestants asked to buy a vowel, Alfredo thought a vowel might be one of the letters, or a vowel might just be a strange English word meaning "prize." And this was America, the home of George Washington and *Wheel of Fortune*; the home of the Statue of Liberty and *Family Feud*. If anything, America stood for liberty, equality, and prizes for all.

In fact, Alfredo tried to wake up the new drunk to see if he'd lived long enough in America to know if *vowel* meant "prize." The drunk did wake up, but he had no interest in vowels. He began immediately bragging about friends of his who had stolen the Virgin Mary stamp machine.

At first, Alfredo thought the drunk was still drunk. There was no such thing as a Virgin Mary stamp machine.

"You're drunk," Alfredo said.

"Of course I'm drunk. I'm a drunk," the man said. "If you're sober, you're not allowed to be a drunk."

Only a drunk would say that. Alfredo tried ignoring everything the man said, until he realized from the man's endless chatter that actually there had been a stamp machine in the post office with a likeness of the Virgin Mary. Alfredo was stunned. He had heard of such miracles when he was a boy, and now he was in the same town where such a miracle had happened. It would be a horrible sin to know of such an offense against God and tell no one. So he had to get the attention of the police.

"Have you driven a Ford lately?" Alfredo yelled down the hall, but no one answered, except the drunk.

"I wish you'd shut up," he said, and lay back down on his bunk to sleep.

Alfredo tried to get someone's attention again.

"I'd like to buy a vowel, Miss Kitty," he yelled.

"Shut up, or I'll cut your throat when I get a knife," the drunk said, and put a pillow over his head.

A little more quietly, Alfredo called: "Denorex tingles. Head and Shoulders doesn't."

One of the officers did come down the hall and say a lot of English things Alfredo couldn't understand as Alfredo urgently pointed behind himself at the drunk and gestured wildly and said, "¡Español! ¡Español!" as if maybe the officer would realize he needed someone who could speak Spanish. Alfredo waited anxiously in his cell after the officer walked away, and Alfredo prayed to the Lord: *Please, dear Lord, make them understand I know where the Virgin Mary and all of her stamps are.*

And finally Sgt. Mondesi did come, and Alfredo whispered to her through the steel bars, "This drunk here says he knows who stole the Virgin Mary."

Chief McLemore was notified at home of the important new drunk in jail, and he drove back to the police station that night to interrogate him, with Sgt. Mondesi as the translator. The drunk was taken to McLemore's office, since the police station was too small to have an interrogation room, where Sgt. Mondesi gave McLemore the drunk's driver's license. McLemore read the name on the license.

"Jesus?" he said. "Jesus stole the Virgin Mary stamp machine?"

"*Hey-seuss,*" Sgt. Mondesi said.

"I know how to pronounce it," McLemore said. "Well, go ahead and start asking him what he knows. Read him his rights, first."

After Sgt. Mondesi explained Jesus Villalobos's rights to him, Jesus responded.

"He said he wants to see a lawyer," Sgt. Mondesi said.

"Tell him it's night. All the lawyers are asleep," McLemore said.

Sgt. Mondesi translated that, and translated Jesus' response.

"He wants to know if you can wake up a lawyer."

"That would be rude. Tell him he doesn't have anything to fear but fear itself, and the fact that I'll break his spine in half if he doesn't answer your questions."

"I can't tell him that."

"I know. Tell him . . . tell him if he helps us recover the stamp machine, he won't be charged with a serious crime."

That was translated, and Sgt. Mondesi said, "He wants a beer and a cigarette."

"Go to the store and get him some."

Sgt. Mondesi did so, and Jesus was drinking a beer and smoking a cigarette as he told Sgt. Mondesi everything he knew about the Virgin Mary.

32

It seemed like the summer was almost over. The newspaper said the Virgin Mary stamp machine would be returned, and Alfredo would be deported. Kenlow was out there somewhere. But today it seemed like he wasn't real either. Maybe everything was going to be all ordinary again and Eva could go back to her normal life. But she couldn't remember what her normal life was. She remembered various things she'd done, such as wake up, eat breakfast, and go look for dinosaur bones or something. Or else she and Ava would ride their bikes or go fishing at the sewage treatment plant or play baseball, or maybe watch TV. But all of that seemed so distant and strange now, as if those were the remembered activities of someone who used to be Eva and who wasn't Eva anymore. It was like that part in the Bible where this guy said "vanity of vanities; all is vanity," as if everything you did was a waste of time. Eva was beginning to understand that, although she didn't especially want to.

Most of the Bible was so somber that Eva thought if you finally understood it, it meant most of your brain was replaced by Scripture, and you'd never have a normal thought again. It'd be like a few of the people at church who could always quote Scripture no matter what. You'd just be a walking Bible tape recorder, like someone pushed your Play button and it got stuck, and all your life you repeated everything you ever read in the Bible. It was like at a church breakfast one time where this man was sitting at the table with Eva and Ava and their mom and dad, eating scrambled eggs and English muffins, and the man said, "The Lord gave us eggs, and the Lord gave us muffins," and Ava looked at him and said, "Is he in the kitchen?"

It just seemed a little too weird to always be thinking about religion, which was partly why Eva was worried about beginning to understand that saying about everything being vanity. If she started understanding parts of the Bible without even trying to, maybe her brain was starting to be replaced.

But another thing it maybe meant about everything being vanity was just that Eva was growing up. It could be that. She hadn't started out the summer with any plans to grow up. She couldn't recall any plans at all. But now it occurred to her that so much of how she'd lived her life was just vanity.

Not all of it. Maybe some of it was vanity, and some of it was just fun. And maybe that was a sign that you were growing up: when you sat around brooding and sulking and wondering about too much, like she was doing now. It seemed as if maybe you had to have some purpose in your life. Like Alfredo. He'd been a purpose for a few weeks. And now there wasn't anything more to do, and Eva didn't have a purpose anymore.

She looked around the front yard for a purpose. Maybe she'd see a purpose lying in the grass. No matter how hard she stared, it looked like there was just grass in the grass. She looked up at the sky, at some fat white clouds floating lazily along, and there wasn't any purpose up there, either. Looking up at the sky, toward all of the empty black universe beyond, made her think about God, and how come he never talked to anybody anymore. In the Bible, he talked to people all the time. He sent them angels and omens and manna and curses and locusts. He was always sending something.

Across the street, a UPS van drove up and parked. It made her wonder if God would ever send anything by UPS. Everybody thought God was in the sky. If he was, you'd think NASA would have gotten a photograph of him by now. At the grocery store one day, there was an issue of that magazine called the *Weekly World News*, and on the cover was a picture that was supposed to be a photograph of Heaven floating around in outer space. Eva's mom said it didn't look like Heaven. She said it looked like a casino in Las Vegas. She said she didn't think there'd be any slot machines in Heaven. Probably not. Heaven seemed pretty somber. People always talked about Heaven as if you went there when you died and met all your relatives and friends who'd already died. It'd be like there was this great big crowd wandering around in Heaven, and then when someone new came along, someone in Heaven who knew the new guy would say, "Well you finally died. We were getting impatient." And then, the truly strange thing was if people from different centuries died and all of them went to Heaven, you'd be up in Heaven with Neanderthals and Vikings and Philistines and Huns and Assyrians and Romans and conquistadors and Aztecs and Mayans and all the vanished civilizations that used to conquer each other. It seemed like a few of those groups would try to conquer Heaven. And then God would have to kill them again.

She heard the front door open behind her, and heard little footsteps coming across the porch toward her, and it was Ava. She looked down at Eva sitting on the steps and said, "What we gonna do today? Go look for bones?"

"Vanity of vanities; all is vanity," Eva said.

"I know," Ava said, and bit into a piece of celery. "We gonna go looking for bones?"

"I'm tired of bones."

"Okay," Ava said, chewing loudly on the celery, as if nothing mattered, and so what?

The girls sat together without talking, both of them staring at different parts of the street, as if that was what the world was for—just to be stared at. Eva thought that was one of the worst parts of being alive, where all you did was sit still because you didn't know what to do. Her dad called it ennui, this French word. It meant you were tired of everything and felt useless in the world.

"I have ennui," Eva announced.

"Can I have some, too?" Ava said.

All day long at the store, Kenlow had been feeling sullen and restless, as if something big was going to happen but he didn't know what. When another customer came up to the checkout counter and Kenlow rang up their bill, it was $6.66.

That was it: 666! It was an omen. Just like in the Bible. It meant the apocalypse.

It also meant the customer needed change, which Kenlow gave to him. And he ripped off the sales receipt and kept it, placing the $6.66 omen in his pocket. Then he fumbled around in his agitated mind for the particular meaning that $6.66 held for him. In the hour remaining before Kenlow got off work, he imagined and reimagined the countless possible meanings the $6.66 held for him. He broke into a cold sweat when he thought it meant Satan himself had sent a message to him. But then, he didn't know what the message *was*.

When he got off work at four in the afternoon, he had at least decided that whatever he did would be his final message to the town. He kept trying to decipher the message on the register receipt. Whatever it meant, it had to be bigger and more distressing than any of the fake satanic things he'd done so far.

And so he went into the wilderness, like an unknown or unnamed character from the Bible going forth to fulfill a prophecy. He walked to the old house where Alfredo had lived and saw it covered with darkness in the afternoon shadows, like a fortress of evil. No one was there. Kenlow couldn't see or hear any birds or other animals nearby, as if they all had sensed Kenlow's approach and fled, like the wilderness itself was aware and afraid of Kenlow. For a moment Kenlow thought even the bugs had been scared away, but then a little cloud of gnats flew toward Kenlow's face, and he was forced to suppose that everything was capable of fear except gnats.

Kenlow carefully took off his backpack and set it down upright on the decaying front porch, so nothing would fall over in the backpack. He took the can of red spray paint, shook it up real hard, and began spraying the omen on the front wall of the house. He made the dollar sign about two feet tall. Then he sprayed the three sixes with the decimal point. *That* would be shocking enough for the whole town. Some stupid people would think it meant the house was being sold for six dollars and sixty-six cents, but smarter people would realize its satanic message.

Then he went inside the house, which, even though he'd associated himself with satanic powers, still made him nervous. He feared running into a real satanist. He stood still in the dark front room, listening for any sounds that might make him run away. Nothing happened. No one came at him. There was no sound at all. Feeling safe from the evil that he pretended to represent, Kenlow put the backpack down on the floor and shook up the spray paint again. He slowly sprayed a large pentagram on the floor, about eight feet wide, which you could barely see, as it was dark except for some sunlight that came in the front door and the broken front windows. Then Kenlow took the leftover chicken bones he'd been saving from his lunches for two weeks and put all the bones in the middle of the pentagram. It made a pile about six inches tall. On top of the bones, he put a ten-inch slice of kielbasa, not because kielbasa seemed evil but just because he had some. Next to that, he put four pig's feet on the pile. Pig's feet didn't cost very much, and it looked good to have real animal feet in the pile.

That was it, except for the final thing that made Kenlow's pulse go faster with a sense of fear and exhilaration at the fantastic horror he was about to commit. He took the gallon jug of gasoline out of the backpack and slowly dumped gas all over the bones and kielbasa and pig's feet. A lot of the gas spread out across the floor and seeped down through cracks in the floor. Kenlow made sure none of the gas got on him or his backpack. If he'd calculated things correctly, the fire would just burn real brightly in the middle of the floor for a few minutes and then go out. People who came by the house would see the new omen painted on the wall and could see the scorched bones in the house, as if a genuine animal sacrifice had been made there. No one would think Kenlow was a goddamn gardener then.

Kenlow moved over to the doorway with a sheet of a newspaper rolled up and ready to be lit and thrown on the gas. He wondered if he should have a ceremony first, or say some satanic things. The problem was, he'd never really studied satanism, so he didn't know any satanic things to say. Still, there was no one around, and he had a little bit of time to try and think of something. The only thing slightly evil he could think of was a fragment of some witch's spell he had heard on a TV show.

"Eye of newt," Kenlow said. He tried to remember the full incantation, and said, "Eye of newt . . . lizards and beetles . . ." All he could think of next was Paul McCartney.

"Screw it," Kenlow said, then lit the newspaper with his cigarette lighter and tossed the burning paper onto the pentagram. The gas made a wooshing sound, and yellow and blue flames raced across almost the entire floor. It made Kenlow stumble backward onto the porch, where he stared with delight and fear at the fire all over the inside of the house. He thought the flames would die down, but they didn't. The floor caught on fire. Kenlow had an impulse to run, but he had a stronger impulse to watch the fire. There was still no one else around, so he decided he had enough time to watch the flames move up to the roof of the house before anyone might see the fire or the smoke, and *then* he'd run away.

Maybe the old wood was so decayed and dried out that

it burned a lot faster than Kenlow thought was possible, because within about four or five minutes, the roof of the house was on fire. A big dead tree right next to the house caught on fire, and then that fire spread to the limbs of another dead tree. Little pieces of burning branches and twigs dropped to the ground, and then, in an unpredicted piece of cataclysmic good luck for Kenlow, the ground itself was on fire. He realized that not only were the house and two dead trees burning, but all of the dried leaves and twigs and branches and bushes on the ground were going up in a little wave of flames that crackled and smoked and jumped forward to the next section of forest to burn. It was as if Hell rose up through the ground and started to set the whole forest on fire. Kenlow admired his personal apocalypse until he saw that the fire on the ground was slowly moving toward the trail he needed to use to get out of the woods. He grabbed his backpack and started running down the trail, slowing down every few seconds to look behind him at the flames and smoke advancing behind him.

Eva and Ava were digging in the soft dirt beside the stream, where Eva hoped a dinosaur fell down and died millions of years earlier, when she smelled wood smoke. She stopped digging and sniffed the air again. As soon as she glanced toward the woods, she saw a wide plume of white smoke down by the old warlock's house.

"It's a fire!" she said. "A forest fire!"

"Uh-oh," Ava said. The girls stared at the smoke for a few seconds. It was getting thicker, and they could see little patches of orange flames through the trees.

"We gotta run, Ava! Let's go!" Eva said, picking up the shovel and yanking Ava's hand as the girls ran along the edge of the stream toward the trail. It was about half a mile to their house, and Eva worried that the fire might move through the woods ahead of them and set the trail on fire.

"I'm tired," Ava said as she ran.

"We gotta keep running," Eva said, slowing down just a little bit so Ava could catch up. The girls seemed to be running about half-speed, which Eva judged was fast enough to stay well ahead of the fire. Just then she heard the distant sound of a siren, and then another siren, so maybe the fire department was already on the way. Eva stopped briefly to catch her breath, and as she and Ava rested, they looked off toward the white smoke spreading out over the tops of the trees. There was more smoke than when they first saw it, and there was a faint crackling off in the woods, as if you could hear the trees burning and popping as the fire got closer.

"We have to go on," Eva said, and the girls were running again.

Kenlow had gotten far enough ahead of the fire that he felt comfortable in stopping on the trail and looking back to enjoy the sight of the white smoke expanding across the sky. He stood there for a while, listening to the crackling sounds getting closer to him, and he watched with anxiety and wonder as the small patches of flames visible through the trees became larger and closer. There in the forest, where everything already seemed very dense and closed in, it appeared to Kenlow as if all of the world were on fire. He liked it. He'd never before been responsible for so large an event as a forest fire. It would have been more satisfying to Kenlow if the fire weren't still moving *toward* him. He had to start running again, wondering how much fame and glory this would result in.

As Kenlow accelerated down the trail, he looked back one time, and then noticed through his peripheral vision just as he turned his head forward again that there appeared to be a large hole in the trail exactly where his left foot was going to land. His foot went down into the hole too suddenly for Kenlow to change directions or even slow down. As his body simultaneously went down and forward, Kenlow felt an unbearably sharp jolt in his left ankle, a jolt that would have made him scream, except exactly at that instant, his head slammed down onto the trail, making it impossible to scream just yet. He lay there, stunned and unable to move right away as an intense pain welled up in his ankle.

Eva and Ava came running out on the trail just a few feet behind Kenlow, where the two trails converged, and the girls abruptly stopped to look at Kenlow lying on his face with his left leg bent down in one of the holes that Eva and Ava had dug earlier in search of dinosaur bones.

"Guess we forgot to cover up that hole," Ava said.

"Looks like it," Eva said, staring anxiously at Kenlow, the last person she'd want to see anywhere.

Kenlow was moaning and didn't seem to notice the girls right away. His left leg appeared to have been bent at the ankle, as if maybe it had snapped.

"That's that guy!" Ava said, finally recognizing Kenlow.

"I know," Eva said.

The girls watched Kenlow rocking from side to side on the trail as he moaned, and then they looked off at the fire moving toward them. The whole woods smelled like fire. The sky directly above the girls was getting dark from the advancing smoke.

"I think I broke my ankle," Kenlow groaned.

"That's good," Eva said. "Now you can't chase us."

"But there's a *fire* coming," Kenlow said.

"Did *you* start the fire?" Eva said, no longer very afraid of Kenlow because he was too injured to hurt her or Ava.

Kenlow grabbed his leg with both hands and moaned some more.

"Well did you?" Eva said, feeling a litle bit superior to Kenlow in his weakness. Also, she couldn't think of Kenlow being near a forest fire without imagining he'd started it.

"Of course I didn't!" Kenlow yelled and then rolled back and forth on the trail for a few seconds.

As scared as Eva was of the fire, which was visibly

nearer and still advancing, she felt an odd impulse to cause some pain now to the boy who'd bullied her. The easiest way to cause Kenlow some pain was to simply stand there and do nothing to help him get away from the fire. There was time. She just looked at Kenlow. She stared directly into his eyes, so he'd be forced to see that she wasn't afraid of him, and he'd be forced to realize that now *he* was the one in danger. Possibly that was immoral or sinful, but Eva enjoyed it.

"You've got to help me up," Kenlow said.

"No I don't," Eva said.

"But I'll get burned to death!" Kenlow said more loudly. He looked behind him at the fire, which seemed to be steadily moving toward them.

Ava was puzzled by Eva. She looked at her and said, "We gonna leave'm here?"

"You can't!" Kenlow yelled.

"We could," Eva said.

"I'll kick your ass!" Kenlow said, almost starting to cry. He tried to crawl down the trail, but the pain in his leg was so severe that he immediately stopped moving. He pulled up his pant leg and saw a bloody tear in his flesh where part of the bone stuck out in plain view. Panic and dizziness flashed through Kenlow, and he passed out on the ground.

"I think he passed out," Eva said.

"How can you tell?" Ava said.

"He's not cussing at us."

The girls stared at Kenlow, all curled up in the dirt like a dead armadillo.

"Fire's coming," Ava said.

"I know," Eva said.

"What we gonna do?"

"I'm thinking."

Eva stared at Kenlow and wondered what Jesus would do. Jesus would probably forgive Kenlow for his sins and carry him away from the fire. Jesus was nicer than Eva. Eva wasn't ready to forgive Kenlow for *any* damn thing. And although Jesus might carry Kenlow from the fire, Jesus was stronger than Eva. As skinny as Kenlow was, he still looked pretty heavy. Eva couldn't possibly carry him down the trail.

"We could try to drag him," Eva said.

The girls began dragging Kenlow along the uneven trail. They were about one hundred yards from the clearing at the edge of their neighborhood. It was extremely tiring, especially for Ava, and so Eva tried to drag Kenlow even harder to make up for Ava's weakness. They'd dragged Kenlow and his backpack about thirty feet when they stopped to rest.

"He's too heavy," Ava said, and let go of Kenlow's arm, making it plop down in the dusty trail. "I have to go to the bathroom," Ava said.

"We don't have time for that," Eva said, letting Kenlow's other arm drop to the trail while the girls caught their breath and stared back at the burning bushes and trees.

Kenlow groaned. His eyes opened. "Goddamn it! My leg!" he said.

Ava was shocked. "He said *goddamn*," she said. "*We* can't say that."

"We've got to keep dragging him," Eva said.

"We also can't say *shit*," Ava said.

"Start dragging him, Ava."

"And we can't say *bitch*, either," Ava said.

"Grab his arm," Eva said, and the girls grabbed Kenlow's arms and slowly dragged him forward, just a little bit slower than before. They still had a long way to go, and it looked as if the fire was picking up speed on them. Little trails of white smoke wafted along ahead of the girls, and some of the smoke went right over them, making them start to cough now and then, which slowed them down even more. When they stopped to rest again, the edge of the fire was about fifty yards behind them. Off toward the neighborhood, they heard sirens, pretty loud now, as if fire trucks were out at the edge of the woods, but they couldn't see or hear any firefighters coming toward them. Everywhere they looked behind them, different parts of trees were burning, but mostly it was the bushes and leaves and branches on the ground that rapidly caught fire and seemed to surge forward at them, as if the fire knew where the girls were and was chasing them.

Kenlow was trying to crawl, now, but it didn't work. "Oh, fuck," he groaned.

"We can't say that word either," Ava said.

Eva stopped. She looked at Ava and said, "Let go."

It was an interesting moment, where Eva had the choice to save Kenlow's life or just leave him there. He wasn't a very nice boy at all. He appeared to be nothing but mean. If there hadn't been a fire in the woods when Eva and Ava came across Kenlow, he might've hurt them then, just like he threatened to. So it was like saving someone who only meant harm and who might still do that after the fire. Like saving the one person who'd be your enemy.

Eva looked at the fire through the trees. It was a wall of darkness and smoke, with flames around the edges. Eva estimated that if she left Kenlow there, the fire would get to him in about five minutes. It might just burn on past him on the trail without touching him, since the trail was all dirt and wouldn't burn. But maybe some burning branches or something would fall on him, or maybe the flames next to the trail would be so hot it'd still burn Kenlow's skin, like a roast in an oven.

But she couldn't really leave him there. She was only pretending to have that choice, so while it looked as if she were thinking about it, Kenlow might grovel. Eva had never seen anyone grovel, except in a movie. But it didn't look like Kenlow knew how to grovel. He just lay helplessly in the dirt, cursing and moaning, which was kind of close to groveling. And Eva remembered this part in the Bible that said you're supposed to love your enemies. She didn't want to go *that* far—to actually *love* Kenlow. That was one of those parts of religion that, no matter how stupid it sounded, people always quoted it. Well, maybe she wasn't going to love Kenlow, but she'd at least keep dragging him down the trail, which she decided might be humane without seeming too affectionate.

"All right," Eva said. "Grab his arm again. We'll keep dragging him."

And so they dragged Kenlow along, becoming more tired with every step. The fire moved right along with them, gaining more ground and flaring up in spots, where something would instantly ignite and the flames would shoot straight up in the air a few feet, as if the fire was lurching at the girls, like it knew they were getting too tired to go much farther and so the fire was speeding up to kill them all for no reason. Kenlow stopped moaning and started coughing. Then Ava started whimpering and coughing from the smoke.

"He's too heavy," Ava said, and let go of Kenlow.

A crashing, tumbling noise came from somewhere in the trees, like maybe a tree falling in the fire. So much smoke and sweat kept getting in Eva's eyes that she couldn't see for more than a second or two without wiping her eyes. She was trying to decide if she should yank on Kenlow one more time, or just grab Ava and start running, when she heard some men yelling nearby, and then there was a firefighter on the trail with his oxygen mask and a helmet on, staring through the smoke as he held a big hose and sprayed water all around the girls and Kenlow and finally all *over* them, as if he hadn't seem them yet. The force of the water knocked Eva and Ava down beside Kenlow, and it was all cool, then, and Eva looked up through the smoke and the water at the firefighter's oxygen mask, which was shiny and hid his eyes, as he sprayed more and more water over everyone's heads on the trail, as if God had come through the smoke with an oxygen mask on, his face still as concealed and unknown as ever.

After some other firefighters came up the trail and carried Eva and Ava and Kenlow up to the edge of the trees, where all the fire trucks and police cars and the girls' parents and a lot of spectators were gathered near the long, swollen fire hoses that trailed away toward the woods, Eva was a little bit stunned. She wasn't physically hurt. She just felt stunned. She looked at Kenlow as he lay on a stretcher while some woman from the ambulance put a splint on his broken ankle. In his pain and fear, Kenlow didn't look so evil. He didn't look like an enemy. He just looked like a boy who was afraid of what the world could do to him.

There were police there. Eva could walk up to them and say who Kenlow was and they'd probably arrest him. But she wondered if in his fear, Kenlow had changed while he was being dragged away from the fire, and he wouldn't want to hurt her anymore. She wished there were a different thing, something a step below forgiveness, that she could give Kenlow. For example, it seemed like a good idea— but she couldn't recall any instance in the Bible—where Jesus, instead of telling people to "Go, and sin no more," said to them, "Go, and you're on probation."

So Eva seemed stuck with the idea of complete forgiveness. She walked over toward Kenlow, trying to persuade herself to forgive him, but a police officer was already standing next to Kenlow, holding an empty plastic jug.

"We found this jug in your backpack," the officer said. "Can you explain why you had gasoline with you in the woods, or would you like to speak with a lawyer?"

A television reporter and a man holding a TV camera walked through the crowd right up to Eva, and the reporter said to Eva, "Are you the one who helped save the life of that boy on the stretcher?"

"Didn't mean to," Eva said.

c·h·a·p·t·e·r
33

People from three television stations and at least five news-papers were in the little lobby of the police station to listen to Chief McLemore simultaneously announce how his po-lice department arrested a teenage boy for setting the forest on fire and how the police and an illegal alien recovered the Virgin Mary stamp machine. He dealt quickly and briefly with the facts about Kenlow, simply giving his name and age and saying that sufficient evidence existed for the police to hold Kenlow in custody in relation to the forest fire and other unspecified charges associated with the recent outbreak of alleged satanism. McLemore pushed all that aside in order to get to the more satisfying topic of recov-ering the stolen Virgin Mary stamp machine. Standing to the left of Chief McLemore were a few FBI agents and postal service inspectors, who seemed a little bit disap-pointed that it was Chief McLemore who found the stamp machine. Standing to his right was Alfredo, who stared with his usual boyish glee at the TV cameras.

"Last night, at eight fifty-three P.M.," Chief McLemore said into the group of microphones in front of him, "offi-cers from the Waxahachie Police Department raided a farm-house on the outskirts of Waxahachie and recovered the so-called Virgin Mary stamp machine. The stamp machine was found in a barn, where we believe local people were being charged admission to go look at the stamp machine and pray for miracles. Three men have been arrested and will be arraigned on federal charges. I haven't been told what all the charges will be, but they'll include theft of federal property and maybe selling religious miracles without a license.

"I need to point out that the recovery of the stamp machine was made possible because a prisoner in our jail, a man who'd been arrested for drunk driving, knew where the stamp machine was and gave that information to another one of our inmates here, Mr. Alfredo Santayana," Chief McLemore said and put his hand on Alfredo's shoulder. "Mr. Santayana is being detained as an illegal alien, and while he was awaiting his imminent deportation to Guatemala, he had a serious enough interest in law and order to alert us to the location of the stolen stamp machine. I think it's worth noting that Mr. Santayana freely helped us recover the famous Virgin Mary stamp machine even though he was promised no reward for doing so, and even though he still faces deportation in a few days. He's the most civic-minded illegal alien I've ever heard of, and I think it's an embarrassment to the United States of America that we could reward this decent man by kicking him out of our country."

Rev. Schindler was so depressed and ashamed of Kenlow's arrest for arson and satanic threats that he had no interest in completing his next sermon, which was to be titled "Identifying the Subtle Signs of Satan." In this case, Satan had been in the kitchen having *dinner* with Rev. Schindler, and he hadn't even known it. Instead of exorcising the jail, he should have exorcised his kitchen.

After Kenlow was placed in his parents' custody, Rev. Schindler made Kenlow stay in his room all day, mostly so he wouldn't have to look at him. This was the most disabling injury of all: to have been a minister for his entire adult life, and then find that his own son was a satanist or a mock satanist.

Rev. Schindler spent most of his time shut up in his study, where he wouldn't have to answer any of the phone calls from his bewildered church members and where he could be depressed in complete and painful privacy. As agonized and unruly as his thoughts were, he wondered if, like in the Old Testament, he should build a pyre in his backyard and set Kenlow on fire as a burnt offering to the Lord. But even if he piously burned his son to death, the state might not regard it as the legitimate expression of his religious beliefs.

He thought of dressing only in sackcloth and ashes to signify his penance for having raised a bad son, but he didn't know what sackcloth was. He had some old paper grocery sacks around the house, but even if he taped them together to form a garment he could wear, it would say DAVE'S BIG BASTED HEN all over the garment.

As he brooded without rest, he thought that what made everything even worse was that as he warned his congregation of the unmistakable evidence of Satan's presence in town, it was just Kenlow. And when he exorcised the jail, that, too, was based on phony evidence. And yet he'd gotten nearly everyone in his congregation to believe in the immanence of Satan. He had been so convinced that Satan was nigh that he had committed the sin of pride.

It was the only time in Rev. Schindler's life that he felt disappointed that Satan hadn't shown up.

He brooded for a while longer, wondering what he should do. He was too bewildered and depressed to think very clearly. He might want to apologize to his congregation, and maybe write a press release to the public at large saying Satan's appearance had been cancelled. But he didn't want to sound *too* apologetic. It wasn't like people were going to ask for refunds. But he *did* have to own up to the fact that his judgment had been wrong. He could do that. He was ashamed, but he could still apologize to his church and write a press release saying that maybe the end of the world had been delayed again.

One thing he decided to do right away, though, was apologize in person to the illegal alien in jail. He had never been so proud a man that when he realized he was plainly wrong he couldn't admit it.

He drove down to the police station and went inside, where he quietly explained his mission to Chief McLemore, who granted him an audience with Alfredo. Sgt. Mondesi stood beside Rev. Schindler to translate as Rev. Schindler looked through the steel bars at Alfredo and said, "I'm here to apologize for exorcising you."

As Sgt. Mondesi began her translation, Rev. Schindler looked down and away from Alfredo's eyes, wondering if he hadn't humbled himself too much to an illegal alien. But he resisted that thought, remembering that Alfredo was more human than alien. He couldn't imagine how Alfredo might react to the apology the sergeant was translating now, and his face burned with the shame of every foolish thing he'd done recently. He couldn't really think of Alfredo as just an illegal alien. He thought of him now as a decent human whose sense of injustice could come forth at any moment to scald the reverend.

There came a silent pause after the apology had been translated, and Rev. Schindler kept looking down at the floor and burning with shame. At last, Alfredo spoke.

"I'd like to buy a vowel," Alfredo said.

"Is he speaking in tongues?" the reverend asked.

"He's speaking TV," the sergeant said.

"And what does it mean? Does he forgive me?"

"I'll ask him," the sergeant said. She spoke Spanish to Alfredo.

Alfredo looked at the reverend and said, "Beam me up, Scotty."

"Apparently he's been watching *Star Trek*," the sergeant said.

"Does he forgive me?"

"Well if he wants you to beam him up, he probably isn't mad."

c·h·a·p·t·e·r

34

A national wire service story in the paper the next morning quoted some official from the INS as having said that even though Alfredo had shown admirable moral character by helping the police, he was still violating immigration laws and had to be deported.

"By God, I'm not going to stand for this," Eva's dad said at breakfast. "If I have to, I'll go to the jail and handcuff myself to Alfredo. If they try to deport him, they'll have to deport me with him."

Eva had never heard her dad talk so recklessly before. She kind of liked it.

"Maybe we should make this a family outing," Eva's mom said. "We'll all handcuff ourselves to Alfredo and go to Guatemala with him. I think it's time we took the girls to a foreign country."

"You mean Hawaii?" Ava asked.

Their dad stood up from his chair at the table and walked over to the phone on the wall and called somebody.

"Who're you calling?" their mom said.

"McLemore," he said, and everybody watched him on the phone, wondering what reckless things he'd say next. When he asked to speak with Chief McLemore, he was quiet for a few seconds and then said, "He is? Oh, well. That's interesting. If he gets back today, please tell him I called and I'll call again. Thank you. Good-bye."

He walked back to his chair and sat down and said, "They said Chief McLemore went to the INS office in Dallas to sit on somebody until they either let Alfredo go or they suffocate."

Eva thought maybe she should pray again, to help Alfredo get a green card, but she was beginning to see a problem with that. The problem was, she'd already prayed probably hundreds of times in her life for things that never happened. It could have been that some of the things shouldn't have been prayed for anyway. That was true. Like when she prayed for a six-foot-long plastic *Tyrannosaurus rex* skeleton and she didn't get it. You could say a plastic dinosaur skeleton wasn't spiritual. So forget that. But what about when you prayed for peace and you got war? What about when you prayed for Alfredo to find a job and be legal, and he just stays in jail? What about when you prayed your parents would love each other and it didn't happen? Nobody ever could answer those things, like God sat up in outer space with hundreds of millions of prayers racing at him like a gigantic wind, and most of the time, the prayers just raced on by, and nothing happened. Some people said God didn't exist. Eva didn't think that. She thought God existed. She just couldn't tell what for.

She imagined maybe another reason it seemed like most prayers weren't answered was that if God always had hundreds of millions of prayers coming at him, maybe he wanted to dodge some of them, the way you dodge bugs. Or maybe it just took too long to answer all of them, like the prayers got backed up the way things did on a telephone answering machine.

It seemed like, over the centuries, prayers could get so backed up that, like if somebody prayed something in 1900, God just now got the prayer and he'd answer it after you were dead. But this made God seem terribly inefficient, so Eva rejected that idea and realized she had a headache, probably from trying to think too seriously. She knew what some of her friends who went to church would say. They'd say she was having sinful thoughts about God, and so God gave her a headache. Eva wondered about that. She couldn't help but wonder how come God seemed to have such a hard time hearing prayer and answering that, but he could instantly detect a sinful thought and immediately punish it?

Like most of her religious questions, she seemed to have them not with any hope of getting an answer, but only to remind her of how vast her God-given ignorance was.

As she sat listlessly back in the living room, she heard the phone ring and heard her dad answer it and talk quietly, and then he yelled, "Eureka!"

According to her *Young Person's Encyclopedic Dictionary*, that was a town in California, so Eva didn't know what her dad was so excited about. But he sounded happy and was talking loudly on the phone now, saying, "Well that's just wonderful. At least I think it is," and Eva and her mom both walked into the study at the same time to see what was wonderful.

Eva's dad smiled at them and said, "Dolores Galloway found Alfredo a job."

"Well what, *what?*" Eva's mom said.

"Yes. Okay. Yes," Eva's dad said, still on the phone as he wrote something on a notepad. "Well we'll certainly call them in the morning and let them know we've got an employee for them. And I'll call you right afterward to let you know what happens. Bye."

He hung up the phone and smiled at Eva and her mom. He didn't say anything.

"Well tell us!" Eva's mom said impatiently.

"Alfredo's really got a job?" Eva asked.

"Here's the deal," her dad said. "Dolores Galloway works in the office of state senator Rachel Bowie, who's a descendant of Jim Bowie. According to Dolores, Senator Bowie was watching CNN and saw the story about Alfredo helping find the Virgin Mary stamp machine, and she just thought it was awful that a law-abiding illegal alien could be deported after helping his own captors locate the internationally famous Virgin Mary stamp machine. So when she found out Dolores went to our church and that we were trying to find an appropriately repugnant job for Alfredo, *bingo* . . . she knew of one.''

''What? What?'' her mom said.

''Senator Bowie is the head of some state subcommittee on highways and transportation, which of course has thousands of jobs, and so Bowie happens to know of the one job in the state that's so detestable that almost nobody wants it.''

''Oh, Lord,'' Eva's mom said. ''Hurry up and tell us the good news before we realize how bad it is.''

''Well I don't know the precise job title,'' Eva's dad said. ''Dolores didn't say. But let's just say Alfredo will have a job in the state highway beautification program.''

''You mean he'll pick up litter?'' Eva's mom said.

''Biodegradable litter.''

''What kind of biodegradable litter?''

''The kind that has four legs and armor plating.''

It was quickly arranged for Eva and her family to meet Diego Guerra at the jail to tell Alfredo about this new opportunity for freedom. Everyone stood anxiously in Alfredo's cell as Diego Guerra spent about twenty seconds explaining in Spanish that Alfredo could now live as a free man in the United States and work toward actual citizenship because he'd been offered a job picking up dead animals.

Alfredo looked confused. He asked a question. Diego Guerra turned around toward Eva's parents and said, ''He wants to know if that's how you become a citizen, by picking up dead animals.''

''Tell him it's just a job, and he'll get paid for it,'' Eva's mom said.

Diego Guerra explained that. Alfredo still looked troubled, and asked another question. Diego Guerra said, ''He says he wants to know what you do with the armadillos after you pick them up.''

"As far as we know," Eva's mom said, "he'll put the dead armadillos in a truck or something so the animals can be disposed of.''

Diego Guerra told that to Alfredo, who nodded his head slightly and asked another question. Diego Guerra said, "He wants to know why there are so many dead armadillos in Texas.''

"Because they're careless," Eva's dad said.

Alfredo said a few things in Spanish, and when he was through, Diego Guerra said, "He wants you to know that even if he has to pick up dead animals whose stench will cause his stomach to violently tremble, he thinks you are the kindest people he ever knew. He also says he would be very honored to pick up United States of America dead armadillos, and he hopes he gets to wear gloves.''

Everybody was so glad that Alfredo was finally going to get his green card, which was really pink, that a big Green Card Day was being planned at the church by the Strategic Air Command. Really it was the Social Action Committee at the church, but it had the same initials as the Strategic Air Command, so a lot of people called it that. There were only a few days to plan for Green Card Day, but everything seemed ready when the church service was over at noon on Sunday, and all the people went outside to the lawn, where there were picnic tables all covered with big gobs of fried chicken and sliced ham and corn on the cob and potato salad, with also a table that was supposed to have Guatemalan food, but it seemed as if nobody knew what Guatemalan food really was, so the Guatemalan table had Mexican food, like refried beans with chiles, and homemade burritos, and something called black bean soup, which Eva had never heard of before and which looked to her like liquid tar with beans in it. Someone said they were going to have armadillo steaks. Eva never saw any.

It was a big crowd out wandering around the tables, including just about everybody who ever had anything to do with Alfredo, like the state senator who nobody knew and who was supposedly related to Col. Jim Bowie, and like Chief McLemore, who was completely dressed up in a formal police chief's uniform with white gloves and a revolver. It was as if he never could tell when he might need to shoot someone.

A lot of the people kept going up to Alfredo wherever he was and introducing themselves, and although a few of them knew Spanish, most of them didn't, so they just took turns saying things neither of them understood and smiled about it. Mostly, everybody ate a lot, which you could do without knowing two languages, and one of the church women brought an acoustic guitar with a strap on it so she could wander around in the grass playing Guatemalan folk songs whether you wanted to hear them or not. That was one of the strange things Eva was learning about how adults acted when they got in a social group. There was always somebody who'd do something playful or cheerful like that, as if everybody was always supposed to like the same things at the same time, when probably they didn't.

Then someone from the Strategic Air Command came walking across the grass holding this great big pink doll thing in the shape of an armadillo with a rope fixed on the center of it, and the rope was attached to a long pole. Eva wondered if somebody thought it was funny to give Alfredo an armadillo doll, which possibly it was. But then when the person went up to Alfredo with the doll and began explaining things to Diego Guerra—who explained them to Alfredo—everyone knew the armadillo doll was a piñata, and there were prizes in it for Alfredo. Alfredo smiled like a boyish boy, as if no matter how bad his life had been anywhere, the only thing that mattered was what was going on right then.

Eva's mom stood by Alfredo and gave him a blindfold. Alfredo held it up to his nose, as if he were going to blow his nose. Diego Guerra stopped Alfredo and told him it was a blindfold. Alfredo nodded his head and was laughing as Eva's mom tied the blindfold over Alfredo's face so he couldn't see, and then Eva's dad took Alfredo by the shoulders and turned him around and around a few times, to get him a little bit dizzy and so he would not know where anything was. Then Diego Guerra handed Alfredo a long, thick stick and explained more things as the person with the armadillo piñata raised the piñata up on the rope and the stick so it swayed a few feet in front of Alfredo.

Everybody in the crowd stood back, so Alfredo wouldn't whump somebody in the head when he started swinging his stick. Everyone cheered as loud as if they were at a baseball game or a carnival while Alfredo stepped forward and swished his stick so fast through the air you could hear a high-pitched woosh, which made a few people twitch and move back even more. Alfredo wooshed his stick a few more times, like a blindfolded samurai warrior swinging his sword at invisible enemies. But with the next woosh, Alfredo and the man holding the piñata stepped toward each other at precisely the right time, so Alfredo's stick smacked straight into the butt of the armadillo and broke it right open, spilling out this little spray of prizes onto the grass. Everybody cheered and clapped as Alfredo pulled his blindfold off and got down on his hands and knees in the grass to look at some apples and oranges and wrapped pieces of candy while the piñata man reached his hand inside the busted piñata and scooped everything else out so it dropped in the grass in front of Alfredo. Eva squeezed up to the front of the crowd near Alfredo and saw all the prizes. One of them was a light blue surgeon's mask, which Diego Guerra put on Alfredo's face over his nose and mouth, explaining how it could be useful in blocking out unpleasant odors in Alfredo's new job.

Alfredo kept the surgeon's mask on as he picked up a green card from the grass. It wasn't a real green card. Just a fake. The real one would be pink, of course, and it would take a few days to get that one. But Alfredo waved the fake green card at everybody and pulled down his surgeon's mask so he could clearly say something in Spanish that almost nobody understood. But Diego Guerra explained it.

"He said now that he's legal, maybe dead animals won't smell so bad."

Still in the grass in front of Alfredo was a key ring with a key on it. Alfredo picked it up and said something to Diego Guerra. Diego Guerra laughed and said, "He thinks somebody lost their key. He wants to give it back."

Almost nobody else knew what the key was for, either, but Diego Guerra did, and he said, "Alfredo doesn't know this yet, and I'll explain it to him, but the key is for an apartment. An anonymous person from your church found Alfredo a place to live, and paid the first three months' rent. So that's the key to the apartment."

Diego Guerra squatted next to Alfredo in the grass and told him about the key. Alfredo stared at the key for a long time, like it was an astonishing artifact from an ancient temple, as if it could be gold, or an emerald, as if it were far too valuable to suppose he should even touch it. His gleeful smile began to vanish, and he looked perplexed, and then sad, as he held the key up near his face and just stared at it. Eva could see the tiny outlines of tears going down his cheeks, and all of the talking and laughing around him died away softly, and there were other people crying and acting as if they weren't. Eva had to blink and rub her knuckles against her eyes to get her own tears away without knowing why anybody was crying, why nobody was saying anything at all, like you just had to cry because there was something good in the world, and at first you could hardly imagine it was there. But it was. And so you cried.

Alfredo used his blindfold to wipe the tears from his eyes, and he looked at everyone gratefully.

"Kotex understands," Alfredo said. But it didn't seem to bother anyone. They were laughing and wiping their tears and blowing their noses, and it was all cheerful again, in a kind of delicate way, as Alfredo held his new key in one hand and stared at the blank, blue sky, like he was wondering if God gave him the apartment and his green card and a job.

"It was us," Eva thought. It bothered her to think that everybody had prayed and prayed for help for Alfredo, and when nothing happened, they had to do it themselves. She looked in the sky at about the same spot where Alfredo had been looking, and all you could see was the ordinary sky, like if God was up there floating around, he was camouflaged. She didn't want to think God hadn't done anything, but you couldn't tell that he had. It was something that never got solved, what God's job was. As Eva tried to figure it, there had to be some kind of occult, magical way that, when you prayed over and over to God, God did exactly what you asked for by having someone else do it.

That was believable enough to Eva, although she knew this was frighteningly close to being an atheist. But she wasn't thinking God didn't exist. She was only wondering if he ever *did* anything.

Eva kneeled down in the grass beside Alfredo to help him pick up all the candy and stuff, while listening to Alfredo and Diego Guerra talk in Spanish. Then Diego Guerra said, "He said he thinks the Virgin Mary answered his prayers."

Eva wondered how that could be true. The Virgin Mary couldn't even stop her own stamp machine from being stolen.

Then Diego Guerra said to Eva, "And I said to Alfredo, 'So you think the Virgin Mary got you an apartment? I don't think the Virgin Mary is a landlady. She works for the postal service, now.'"

$c \cdot h \cdot a \cdot p \cdot t \cdot e \cdot r$

35

Out on the side of the highway at sunrise, with brilliant beams of sunlight flowing delicately through small breaks in the nearby trees so you had to think of the glory of the world, Alfredo stared down at his first dead armadillo. He put on his surgical mask.

"You going to operate on him, doctor?" said Esteban, one of the Spanish-speaking workers in the group with Alfredo. "It's too late for surgery. He's dead."

Alfredo felt himself blushing. He said, "No. This mask is a gift from the Americans who helped me get this job."

"Someone *helped* you get this job?" Esteban said to the other man, Carlos. "It must be someone who doesn't like you."

"No. They were very nice to me," Alfredo said. "They helped me get my green card, and they gave me this doctor's mask so I wouldn't have to smell the stinking stink of all the stink that stinks."

Then Alfredo made the sign of the cross in front of his surgical mask as he unhappily looked at the dead armadillo.

"Are you going to pray for the armadillo's soul?" Carlos asked. "I've never heard a prayer for an armadillo before. What's it sound like?"

Alfredo briefly wondered what you'd pray to God about a dead armadillo. *Please take this armadillo into Heaven, where there are no cars.* He stopped thinking that and said, "No. I'm not praying for his soul. I'm just thanking God I have a job."

"So you think God got you this job?" Esteban asked. "I guess God doesn't like you, either."

They all three laughed, the way people can be amused by the shared lowness of their lives. Then they looked back down at the slightly squashed armadillo, as if eventually someone would have to do something with it.

"You're the new man. You get to pick up the first dead animal of this lovely morning," Esteban said to Alfredo.

Alfredo didn't move.

"Go ahead and pick it up, doctor."

Alfredo touched his surgical mask, as if making sure it was on tight, and then he looked carefully at the armadillo about three feet in front of him.

"It looks like he almost made it across the road before he got hit," Alfredo said. He walked over to the edge of the asphalt road, examined the road for a few seconds, then said, "It looks like he was just barely hit by one edge of the car. The car probably didn't slow down."

"Who are you—Kojak?" Esteban said.

"I think he's Columbo," Carlos said.

Alfredo smiled behind his surgical mask, happy that his new friends knew American TV as well as he did.

"Well, Kojak, we're not supposed to solve a goddamn killing. We just pick up the animals and throw them away," Andres said.

"I feel bad for him," Alfredo said.

"You don't get paid for feeling bad. You get paid for picking him up," Esteban said. "Use your hands or use your shovel."

Taking a deep breath, Alfredo put the wide, flat blade of his shovel under the armadillo and started to gag.

"You already gagging on the first one?" Carlos asked. "This gonna be a long day."

"Okay. I'll be fine. Here I go," Alfredo said, putting the shovel all the way under the armadillo and gagging again as his eyes began to water.

"You glad to be in America now?" Esteban asked.

Alfredo didn't know how to gag and say yes at the same time.

There was some talk that Kenlow would go to a reformatory, whatever that was. But first there'd be a trial and Eva would have to be a witness, meaning she'd sit up by the judge and have to point out Kenlow as the boy she ran into in the woods during the fire, and she'd have to say he was the one who threatened her after she saw him in the woods near the pentagram with Vienna sausages, and so on. It made Eva feel sort of awful, that she could put some boy in a boy's prison. Some of what he did you could maybe say was evil, and some of it didn't seem all that bad. Maybe he needed counseling or a psychiatrist, like Eva's mom said. Her dad was still a little bit mad about Kenlow starting the fire and endangering Eva's and Ava's lives. He said maybe Jesus could forgive Kenlow, but *he* didn't have to yet. That surprised Eva, who thought her dad would be the one going around talking about forgiveness. But it just meant he loved Eva so much that he didn't want anybody to hurt her, and so that was good to know. Eva was told that maybe they could just put Kenlow in jail for a few weeks, and then have him do community service, like pick up dead animals for the highway department. Eva was appalled. That meant they could punish Kenlow by having him do the same job that was supposed to be a privilege for Alfredo. She didn't want to think about that. She also didn't want Kenlow in a reformatory if it meant he'd just get meaner in there and he'd come looking for Eva when he got out. If that was justice, where bad people were made worse, Eva wanted to avoid justice for the rest of her life. She had it in her mind that when she went to court, she maybe wanted to forgive Kenlow, and ask him to go see a psychiatrist. Mainly, she just wanted to stop thinking about it all and be the girl she used to be earlier in the summer.

She sat quietly on the front porch, watching the morning sun spread across the shadows as a praying mantis crawled into view on one of the bushes beside the porch. It was peculiar how the big green bug looked as if it were holding its arms in prayer. The mantis looked pious and worshipful, like a nun, and you could wonder exactly which prayer it was saying until it jumped forward and grabbed a grasshopper with its prayerful arms and began chewing the grasshopper's head off. The praying mantis didn't look very religious then.

Eva moved away to the end of the porch so she wouldn't have to watch the devout praying mantis gnaw on a squirming grasshopper. Sometimes the peacefulness of nature was pretty brutal. She stared again at the morning sunlight until an old sorrow stirred in her, and she wondered if her family was working or failing. By habit, she almost immediately prayed for her parents to love each other again, but she couldn't quite pray. It seemed like too many of her prayers were unanswered, as if saying anything to God was this strict religious contest where you had to pray exactly the right thing in exactly the right way, and if any detail of the prayer was wrong, you'd be ignored again and suffering would descend on you like a mist. It seemed strange and even unfair that maybe God helped Alfredo get a job and a green card, which Eva had prayed for, but God wouldn't help her parents love each other, which Eva had prayed for long before she met Alfredo. Nothing was fair. Nothing made sense.

But people prayed anyway. Like if, by accident, you might say the right prayer, or God might be in the right mood to answer one. So Eva decided to say one more prayer to Ted Williams.

Dear Ted Williams:
I know I can't get everything I ask for, and I'm not asking for that. I just wish my parents would love each

*other again, so no one would have to be sad anymore
and have several of the symptoms of depression like
they show on that TV commercial we see all the time.
I won't pray for anything selfish again, like video
games or anything. I just wish my parents would love
each other, and we wouldn't be alone again. I hope
you get this prayer, and think about it. Amen.*

And then the prayer went on its way to some unknown
spot in the universe, where it might be analyzed and graded
and considered in the lottery.

Eva went back inside the house and got Ava and some
fishing poles. No shovels. She wasn't in the mood to go
looking for bones anymore and risk finding another person's skeleton, even if she found Lewis or Clark. She and
Ava took a trail that wouldn't go anywhere near the burned-
down warlock's house or the rest of the blackened forest.
She just wanted to go fishing. They brought some iced tea
with them to drink while they fished at the sewage treatment plant.

"What kind of fish will we catch?" Ava asked.

Eva thought about it for a while, trying to recall the
names of some freshwater fish.

"A crappie," she said.

It made Ava rock sideways as she giggled.

They fished for a while, catching nothing, which was the
tradition. Ava looked over at Eva and said, "Did Alfredo
ever buy a vowel?"

"No. We just gave him some consonants," Eva said. It
was an odd question, so it required an odd answer.

It seemed like the summer had started again. There were
flies everywhere. Ava slapped her hand on the bare skin of
her knee and said, "Where do all these damn flies come
from?"

"Don't say 'damn flies,' " Eva said. "Say 'house-
flies.' "

"Well they're not in the house. They're out *here*," Ava
complained.

"That's because they haven't found a house to go into yet," Eva said, explaining the world as usual, while the girls contentedly held their fishing poles over the fragrant lake.